MW00437783

Also by Joe Moore

Faith, Hope & Reindeer

2nd in the Santa Claus Trilogy

Believe Again,

The North Pole Chronicles

1st in the Santa Claus Trilogy

By Joe Moore

as told to by

Alfie Newsworthy

Published by The North Pole Press

Published by The North Pole Press

Smoky Mountains, Tennessee
ISBN-13: 978-0-9787129-3-8

Cover design by Mary Moore
Photo by Senior Airman Joshua Strang

Copyright © 2013 by Joe Moore

Library of Congress Catalog Number
2013900359

Printed in the United States of America

Dedication

To My First Grandbaby, Jameson,
and to all the children, young and
old, who believe in Santa Claus.
You are the real reason Santa
Claus exists.

Childhood is the world of miracle and of magic:
it is as if creation rose luminously out of the night,
all new and fresh and astonishing.

Eugene Ionesco

Acknowledgements

My lovely wife, Mary, is my constant beacon and best friend. She sees me through every difficulty and loves me without question. She is the reason this book exists and quite frankly, why I am still around on this earth. She designed the look and feel of this book and has made it a masterful expression of my thoughts and words. Thank you, sweetheart.

That said, many other people have helped me create this book, and I appreciate and give thanks to the effort of every one of their contributions.

To my dearest friend, Fred Selinsky, who praised *Faith, Hope & Reindeer's* every page and idea, thank you for spurring me on and giving me a few good ideas which I gladly incorporated into this novel.

To my many friends and assistants with the editing, cleaning and correcting, bless you all. Especially Tracy Lewis Shepard and Toni Garland, who cleaned up so much of the grammar and mistakes in this book. I now know what kind of craftsman it takes to polish a rough diamond into brilliance.

To my friend Judi McNair, who also assisted in the cleaning and editing, my best regards and thanks. And to my friends Randy and Terry Ann Fritchman, who have seen Mary and I through so many struggles, and are always there to lend a hand to get us through, thank you for being our best friends.

Also special thanks to my dear friend Robin Webb who helped make this book a reality and keep Mary and me from losing our minds. Bless you for your help and guidance.

So many talented souls help me get my message across to make you, the reader, pick this up in the first place. Thank you all immensely for seeing this novel through my eyes, and putting my image forth so succinctly.

Preface

It fell to me to keep the history of our land and people. I was asked since I had helped run a newspaper office among the tallfolk. My name is Alfie Newsworthy and I am the official historian of the North Pole.

Now I arrived after the construction of the dome and years after the settlement began, but before the first Santa Claus. Oops, excuse me, I am getting ahead of myself.

What follows is a history of the North Pole including how we were able to tame this inhospitable climate, and make a paradise where hardly anyone else would dare tread. It also explains why we are here, what we do and how the true story of Santa Claus began.

In many meetings and conversations that took place, I was present, although I may not identify myself as being there. Council meetings and the like were always recorded for posterity and were turned over to me for the reason of making a historical account.

Many things are easily proven and some things, while not so easy to prove, are true nonetheless. We believe in sincere speech at the North Pole and invoke it everyday. You'll understand what I mean shortly.

So for those who seek the truth and history of Santa Claus, and all the elves of the North Pole, I invite you to pull up a chair and get comfy. It is quite a story, or more exactly a Chronicle of the North Pole.

Chapter One

All the best things in the world can be found in the eyes of a child.

- Forrest Hedemup

The Beginning

Long before Santa Claus moved to the North Pole and became world known, the North Pole began, and was run, by the elves. We had come to the top of the world after being treated poorly by bigger people. It was not so much that we were beaten or kicked, though occasionally that would happen, but because largely we were just ignored or dismissed. People didn't take us seriously, if they took us at all. They all thought that since we were small, we couldn't be very smart. Nothing could have been further from the truth.

So we had come from many lands, each hearing the promise of a better world. Elves came from every continent, and like the tallfolk we lived among, were every shape, color, with pointed ears and round, some short and others taller. Though unlike the tallfolk, most of us are around four feet give or take a few inches. We spoke different languages, had different stories and legends and brought various hopes and ambitions. When things had become unbearable in the country where they lived, those elves would pack up their belongings, and hoping the stories they heard were all true, would make the arduous trek to the frozen north.

Now I am not boasting here, but sincere speech needs to be spoken. We are far smarter than the people we had lived amongst. And once we banded together, we found that together we bordered, or even exceeded, genius. As anyone knows, two people are smarter than one, and four are smarter than two, and so on. But with the elves, as we increased our numbers, our collective smarts geometrically progressed and became nothing short of brilliance.

In addition to being much brighter than most tallfolk, we have a very peaceable nature to ourselves. Rarely do we ever have a disagreeable day. We find great joy in working with each other. We have a strong sense of accomplishment in everything we do together. On the rare occasion we do disagree on something, we work it through with compromises, or when in doubt we just bring in a couple more opinions from other elves, until we can agree on a particular course of resolve.

Because this land was inhospitable to others, we were not only left in peace, but were able to build a large settlement. We advanced our discoveries much faster than the outside world and began constructing marvelous inventions and ways to accomplish things and tame our new land. The developments we came up with would have given any other country pause. Soon we were centuries ahead of any other civilization.

Being friendly and forgiving by nature, we not only don't hold a grudge against bigger people, but found their children wonderful in their overall innocence and curious nature. This is something that has always been particularly endearing to every elf. We like the fact that through playing, many children learn how to get along, and learn good lessons from others. All of us elves wanted to encourage that playtime for children.

It was Carrow Chekitwice who first suggested that perhaps the elves could build some things for the children to play with and enjoy. Again, while we elves were genuinely not against tallfolk, as they came to be called by us, we still avoided them as much as possible. Of course even with our collective smarts, we have to deal with the tallfolk from time to time. We need many goods and occasionally some services from them, because even with all our advances, the North Pole could not provide all our needs. But we elves had plenty to trade in order to get what we needed.

Not the least of which were our wonderful toys that would often touch a heartstring of the tallfolk and cause them to remember, even if just for a moment, what it was like to be a child. And the tallfolk wanted to give these toys to their own children, which of course was what we elves wanted, too.

Because of our advances, tallfolk often would be happy to trade for what we produced. Much of it had never been seen before, and often we would be decades ahead of their own inventions and tools. Soon our products became in high demand among them. But problems developed as some of the inventions that were traded became used in ways that we had not intended.

Our products were constructed and used against other people and changed from our initial designs. Wars came about because of our advances to the tallfolk and their misuse. So the Council of Elves decided that we needed to carefully trade only the tools and advances that the tallfolk could handle at any particular time in their development. Many products and innovations would have to wait until the Council thought the tallfolk would not use them for destructive rather than constructive purposes.

Meanwhile in the Arctic, our innovations kept being developed at a breakneck pace. We had not only learned how to tame our harsh landscape, but we had developed a dome to help handle the often frigid blizzard conditions and make the Pole much more livable, even enjoyable. We had become partial to cold weather, and liked the snow, we just preferred it in less amounts and more gently falling. Once under the dome, we kept the inner living area around the freezing mark, and opted not to make it too much warmer as we always felt more sluggish and less inclined to get things done when it was too warm.

Of course we also developed a more seasonal climate including spring, summer and fall. To date we are always enjoying beautiful days and can control the sunlight artificially because sometimes it disappears altogether for many months in winter. But even more important than the climate, in developing the dome which is several miles across, we had constructed a barrier that became impervious to both outsiders and natural disasters, even meteorites.

During our development we had also discovered an interesting side affect to living at the North Pole. We lived much longer than our tallfolk counterparts. And not just by a few years, but decades and even centuries. With each new generation, we lived longer and longer. It was learned that because of the strong magnetic properties of the North Pole, it resulted in elves eventually living hundreds of years instead as a normal lifetime.

Since we were now so long-lived, we became master craftsman in nearly any activity we pursued, often spending several decades working and perfecting our craft. We had eventually abandoned the traditional way of being named outside of the North Pole. Many forsook their old last name and took on new ones, often adopting something pointing to the craft they were particularly good at.

Before long, only first names were given to newborn elves, and they were allowed to pick their own surname when they felt the time was right. Few ever changed it once chosen, but some waited nearly a century before making the decision. I came up with Newsworthy to reflect reporting facts and history throughout our culture.

Occasionally some elves would want to make a

change for a time and move back south for a while. Some wished for their old geography, and were allowed to work on behalf of the North Pole in other areas although they could return whenever they wished. The only requirement was that they could not disclose the elves culture, or location, to the tallfolk. They were especially not allowed to bring any of them to the North Pole, and had to keep the advancements of the elves secret.

This went on for a great many years, and while elves were kept abreast of what was happening in the other lands, we often just shook our heads and kept enjoying our quiet peace in our secret habitat. Many of the elves that worked in other lands would load up a bag of toys and take them to the children of the area they visited. Also, some elves would take a handful of toys and sweets to children of the tallfolk they traded with, and leave them quietly in various places where they would eventually be discovered.

As a matter of course, the elves would say nothing about the gifts and would just leave them secretly. Occasionally a bag of toys would just appear in an area where children were known to gather and play.

Unknown to any of us at first, one particular tallfolk was doing the same thing. He had come from a long line of very generous people that began with a former bishop of early Christianity in Turkey of Middle Asia. That bishop had been anointed to sainthood for his deeds and love of children. This good man, and then his ancestors, had already begun to have many tales told about them.

The bishop of Turkey's lineage spread into other European lands as did their influence. The ancestors had turned up in Italy, France, Germany and the Netherlands. Each had begun many traditions in the lands they traveled, all culminating in events geared around the birth of the Christ child, just as their Bishop forefather had done. They had begun to be known by many names in each land they traveled like Papa Noel, Pere Noel, La Befana, Babbo Natalie, Sinterklaas and others.

Lately, many of the toys we elves had left for children had been credited to this tallfolk. This never bothered us as it had taken the eyes off us, and left us to give our gifts in peace. A couple times the elves were actually pointed to as the gift-givers. We just said nothing and walked away. We did not need the attention of the tallfolk for the gifts left behind.

Finally one of our own came up with the idea to approach the tallfolk gift giver and ask if he would help us distribute our toys to the children, as he seemed to be doing it anyway. Denny Sweetooth, one of our members of the Council of Elves asked about enlisting the stranger for help. Immediately a great debate ensued over whether or not to break our own law and allow the stranger to visit the North Pole, and to witness the wonders of the elves and our land.

After all, he was a member of the tallfolk. Many argued that it was wrong to say that none of the tallfolk could ever be trusted. The others argued that dire consequences would take place if this was allowed to happen. In the end, and by a single vote, it was agreed that the elves would send a delegation to meet with the man. During this meeting, if the delegation agreed, they would invite him to the North Pole.

They had placed on this delegation some of their best and brightest including Carrow Chekitwice - who was known for his leadership and careful ingenuity; Denny Sweetooth – whose suggestion it was in the first place. Also, though Denny was a baker and chef by trade, he was known for his big heart and wise Council; Forrest Hedemup – who was in charge of all the animals and training in the North Pole and a lover of all creatures; Whitey Slippenfall – who was not only one of the elves that made the North Pole habitable, but was in charge of the defenses of the Pole, namely its protective dome, and finally, Ella Communacado – who was the chief information elf in charge of communicating with the elves outside of the North Pole.

Carrow was an ancient elf who had helped design and build the village in the beginning. He was slightly taller and thinner than many of the elves with a beard that ran all the way down to his knees. His face carried a lot of wrinkles and the elves weren't sure if it was due more to his age, or his stern nature. Carrow always seemed to be frowning and studying things, whether village plans or simple toys, with the same unending scrutiny.

At the opposite end of Carrow, Denny Sweetooth

was always smiling and jovial. He was as round as he was tall, and looked like a dwarf even to other elves. Denny's passion was food. Cooking it or eating it didn't matter. He just loved being in a kitchen and near it. But he also was known to have the biggest heart in the North Pole and was always offering counsel and help to others with their concerns, which often were many. Like Carrow, he served on the Council of Elves and was an important member of the community, and one all the elves trusted.

Forrest Hedemup was chosen for his stamina and strength. While no bigger than an average elf, he looked like a ranch hand and was stronger than most elves. He carried large bundles with no effort, and could handle himself with tallfolk if the need arose. He was chosen to help keep a protective eye on the delegation, and to assist with the animals they would need and their load. A good looking young man by elf standards, he was one of the few blond elves with deep blue eyes.

Whitey was aptly named, as he sported a full head of white hair that looked as white and big as a snow bank. He had piercing green eyes, and like Carrow, was taller than most of his village. Whitey was the protector of the North Pole. He handled the defenses and also the security within the Pole. Very rarely did anything untoward happen in the village, but if it did, Whitey was called to the scene. His keen senses were known throughout the village, and he had a great capacity for sensing what was right from wrong. It was for this reason, as much as any, that he was chosen for this important mission.

If Whitey was known for his intuition, Ella was known for being able to put thought into "sincere speech" as we elves call complete truth. A pleasant looking woman with dark hair and dark mysterious hazel eyes to match, she was one of the more desirable ladies of the North Pole, and was often sought after by the single men of the village.

What made Ella important (and sometimes even feared by less sincere men) was her ability to see through to the truth or make sense of any garbled discussion and put it into words that everyone could grasp. There are some that just have a difficult time talking with others. Ella could understand what they meant and spoke their thoughts in a concise manner. Just in case this tallfolk began saying things insincerely or without clear meaning, Ella would be there to interpret.

When these intrepid five left the North Pole on their quest, it was an unusual time in history. As they headed for the Netherlands, Ella explained to the others that this was a time of turmoil in England. As they all knew, the English had colonies throughout the world, on every known continental land mass, but one of these colonies was rebelling against their home country and England was embroiled in a war with their own people.

Apparently Americans, as they were calling themselves, had decided they no longer wished to be ruled by England and wanted to be free and independent. The other elves felt an instant kinship to these people, as they had traveled to the North Pole for similar reasons, though elves would rather leave for places unknown than to create war on others for something as unimportant as land.

The troupe had spent most of the fall, and part of the winter, searching for their quarry through the Netherlands. He was known to be in Amsterdam for a time, but they were not sure he was still around. It seemed the man was anxious to avoid recognition and attention, just as the elves had done. Many times they were told that yes, someone had been by and left some food stuffs and toys, but he was gone before they could even thank him. They had been given a vague description of the man but other then sporting a full white beard and mustache, and being of large and strong build, there was little else to distinguish him.

They finally caught up with the man they sought outside of Eindhoven in the south eastern part of the Netherlands around mid-December. They found him on the road heading out of town. He looked like a peddler and was carrying a large pack on his back. He had a long beard, hair and mustache.

But what the elves also saw was that his eyes twinkled, and he had the reddest cheeks Ella had ever seen on a tallfolk. He called himself Kris, Kris Kringle, and had a very pleasant demeanor about him. He was surprised when approached by the small band. While being of average height himself, he had not seen such a small group gathered together before. They said they would like to talk with him and invited him to dine with them at the local tavern.

Kris at first thanked the group, but told them he had to get his possessions to Tilburg, as he had children waiting for him. The elves pressed him further and said that what they had to say to him may help him reach a great many more children than just in Tilburg and Eindhoven. They also explained that they had been seeking him for months and throughout the country. Kris finally agreed to have lunch with them and they all went to the tavern.

Once they sat down, it was an awkward beginning, as the elves didn't quite know where or how to start. They had spent so much time searching for the man, but never truly discussed how they would initiate the conversation once they found him. They were still apprehensive about sharing too much of their life in the North Pole, in case they decided against asking this stranger to join them, so they tried to speak in generalities. Likewise, Kris wasn't sure what business they wanted with him, and while he was polite, he was a little impatient to continue on his way.

They found common ground when Ella asked Kris why he traveled around giving gifts to children and then watched as Kris' eyes lit up immediately. He explained that his ancestor had instructed as far back as 300 A.D., on how God so loved the world that he gave the greatest gift of all to the world. A child, a simple gift that would forever change much of the world and its beliefs. As Kris was the tenth descendant of the great St. Nicholas, he wanted children to know that they were still loved. So like his forefathers before him, he brought gifts to as many as he could, and especially during December to remind them of God's gift. He said that between making, securing and delivering the gifts, his efforts filled the entire year, but it was around Christmas when he tried to have the biggest impact.

He explained that many children lose their innocent nature too soon, and he wanted to help them keep a little joy even if just during his one visit each year. The elves and Kris got into a very animated and spirited discussion about children, and what made them the most special of all God's creatures. Forrest talked about how the best of any creature could be found in the eyes of a child. Denny regaled his stories about the joy of a child's expression in every sweet cake he gave them. Even Carrow who is normally of a stern nature, talked about the wonderment of a child as they handled one of the carefully constructed toys they were given.

The elves saw in Kris the virtues they had hoped; a strong and loving heart, a child's amazement of the earth and heavens, an innocence untarnished by the hardships of the world, and a vitality and enthusiasm that seemed boundless. With an indiscernible nod to each other, the elves began to talk in hushed tones about a wondrous land that was built almost entirely to serve children. They told Kris of their mission to find him and invite him to the

North Pole.

Kris listened enraptured about the amazing things they were saying about the North Pole. Of course he had many misgivings about making such an argent journey to such a faraway place and during such an inhospitable time. Also, if he went he would need to bring his wife, and there were still the children in Tilburg that needed their toys, and what of Christmas coming? This time the elves were ready and met each of Kris' concerns with a solution.

It was finally agreed that first, they would assist Kris in delivering his toys to the children in Tilburg, then they would meet his wife and discuss the North Pole in more detail with both of them. Finally, if they both agreed, the elves would send another delegation to the Kringle's after Christmas, and they would all make the journey then. The elves promised to bring very special clothing that would keep them both safe and warm during the trip.

After spending a great deal of time on the journey to Tilburg with Kris and then meeting Mrs. Kringle, the delegation was even more certain that they had made the right decision. Ann Marie Kringle was warm and enchanting with an easy smile and laugh, like her husband. They both seemed so very...jolly! They were comfortable to be around and they had an easy spirit wrapped in a blanket of endless faith. All had agreed to the plan as laid out by the elves and set the date to begin right after the Epiphany, on January 7th of the New Year.

This accord would change history around the world

for billions of children everywhere.

Chapter Two

If people would only credit our minds instead of our stature, the world would find us very tall indeed.

- Frederick Salsbury

The Journey

On January 7th, 1780, just as promised, five elves knocked on the temporary home of Kris and Ann Marie Kringle. You see, Kris and Annie, as Kris called her, moved around so much through so many countries that they never had a permanent home. This was all about to change.

The elves on the other side of the door were different than the first group that Kris and Annie met.

Apparently it was decided that since the trip would take a good period of time, that elves skilled in other developments should accompany the Kringles during their trip up North. One of these was Carrow's wife, Ulzana Stitchnsew who was an accomplished seamstress and tailor. Ulzana looked weathered and wrinkled, but Kris sensed the strength in this woman and thought many people would misjudge her age and willingness. She walked slightly bent but her eyes were sharp and clear, and her movements succinct.

She presented travel clothes to the Kringles. They were beautiful and seemed quite warm. Ann Marie got a heavy full length dress of green velvet with fur lining around the front, bottom and pockets. It came with an extensive overcoat to match and a heavy fur hat.

Kris received a heavy bright red woolen pair of pants and matching coat. His too, was trimmed in fur in the front and around the pockets. He joked that the bright color would certainly draw looks from everyone. He also received a matching overcoat and very heavy fur-lined boots that went all the way up to his knees. He thought they were a little tall for his comfort and rolled the tops down to around his calves. The inside fur of the boots matched the fur on the coat.

His hat was long and came to a point with a tassel. Ulzana said that her husband was vague on how big Kris' head was, so she thought she would leave plenty of extra to trim off. Kris thought the extra material was fine and said it would do nicely to cover his face. With that, Ulzana pulled a long strip of fur from her bag and with remarkable speed that belayed her age, sewed it around the bottom of the hat to match the ensemble. She said it should keep Santa's brow and head warm.

The other elves that accompanied them on their journey were Stacey Buttons, the elves best doll maker; Jamie Hardrock, the chief miner who supplied the settlement with coal for their fires; Willie Movinmuch, the elves principal transportation specialist; and me, Alfie Newsworthy, the elves historian and record keeper.

Stacey was as spry and bouncy as Ulzana was old. She always talked in excited tones and the Kringles almost got the feeling that she was brought along for enthusiasm and comic relief. She had red hair that fell just past her shoulders and a clear, smooth face that showed a few freckles. Ann Marie thought she looked like a doll herself and wondered if she patterned her creations after the mirror image of herself.

Jamie looked somewhat like the Leprechauns Kris has heard about in Ireland. He also had red hair with a round red beard to match. He had a brightness to his eyes that showed he enjoyed life and was pleased to be here. He spoke with a bit of a brogue as well, but could make his meaning plain. His hands and nails were blackish from his line of work, but he was clean overall and there was no soot or dirt on his clothing. Like Forrest from the last group, Kris sensed that Jamie was here as much for the load bearing as for the leadership.

Now how to describe me while we are at it? My face is a series of angles and points. I have a long nose, a distinctly pointed chin, pointed ears and even my head seems to come to a point. I have great tufts of white hair that are undisciplined and seem to go every direction. I also wear half moon glasses that I need if anything on paper is presented to me.

Willie Movinmuch has short cropped brown hair and a thin mustache. He has an unmistakable intelligence that you could tell existed just by looking at him. His eyes are keen and miss nothing, and while he is somewhat unremarkable in his features, there is something that draws you to him just the same. He moves with deliberateness and is very sure of everything he does. Kris found him fascinating, and had a hard time to not stare at this elf.

Willie asked Kris if he and Ann Marie were accomplished riders, which they were. Kris said he often would take a boat to Spain and then ride a great steed up into France, Germany and so on for his deliveries.

We had arranged two horses for the Kringles, and Willie had constructed a cart and secured donkeys to carry the elves and the Kringles other belongings. We said that because of the great distance we would be traveling that we may be gone for quite some time. Once the cart was loaded and secured, we all set out across the landscape riding ever north.

During the trip we discussed many things. The topics ranged from the making of toys, gathering of foods and sewing clothing for the children, to more complicated things. Such as the items we had at the North Pole, and what needed to be continually imported, to some of our modes of transportation, which were different from their land. Willie used the word "outmoded" on more than one occasion.

Willie said that some amazing things had been constructed up north, but he would wait until they got there to explain, as it probably wouldn't make too much sense to them now.

I relayed the story of the great migration of the elves to the North Pole, and how so many were pushed to go there at the very same time.

Kris offered that maybe God put the thought in their collective heads as he had with the Jews during the exile from Egypt. I shrugged and said whether God or a collective consciousness, we all seemed to be motivated to make the change and head to the same destination.

"Good thing too," stated Stacey, "otherwise we might have frozen to death before we ever built the first building."

Annie asked how they survived during that first year and since, especially during the harsh winter?

Jamie said that they all brought everything they could carry or drag with them including livestock, tools and possessions.

I said, "Yes, we shared everything and it was quite a communal project from the start." After a period, I explained we had learned many secrets of the North Pole, and with our collective ingenuity we were able to begin amassing many things to make our lives more bearable.

"Believe it or not," said Stacey, "We have a few months that are reasonably temperate reaching 16 to 21 Celsius [60's to 70's Fahrenheit]. Of course we don't announce that fact very often to outsiders."

When we had reached a town called Zevenbergen, north of Breda, we arrived at a dock on one of the inland rivers, there was moored a small ship guarded by two of our other elves. Skippy Seaworthy, the captain, was making nautical preparations and his first mate, Hardy

Wavebreaker, was attending to the lines and manning the single sail of the ship. Kris commented that a lone sail would probably take them forever to reach the polar ice cap. We all just looked at each other and grinned.

After everything was stored and everyone made comfortable, Hardy cast off the lines and pushed the boat away from the dock. Once we were far enough away from the shore and out of sight of land, Hardy lowered the sail.

Suddenly with a loud noise that caused both Kris and Annie to leap to their feet in terror, the ship began sailing under its own power and very quickly, too.

Willie came to the Kringles aid and told them to be calm, that the elves had discovered a form of combustible power that made almost every transportation mode much faster and easier to move products and food across huge expanses with minimal fuss and time.

I came up to Willie and excitedly said, "Tell them about the livestock and the winged machines."

Willie said, "I think we should wait until later."

Kris interjected, "It sounds like we have a great deal more to learn than what I first thought, and perhaps you should clue us in on anything you can. What are winged machines and what about your livestock?"

Willie shrugged, "Well we find when we give certain feed to some of our livestock they seem to become weightless and begin floating through the air. We haven't figured out what value that has right now, but it is kind of fun to watch, and it makes it easy to move them from one pasture to another. We also have discovered the power of flight and have large aerial machines that can move products and people from one area to another through the sky."

Kris said, "Surely you are mocking us now, trying to see just how gullible we are. We know if such machines were in use we would have heard about or seen them."

"There are a great many things we hide from the populations of other countries," commented Jamie, who had just walked over to our group. "And there is a great expanse we must cross to even see any other inhabitants, which keeps many of our inventions protected from prying eyes."

Kris laughed and said, well that may be well and fine, but they will never get him to move through the sky, that was the bird's domain and he was happy to leave it to them.

Willie shuffled his feet, cleared his throat and said, "Well then you are going to have a very long walk, because that is how we intend to get you to your final destination."

Kris looked crestfallen as if this whole trip had been in vain. He looked over at Annie who was grinning like a Cheshire cat.

"Oh, imagine Kris, being able to fly like a bird and see things as God sees things!" She was clearly animated at the thought and went on, "I am certain that these clever folk would not risk our lives after taking us so far if it were not perfectly safe."

Willie jumped on her words, "Absolutely not! We have been using these for many years with nary a mishap!"

Jamie and I glared at Willie, and tried to settle the look of concern that came over Kris' face at the word 'nary'.

"What he means," I quickly said, "is that these are quite safe and we worked the problems out of our machines long ago."

"Look at what they did to this craft," said an excited Mrs. Kringle, "The advances these people have made are astounding. I can't wait to get there to see the other things they have invented and created!"

"You won't be disappointed there, lass," Captain Seaworthy said, "I thought I had really come up with something when I put their engines into watercraft, but that was just small potatoes to some of the stuff the village has accomplished. Wait until you see the dome."

"And the manufacturing area," piped in Stacey from the other side of the boat.

"How about the time continuum?" yelled out Ulzana from the bow.

"Alright, enough," I yelled sternly, "We don't want to overdo it before we even get them to the village."

The Kringles were trying to follow along, but couldn't begin to grasp a word of the things these elves were shouting about.

The rest of the voyage was relatively quiet, which

was fine since it hardly took anytime at all to reach our next destination under the swift vessel we were on. The waves became choppy as we approached land, but Skippy and Hardy handled the ship expertly and minimized the effects the ocean was throwing at them. We landed on a deserted but windy beach. The Kringles bundled their coats tighter and pulled their hats lower. Of course, we elves seemed to take this in stride and were almost unfazed by the howling wind.

The Captain and mate bid them a fond farewell and said they hoped to see them on another cruise. As we left the ship the wind blew snow all around us and the ship seemed to just vanish. The wind was blowing so hard we couldn't even hear a whisper from the boat's engine.

The Kringles followed closely behind us as they couldn't see five meters in front of them because of the swirling snow. Something large loomed ahead of them, but they could not make out its features. It was much bigger than the ship we just left. As we got closer, Kris could see that it had wings like a massive bird. He was led to a series of steps and as he boarded the great craft he began to tremble, though not from the cold.

Kris was just plain frightened. Did we honestly think this hulking monster could be lighter than air? As the rest of us took our places as we had done many times before, Annie came up and squeezed her husband's arm saying, "Isn't this exciting?"

Kris just mumbled something to the effect that

exciting wasn't the word that came to mind. He turned to Willie as he approached the front of the craft with Jamie and asked, "Are you sure the weather isn't too bad to try this?"

Willie just chuckled and said, "Heck, this is a nice spring day in the North Pole. Wait until we get into a real blizzard!"

Just then, even with the wind howling, Kris heard a sound that made the engine on the ship seem like a guttural burp. Willie was flipping switches and turning dials. He watched as two huge windmill type turbines began to turn on either side of the big ship, and he gave an involuntary shiver.

Stacey said, "Uh, Kris you may want to take a seat until we arrive. It won't take too long."

Kris stumbled to a chair and sat down. Moments later the big ship began to lumber through the driving snow. Shortly thereafter he felt himself jolt into the air. He closed his eyes and gripped the chair with almost superhuman strength.

After a few minutes, which seemed an eternity to Kris, we broke through the clouds into a beautiful blue sky. Ann Marie was watching out the window and her breath caught in her throat. She gasped, but with excitement rather than fear. The clouds looked like giant cotton balls and floated below them effortlessly.

When Kris finally dared to open his eyes he could scarcely grasp what he was seeing. At first hesitant, he inched closer to the window, where his wife sat across from him glued to the scene outside. As they floated across the heavens they felt a shutter and shake run through the craft and Kris came immediately to his feet. "What was that," he fairly screamed.

"Relax, Santa, that was just turbulence, when cold air hits a warm air mass it causes the craft to make an adjustment between them," said Willie from the cockpit.

"What is that," asked Kris.

"Well cold air moves higher in the atmosphere..." began Willie.

"No, you called me something else, what was it?" asked Kris.

"Oh...well, whether you know it or not you are called many names from all the lands you have visited. I originally hailed from Holland and there they call you Sinterklaas or a loose translation in English would be St. Nicholas, and we say Sinter, Santa or Santee for short."

"Well St. Nicholas was my legendary ancestor, but I am no saint myself," explained Kris.

Willie shrugged and said, "Well whatever you believe, popular opinion has branded you as such, and as Shakespeare said, 'A rose by any other name...' You are called in many countries St. Nicholas or Sinterklaas or its local dialect, so you might as well get used to it if you plan to continue spreading joy to children as you do."

Kris thought about Willie's statement. He was slightly uncomfortable about being referred to as a saint and hoped God would not think it blasphemous, but he felt the rest was a term of endearment. Since he never really made a habit of introducing himself in places he visited, other than as an ancestor to his famous relative, he guessed the various names just grew naturally because they didn't know what else to call him.

Kris noticed the nose of the machine beginning to point down and wondered if they had reached their final destination. He didn't need to wait long to find out as the craft started bouncing around as it fought the winds in its descent back into the clouds.

Everyone else was undisturbed with the rocking and bumping going on. Even Annie seemed relatively calm through it all. Kris finally decided that he would not be the only person showing distress during this crazy ride, and that it was really not much worse than riding a particularly clumsy horse, so he pretended to relax and pull his hat lower over his eyes.

With a bang, the skis of the winged machine touched down on the frozen tundra of the North Pole. The ship taxied across the frozen field for a time and then made an about face and roared back toward what looked like a solid wall of snow.

Kris and Annie became more and more concerned as the machine continued its onslaught toward the wall without slowing.

It was Ulzana who came up to Ann Marie and assured her there was nothing to be concerned about. "We are approaching the dome and we will slip right through it in a moment. We are in no danger." she explained.

Kris couldn't help close his eyes again as they sped towards the dome, sure that the whole adventure was going to end right there.

What he heard next was not a crash, but a gasp from his wife, followed by her saying, "Oh, my great heavens. I don't believe it!"

As the great machine revved down its engines, Kris rubbed his eyes as if they were playing tricks on him. The sight was beyond belief, even after all the things he had recently witnessed with our amazing group.

There were buildings of every size and shape, with brightly colored beautiful stained glass on many of the buildings with architectural styles of every kind and culture imaginable. He found himself gasping at the sight. And everywhere he looked were people no bigger than his companions.

We had arrived at the elves village in the North Pole.

Chapter Three

The power of any society rest on not who is the strongest,
but how all may pull together to accomplish great things.

- Carrow Chekitwice

The Council of Elves

The whole trip in the boat and flying machine took us less time than it did to get from one village to the next in the Netherlands. Kris thought it was truly amazing that people could travel so quickly.

When we exited the flying machine, the Kringles stood trying to take in the sights they were witnessing. Every building has a specific purpose just like in the rest of the world, but the busyness of each structure went at a breakneck pace, compared to the tallfolk's culture.

Even with all the bustle, things came to a grinding halt as the residents looked over our guests.

I said to Kris and Annie, "You will have to forgive them, you are the first tallfolk to ever visit the North Pole. They do not mean any harm or malice."

"Yes," said Ella, "News of your imminent arrival had spread throughout the village before we were packing to leave."

From earlier discussions, the Kringles knew what tallfolk referred to, and of the mistrust and dealings the elves had with big people before moving to the village.

Many of the villagers just stared and whispered to each other at the people before them.

"Well, come on, we will get you situated at the inn. We will have your possessions sent along to you shortly," said Willie.

We walked off with the Kringles in tow. Ann Marie and Kris kept slowing as they looked inside and over each of the buildings they passed.

"Have you ever seen such beautiful work?" asked Annie. "This is the most remarkable craftsmanship I have ever seen. And that is just the structures themselves, imagine what they can produce inside these stores that we can't see?" questioned Kris.

They approached a multi-gabled building with doors befitting a castle and turrets on and around every corner. We opened one of the great wooden doors and ushered the Kringles inside.

There was a large counter albeit short in stature at one end of the vestibule and a huge roaring fireplace at the other. The inside was toasty and the Kringles immediately started pulling off their outer coats and hats. From a corner behind the counter came a seemingly young man who walked to the center of the desk and said, "Ah, so the Kringles have finally arrived. We have your room ready and waiting for you, and I will have Wilhelm take you to it." The young man rang a bell and another elf came out from somewhere behind the wall and walked up to the Kringles.

"Good day mienherr, I am Wilhelm. I shall be pleased to take you to your room," the elf stated.

"Thank you, good sir, we will be happy to follow," said Kris with a slight bow. They bid us goodbye for the moment and went with Wilhelm.

The room was beautiful and featured another large fireplace which held a strong fire that warmed the expanse of the room. Off to the side was a bedroom that contained a separate bathing area. It was as grand as any place Kris had ever stayed, and much grander than most.

Wilhelm said, "Dinner shall be served at 6:30, approximately two hours from now in the dining room downstairs. You will have other guests from the village joining you there and they will discuss your schedule at that time." He then clicked his heels, and with a slight but curt bow, closed the door behind him as he left.

The Kringles were still reeling from the trip and all the things they recently witnessed. "I hope I can be ready in a couple hours for anything else, I feel exhausted to my core," said Kris.

"I think I would like to lie down for a moment," said Annie, "Perhaps we will feel better if we could just quit moving for a few moments." She laid down on the bed and was fast asleep before Kris could return a comment.

Kris just chuckled to himself and decided he better not make himself too comfortable as his result might be the same. He felt he could sleep straight through until tomorrow if he closed his eyes at all right now.

Kris went into the washing station and went to splash some water on his eyes. He looked around for a pitcher, but found nothing but a strange looking device attached to the bowl before him. He had never seen anything like this at all inns he had visited. He almost jumped when he turned the spigot and water began flowing without so much as a pump. "Amazing," he said to himself, "Wait until Annie sees this." Then he noticed the porcelain bowl sitting on the floor next to the sink and began to inspect it as well. When he pulled the plunger and flushed the commode he nearly shrieked. This was amazing, no outhouses for this trip!

After revitalizing himself with the water and relieving himself, he looked outside the window to the street below. He watched as vehicles without the aid of horses or mules moved up and down the street loaded with goods. He saw elves running to and fro into the buildings with great armloads of products. He watched the scene for what seemed to be a very long time when he felt Annie's hand take his shoulder and give it a squeeze. He turned to look at his wife who was smiling and looking much refreshed from her rest.

"You will not believe some of the things I am seeing down there," said Kris, "They have inventions and ways that no one has ever conceived."

"I would imagine there is a great deal more to this place than we will understand for a while," Annie said softly to her husband, "I read a book a few months back by an author named Swift, Jonathan Swift I think. He wrote about a sailor who found himself shipwrecked on another land. These people were tiny miniatures of himself, but had a thriving culture. I feel a great deal like he must have when he awoke to find himself in an entirely different world, amazed by his surroundings."

Kris chuckled and said, "Well they are not THAT small."

Annie playfully hit her husband's arm, "That's not what I meant. It is just that we have been brought to an exciting new world and it seems we have left the one we knew to discover an entirely different one."

"And you make a point. Do you think now that they have brought us here, and now that we have become witness to their advances, will we ever be allowed to leave in peace?" asked Kris.

"I wonder if the bigger question is whether we would want to? They have advances here to make life infinitely more comfortable and easier. Imagine what they may house inside those buildings?" she asked.

"Yes, wait until you see the washing area. You truly may not ever want to leave, ho, ho, ho!"

"Ah, there's that laugh I've missed so much! That is the first time I have heard it in months my husband. I was beginning to think you had lost your humor forever."

Kris smirked, "Well you know I put a lot of effort into getting the gifts put together and off to the children by Christmas. The world can be such a hard place, and to see them smile and laugh even for a moment....," he said trailing off, "I wonder if these inventive people might be able to assist me in my endeavors?"

Annie thought for a moment and replied, "What if we were brought here for just such a purpose? Talking with Stacey Buttons, it sounds as if they have similar prospects to ours and want to give children joy as well."

"That would truly be something," said Kris.

Just then there was a knock on their door. Wilhelm and the elf that was behind the desk were on the other side with the Kringle's belongings. As they carried the trunks inside Wilhelm asked if everything was satisfactory. They both answered enthusiastically that everything was wonderful and the elves said they were pleased.

Wilhelm reminded them that dinner would be ready in 30 minutes and that they please join their party then.

Thirty minutes later the Kringles came down the steps into the vast lobby of the inn. The elf behind the desk, whose name was Gunther Crispenclean, led his guests to the back of the inn where they saw a large banquet table lined by a variety of elves, some of which they already knew. Besides myself, Carrow, Ulzana, Denny, Whitey, and Willie were all there, but many others the Kringles had not met before. Among them were Denny's wife Priscilla, Keeney Eagleye, Randy Woodturner, Pastor Goinpeace, and two of Carrow and Ulzana's sons, Ford and Ezra among others.

The head of the table and the seat on the right were

reserved for the Kringles. Kris took the head chair and sat down. He thanked them all for their hospitality and offered to say grace before the meal began. After everyone bowed their heads and Kris gave a simple blessing, with the Pastor smiling broadly, Kris smiled and said how much they were enjoying their stay.

Carrow was the first to speak for the elves. He thanked the Kringles for making the long journey to their village and said that as tallfolk they were welcome to be the first of their kind to the elves' establishment.

At that opening, Kris asked exactly why they were invited to this propitious location?

Denny jumped in and said that because of Kris' generosity toward others, specifically children, which the elves were hoping to consult with the Kringles as to how their village might better serve the children of the world along with Kris.

"As you now know, there are many advancements that we have made that could assist you in accomplishing our mutual desires. We have asked you here because we found long ago that to share ideas and ingenuity produces amazing results," said Denny.

"If the miracles we have seen thus far are any indication, then your minds are far mightier than mine, and I could do little to improve your lot," stated Kris humbly.

Willie responded, "It is not always additional genius we seek, often it is just a matter of figuring how to proceed. I think the Council will enlighten you in ways you can only imagine."

"The Council?" asked Kris.

Carrow interrupted Willie, "Yes we would like to invite you to meet with our Council of Elves tomorrow morning for an exchange of thoughts and ideas. We have several questions and thoughts that we wish to review with you."

"Perhaps," Denny jumped in, "The Kringles would like a day to collect themselves and have a tour of the village. Mr. Kringle might be better refreshed if he were allowed a day to recuperate from his long trip."

Carrow answered, "I believe it would be better to meet with the Council prior to providing tours for the Kringles and filling their heads with more then can be reasonably absorbed in one day. Once we have concluded our official business there would be more time for pleasantries."

Denny thought to argue the point further but saw Carrow had set his jaw against further discussion on the topic. *You can be of such ill humor sometimes, Carrow Chekitwice*, thought Denny. He shrugged his shoulders and asked Kris if he thought 10:00 tomorrow morning would be acceptable?

"That would be fine with me. Is Mrs. Kringle also invited?" asked Kris.

"That is completely up to both of you," answered Whitey, "With the outsiders of this village the women have little influence, but here we find that many of our brightest minds are of the female persuasion. Ann Marie, you would be a welcome breath of fresh air to our proceedings."

"My, how refreshing!" exclaimed Ann Marie, "I would certainly be pleased to accompany my husband if that is his wish."

Kris took his wife's hand, kissed it, and said, "As the gentleman said, you would be 'a breath of fresh air' that I would welcome."

With that decided, questions were asked and answered about their trip, Kris asked when and how some of the things the Kringles witnessed had come about, more introductions were extended around the table, and a general feeling of ease filled the room.

Early the next morning, there was another knock at the door. Ulzana came by to offer new clothes to the Kringles that "would be more suited to the custom of our village and help you stand out less." She also suggested that a bath would help the Kringles relax before the meeting and showed them how to use the large tub in the washing station.

Kris had begun to argue that baths were not healthy, and Ulzana cut him off immediately and told him that had been the nonsensical musings from his civilization and that the elves had learned long ago that the complete opposite was true. She also advised them that breakfast would be brought to their room shortly to allow them to bathe and dress at a more leisurely pace.

With that she was gone and the Kringles just

shrugged and decided which of them would bathe first.

As with their traveling clothes, they found the new set of clothing fit beautifully and were much more comfortable and warm than their traditional clothes. They were cut in a less traditional style than the stiff tight clothing of the European variety. These more resembled the clothes of shepherds and farmers and were much easier to move in. In fact, they marveled at how easy it was to move in these garments and how well they fit.

At 10:00 sharp they entered the halls that they were guided to from the inn. The Kringles were met at the door by Whitey Slippenfall who asked them to follow him. They entered a large hall with several chairs in the center. Around the circumference of the room was a raised balcony with several elves seated in a semicircle.

There sat Denny, Carrow, Whitey, Ella, and Ulzana along with several new elves. They were then introduced to Britney Clearwater, Frederick Salsbury, Frieda Cutinglass, and Jackson Kilowatt. They were briefly told, as best as possible, what the responsibilities and departments each elf was over.

Britney handled the water works and controlled the flow and melt of ice for the North Pole, Frederick handled commerce with outsiders and controlled import/export matters, Frieda was an artist that designed and produced much of the stained glass and other decorations throughout the village, and Jackson was the overseer of power at the North Pole which included producing fluids and something called current which allowed most of the machinery to run in the village and elsewhere.

The elves thanked the Kringles again for coming to the village and hoped they were enjoying their visit. Denny complimented them on how well they looked in their clothing and joked about how they looked more like elves now.

With a loud clearing of his throat, Carrow said that was enough of the platitudes for there was business to be conducted here, and they should get down to it.

His abruptness caught everyone off guard, and it was Frederick who reminded Carrow that the Kringles were not on trial here, and that they had been invited by this Council. Denny also reminded Carrow that everything that had been said and seen about the Kringles was very complimentary and that they should be afforded all manner of respect.

Carrow, said, "Yes, yes, but we have much to discuss and we need to get to it. We need to decide our course of action going forward, if there is to be any at all."

The Kringles watched in silent contemplation the exchange that took place before them and at Carrow's last statement Kris blanched and said, "Excuse me, 'course of action'? Are we in some type of trouble here?"

With the exception of Carrow they all began to vigorous shake their heads. "Of course not," stated Whitey, who had taken his place with the other members, "We have had many discussions about dealing with the tallfolk, excuse me, your civilization, and are wondering how best to move forward."

Britney sat higher and said, "You see we have many dealings with people of all nations outside our lands, but we also hold most of our accomplishments in check because of misuse with some of our discoveries with your civilization in prior years."

"We acquire many things from tallfolk," continued Jackson, "And we enjoy as you do providing treats and gifts to the children of the tallfolk, as much as we do our own. But we wish to remain anonymous with our presents and are trying to find an equitable way to meet our goals without getting too much exposure or notice from tallfolk."

"You see Mr. Kringle dealings with tallfolk and elves have not gone well in the past, or even recently, for that matter," growled Carrow.

"Please call me Kris, and my wife Ann Marie. And yes, we were informed how you were mistreated before, but not all tallfolk are bad and some are just not well informed outside of their own lives." said Kris, "And children are completely innocent in all this. They have hardships that I suspect your own children are ignorant of, which I am pleased to say."

"Let me ask you this Kris and Ann Marie, you have long been providing for children, and in many lands, how do you accomplish this?" asked Britney.

Kris shuffled his foot a little and started to speak, then stopped. They waited as he tried to formulate his answer. He tried to begin again and paused.

Whitey said, "Before you speak, Kris, let me caution you. The principle policy of this Council, and all that come before it, is that we invoke the law of "sincere speech". This simply means that there is no embellishment, omissions or outright lying allowed in this hall. If you are discovered not being of sincere speech and are an elf, you can be punished up to and including banishment from the village. While you are both from outside our walls, we expect you to honor our laws."

"Kris never lies and he's very rich," said Annie flatly.

"I'm sorry?" said Frieda.

Annie went on, "Kris' family has always been wealthy, which was why his ancestor began giving gifts and helping others. The Bishop of Myra was an orphan, but his parents were wealthy beyond measure. It all began with the Bishop dropping gold into stockings of a poor merchant who had three daughters and no dowries. During that period, if one could not marry their daughters off with a dowry, they would have to be sold into prostitution, so St. Nicholas dropped three bags of gold at night into the daughter's stockings as they dried by the fire.

"St. Nicholas eventually gave most of his belongings and treasure to others but an interesting thing then happened. The more the Bishop gave, the more he received. People began taking up collections to help St. Nicholas, then subsequently his heirs, provide for others.

Many times, noblemen and merchants would force gifts of food, gold and other things upon the heirs of St. Nicholas. Even when Kris' ancestor changed the family name to Kringle to separate the, by then, famous St. Nicholas from his family, it still continued. His grandfather changed the name because of the guilt of all the gifts, certainly not shame, of being St. Nicholas' ancestor.

"This is also why the family kept migrating across many lands. And it continues today. Kris will give gifts to families in need, someone will hear about it and insist to help replace the presents in some small measure. As much as Kris has given, he has received more than he can give. That's why we know that there are many tallfolk, as you call us, that are kinder than you might ever believe."

The Council sat quietly staring at the lady before them. Even Carrow's eyes had softened and he actually began to smile. He looked at Kris and said, "That's some kind of problem you have."

With that the entire room erupted in chuckles and laughter, and when Kris bellowed his Ho, Ho, Ho the whole room exploded further with a new round of guffaws.

Kris related that his bigger problem was trying to gather food and gifts for the children from the towns and villages, as many of them were poor themselves, and could not provide the goods he needed. He said that because of wars and other problems in the various lands, scarcity was now the norm everywhere he went. He said the politics and egos of the ruling classes had caused shortages of every kind. The elves began to look at each other and nod heads and wink as he spoke.

After a few more questions about the types and quantities of the presents he normally bestowed, the Council asked the Kringles if they might be so good as to wait in the foyer of the hall while they had a brief discussion. They did as they were asked, even though they were unsure as to the reasoning or what this discussion consisted of.

About a half hour later, Denny came out to the Kringles and asked them to return to the hall. He sat down next to Mrs. Kringle as Frederick cleared his throat and began to speak.

"Kris and Ann Marie, we have a very successful commerce here in the North Pole, and we have capabilities that we are sure will truly amaze you. We are able to create a supply of goods that could allow you to visit every child everywhere and provide at least a little something to make them happier in their plight. Be they rich or poor, boy or girl, they could receive something to gladden their hearts.

"We would like to discuss how we can help you give to your hearts desire to children. We have some details that must be worked through and we have some thoughts that might make this task you are trying to accomplish easier, but this will take more conversations with certain elves around the village. While we are having these discussions we would like to provide you a tour of the village and allow you to see some things, so that you know what I am saying is sincere speech.

"Our only restriction is that no matter what you see up here, you are not allowed to speak of it in your civilization. This is for two reasons, the first is that we are concerned about what others would try to do with much of what we have already perfected, and the second and more likely, is that we do not wish to see you or your lovely wife locked up for lunacy. We are sure you would be accused of losing your mind and spouting flagrant exaggerations to your world if you tried to describe and explain our machinery."

At this last statement Kris chuckled to himself, assured that Frederick was completely right on that score. He still scarcely believed what he had seen up to this point himself.

Frederick continued, "We wish to invite you both to return here tomorrow afternoon once you have had some time to see the rest of the North Pole and speak with some of the other elves. We will make certain the entire village makes you welcome and answer any questions you may have about our innovations and procedures. We will have some of our own answers and an offer to lay before you at that time."

Denny turned to them and said, "What Frederick is saying is that your wishes are our wishes, and we want you to be our representative to the world to make it a better place for all, tallfolk and elves, alike."

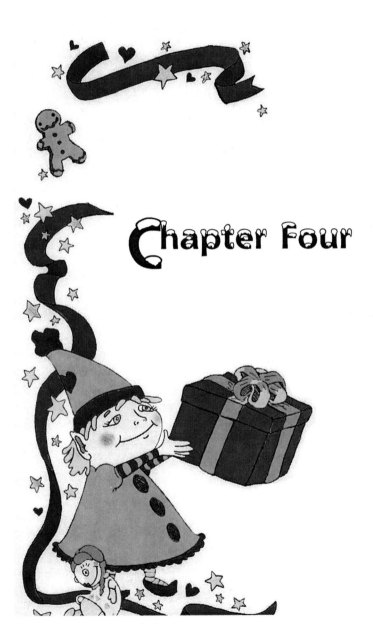

Chapter Four

Santa Claus is anyone who loves another and seeks to make them happy; who gives himself by thought or word or deed in every gift that he bestows.

- Edwin Osgood Grover

The Offer

Before being escorted from the great hall, it was decided by the Council that Frederick Salsbury would be the Kringle's tour guide, as he was most familiar with outside commerce and the importing and exporting of goods with the tallfolk. Frederick was a very pleasant elf with sandy brown hair that just came to his collar and had a wisp that ran over part of his forehead. His eyes were a soft green and like Kris' had a twinkle to them. He was average elf height and solidly built, but not plump.

Frederick stated that he had spent almost as much time in the outside world each year as he did in the village. He had set up warehouses and trading routes through most of the more civilized countries and even in such remote continents as Central and South America and Africa, especially along what is referred to as the Ivory Coast where the North Pole's biggest import – cocoa – came from.

"We import more cocoa to this village than the next three countries, including the Netherlands and Belgium," Frederick laughed, "For what reason I can't explain, but we all seem to have an addiction to the stuff. We drink more cocoa and eat more chocolate than anything else." He shook his head and said, "If anyone wanted to cripple us mentally or economically they would just have to cut off our supply of cocoa and we would be on our knees."

Annie said, "That's funny, Kris has that same affinity, although we don't get that much of it as it is not readily available to many areas we visit."

"Well enjoy as much as you care to here, we have a goodly supply." Then turning to the matter at hand, Frederick stated, "Now where to start. Hmm, I guess the best place would be the manufacturing area."

"I'm sorry what are you referring to, a place or a section?" asked Kris.

"It is an area where we can produce products on a global scale as the need arises," Frederick said in a matter-of-fact tone, "We find anything that has a similar series of movements or parts can be done in a line of workers that we call an 'assembly line' and the task can be repeated an infinite number of times until we have enough finished products to meet the need for it."

Kris and Annie nodded their heads as if they understood, though they clearly didn't.

Frederick said, "Come with me and I'll show you." He took the Kringles to an enormous building that looked to go along a great distance. Even for its size, it still looked whimsical and colorful with multiple roof lines and carved features along its length.

"Behold," said Frederick as he ushered them through the door, "Our manufacturing center."

The Kringles were dumbstruck. There before them were several rows of elves, each row working on different products and pieces. There was a doll line on one, sanding and finishing pull-toys on another, and a third producing horse drawn carriages.

"You make carriages?" said Kris breathlessly.

"We are considered the best carriage maker in either London or Paris!" boasted Frederick, "Of course no one knows they come from here, for practical reasons. We actually have several shops in many of the larger cities, and we are opening one in Philadelphia in the American Colonies later this year."

"But how do you get them down there?" questioned Annie, "Especially through that great expanse. They won't fit on that flying machine, will they?"

"No," answered Frederick, "But we have many other ways to transport them over the tundra besides the air ships. You shall see that later. Just know that whatever we can build, we can also move, including almost anything you can imagine, and some things I scarcely say that you could not."

"I have little doubt of it," muttered Kris. "Are there more of these structures?"

"Yes, we have two more, and we find that is sufficient since we can change out the line and build something else as the need arises in each place. We can take a closer look if you'd like."

Kris just deftly nodded and began moving toward the center line. As he came to the end of the line he looked at racks filled with toy upon toy all made to perfection and painted into different characters, some clowns, some soldiers, some jesters but all brightly colored and waiting for little hands to pull their strings and bring them to life.

"Amazing," said Annie, "Who are they all for?"

Frederick's eyes got wide and he said, "For the children! Wherever we go and what ever country we find ourselves in, we carry bags and bags of these to give to children around the world."

"How many of these can you make?" asked Kris.

"How many children are there in the world?" answered Frederick. "We can do at least one per child, and a few for adults if they are kind to us," he chuckled.

"Impossible," stammered Kris.

"You will find that the word 'impossible' has little meaning up here. For nothing to us is impossible. And we have advances, and have been affected by our environment, more than you could know or believe. For instance, many of us are hundreds of years old and we outlive you tallfolk by centuries."

Kris just stared at the smaller man and said, "Surely you jest! You must be about what...? Forty or forty five?"

Frederick smiled and said, "You are close, I will be 357 this March. And in fact, I was much older physically when I first got here. I actually had a respiration problem when I first arrived that has since disappeared. While tallfolk haven't been here before, I wouldn't be surprised if you don't leave here feeling better than when you arrived."

Annie said, "About all I feel is light headed trying to grasp everything."

"Oh, I am so sorry! I should take you both for some food and maybe we should sit and talk a while before I show you much more," a sincerely apologetic Frederick said to his guests, "How ill-mannered of me."

"Not at all," feigned Kris, "But a little rest and food does sound wonderful."

The trio moved to a smaller establishment between two of the massive buildings. It was similar to a tavern but looked more impressive and many of the surfaces gleamed silver-like around the place.

"This village must be rich if you can afford to make your cookware and stoves from silver," commented Kris.

With a little laugh the elf commented, "They are not, they are actually metal alloys that have yet to be discovered by your civilization. We find that they conduct heat better than iron and can be better insulated to retain heat and cook more evenly."

Kris shook his head and exclaimed, "I may never begin to understand even a fraction of the developments you have here."

The elf laughed and said, "Oh, given sufficient

time you will. But think of the fun you would have learning about them if you decided to take the time to do so!"

Annie smirked and said, "I certainly wouldn't mind learning. These advancements are fascinating to me."

"You always were the adventurous one, my little Annie," Kris said smiling at his wife.

"Is that so, then who is it that has dragged us all around Europe and middle Asia, my husband?" chortled Annie.

Frederick watched the exchange with a broad smile. He was enjoying the playfulness between the couple and felt a warmth toward these two that he had not in his dealings with other tallfolk.

Kris saw the elf staring at them and blushed with a mumbled apology.

"Don't be absurd," grinned Frederick, "I am enjoying watching you both immensely! You remind me of many elves up here, and I am only sorry to say that I do not see such playful spontaneity in my travels among tallfolk more often."

Annie teased Frederick, "Well maybe we are elves that just grew too tall while down south!"

"Probably so," laughed Frederick, "You sure act more like us than them!"

An elf with long braids and freckles walked up to them and asked what they would like for supper.

Annie said, "What is your special of the day?"

The elf giggled and said, "Pretty much whatever you are in the mood for."

Annie thought for a moment while Kris ordered roast beef and Yorkshire pudding. Frederick ordered salmon with capers and asparagus. Finally Annie ordered a roast chicken with stuffing.

All three requested a cup of cocoa as well. The elf smiled and said thank you and moved off.

"What a delightful idea!" exclaimed Mrs. Kringle, "Order what you are in the mood for, but how can they do that, most inns and taverns can scarcely prepare one meal in a day?"

"Again, we have some very unique ways of cooking up here, so preparing many different dishes requires far less effort and time than even one meal in other places," answered Frederick.

Instantly, the young waitress returned with three steaming mugs of cocoa. As they each savored the wonderful aroma and taste. Kris looked at Frederick with a smile.

"Alright," he said, "Explain some of the other advances and we'll try to keep up with your conversation." He was particularly interested in hearing more, now that the needs of food and rest were being tended to.

Meanwhile, in other places across the North Pole Village elves were murmuring to each other and in whispers wondered if the Council would actually propose the things they had heard. Of course as with any civilization, even one so advanced as this, what began as rumor soon was talked about as fact.

Many a debate began across the village as to what the outcome would be from having tallfolk brought to the village. Would this destroy their quiet way of life? Would the tallfolk invade the land and claim the elves advances for their own?

Some villagers had never been outside the dome, but had heard the stories about the evil, warring ways of the tallfolk. Many thought anyone outside the North Pole were barbarians and with no manners or culture remotely close to the elves.

It was already a problem that the outsiders had many of the things they needed for the North Pole, and to have to send many of their own folk to trade and deal with the tallfolk was bad enough...

Others knew better and tried to disseminate the fears of the other elves. They explained that a great many cities and towns were lovely to visit and had wonderful architectural marvels that created the basis of the elves own buildings and that for the most part, the people were good.

And the Council obviously thought that these two

were exceptionally worthy to invite them here in the first place. Further, that if they were going to continue to make advances, that like it or not, they would have to work with the outside world.

Many asked what better way to deal with the outlanders than to have an emissary that was like them, and one that loved children as much as they must be an ideal candidate.

And so while the Kringles were introduced to the modern advancements of the elves, their fate was being discussed outside the walls of the tavern.

"You see we have gone far beyond iron, bronze and the metals you are familiar with, and have developed metals that have much more strength, tensile flexibility and durability than those. We can create almost anything from these metals," related Frederick.

"Add to that the insulation materials we have developed and we can trap and control heat, cold and other elements by just turning a switch and having it powered by current or the odorless gas that we found is in abundance under the Arctic Circle."

The Kringles were in awe at much of what the elf was relaying to them. Kris was asking questions as fast as the elf could explain the principles. Frederick thought they were both extremely bright and were grasping much of what he was saying faster than he suspected most could from their civilization. They also had a wonderment and curiosity that he found stimulating.

Annie finally asked the question Frederick knew eventually would be asked, "Why is it that you don't allow your inventions and wonderful properties to be developed outside the North Pole?"

Frederick had rehearsed his answer several times in his head, but still had trouble answering her at first, "It all began when we were dealing with folks in Asia, China to be specific. We found out that they were having great difficulty moving some of the huge rock to create farmland for their people. Also, they needed better materials to build roads to move their goods through the huge expanse. We showed them how to mix charcoal, sulfur and potassium nitrate together to assist in their quarrying efforts.

"Gunpowder," said Kris.

"Precisely," nodded Frederick, "Within a year they were using it against their neighbors, the Mongols, in newly developed weapons. Shortly thereafter it showed up in other countries and always with the same primary purpose. And in every instance since, when we bring one of our advances to your civilization, it has found its way into military applications."

"If I remember correctly, the Mongols were the aggressors in that conflict, and the Chinese were just trying to protect themselves," Kris said flatly.

"And besides, how could cooking items harm people?" asked Annie.

"Imagine the weapons and ammunition a stronger, lighter alloy could form?" responded Frederick.

"Kris, do you honestly think civilizations are going to continue to war against each other forever?" asked a dejected Annie to her husband.

"Well it has often seemed that way, look at North America and Europe; they have been in one land dispute after another. The Spanish with the French and British, France against Britain, the natives in America fighting the colonists, now Britain against their own people, and all looking to gain the upper hand somehow.

"These folks might be right that it may be better to choose carefully what gets shared and when. But I will also say that because of such motivations in our culture, I am afraid that whether many of these advances are shared or not, eventually we will find ways to make more deadly and far reaching war products no matter what," Kris stated sadly.

"Yes but no reason to help them get there more quickly," added Frederick.

"Perhaps not," admitted Kris.

"Nonetheless, I wouldn't mind learning how to use these wonderful...what did you call them, Frederick?" asked Annie.

"Appliances, because they help us apply heat, cold or water to food to place it at the temperature we wish for," answered Frederick.

"...Yes appliances, just imagine the cookies I could bake for you Papa! And the bread, I could do, all types of recipes," Annie said wistfully.

Kris chuckled and said, "As if I wasn't gaining weight fast enough around you, my dearest."

Just then the elf waitress came up with the various meals and set them before the guests. Frederick asked Kris, "Santa, would you do the honor?"

Santa, as he was called again, bowed his head and gave grace and thanks for bringing them to the North Pole and introducing them to the marvels before them.

After lunch they resumed the tour with Frederick showing them some of the transportation devices used and explaining the power behind them. Frederick explained that the North Pole was divided into three distinct sections. The largest area was the Woodlands where trees of every reasonable species were grown. As they could pretty well control weather under the dome, it was possible to grow trees in the climate they were most used to. This was where they received all the lumber they needed for the variety of things they produced. There was a lumber mill and of course the farming of the wood by lumberjack elves that went on continuously. There was also a green house area to replace the trees taken.

The second area was the manufacturing area where the factories and plants were located. Kris had a fascination with the machinery and asked a good many questions on the fundamentals of the power and how it was generated. Frederick explained what he could and then recommended he talk with Jackson Kilowatt and Britney Clearwater for the rest.

Then Frederick explained about the high area called Mount Elvish where the elves learned their trades, had schools, and also relaxed from their toils. There they could ski, sled, skate, and take up other hobbies like ice sculpting and wood carving.

As Frederick talked, they visited some of the shops and more factories so that the Kringles could see the mechanisms in use and look over the craftsmanship of the products. They also stopped some of the transportation devices so Kris could see more closely their mechanisms and how they were propelled.

Around 4:00 Annie announced that she was quite exhausted from having to take in so many marvels. Frederick apologized again, escorted them back to their inn and asked if they would like to explore some more areas tomorrow.

Annie said more to Kris, "Why don't you go on ahead dear and I will stay around the inn for the morning. I may even take another of those wonderful baths! It is amazing how the hot water comes from that little hole into the tub," and then she blushed realizing her frankness before the elf.

Frederick chuckled and said that he would be pleased if Kris wanted to explore more of the village.

Kris answered that it would be quite pleasant to spend more time among the village and its people. He bid Frederick a good afternoon and then he and Annie retired to their room.

The Kringles had a quiet supper in the dining room alone. While both their heads were filled with the marvels they witnessed that day, their conversation was nonexistent. They were both lost in this new world and contemplated what all this might mean for them.

They retired to their bedroom and while many times they both began to speak of things they saw their words trailed off into nothingness and they settled into a comfortable silence. By 9:00 that evening both were sound asleep in their featherbed and lost to dreams of the North Pole.

The following morning, Kris met Frederick in the lobby of the inn and they again picked up where they left off with Frederick taking Kris from shop to shop, introducing him to the inhabitants of each and demonstrating what each shop produced and how.

After a slower start which included another bath, Ann Marie came into the lobby and found Gunther Crispenclean polishing the cabinet behind the desk.

"Excuse me, Gunther," she said. The elf turned around and smiled at her. "I was wondering if I could see your cooking area and possibly get some teachings on how to use some of your appliances?"

Gunther grinned at her and said, "I don't see why not. I am sure Pierre would be pleased to assist you in your endeavor. Would you follow me?"

They both disappeared behind the wall with the cabinet on it and Gunther brought her to the kitchen area and said to the back of an elf standing over the stove, "Pierre, I have a new apprentice for you to train."

Pierre Gastonlove turned around and looked at the woman towering over him and laughed. "Oh, oui? Mademoiselle wishes to assist me in the preparation of extraordinary cuisine for these unappreciative peasants?" he laughed. He was shaking something in a large pan and seemed to be able to do more than one task at the same time.

"I would be grateful for the opportunity to learn how to master these marvelous tools with a culinary expert such as yourself," exclaimed Mrs. Kringle.

"Aha!" exclaimed Pierre, "Finally, someone who appreciates my genius! Mrs. Kringle, you would be most welcome to join me in my preparations and I shall show you how these tools of my unappreciated tasks work."

"Thank you for your kindness sir. Please call me Annie. And do not hesitate to tell me what you would like me to do," she said in perfect French.

Pierre looked amazed, "Mon Dieu, Seigneur, she also knows the proper speech, what a refreshing assistant. We will speak English for your comfort Madame Annie, but I thank you for the compliment."

"As you wish, Monsieur Pierre," she responded.

Pierre began demonstrating how each piece worked and the pair began preparing several different dishes. After a time, Annie asked if it might be alright to make a batch of her husband's favorite cookies?

As they were mixing the batter another elf came into the area.

"Mrs. Kringle? What are you doing here? You are our guest and do not need to be working in the kitchen!" Denny Sweetooth was horrified at seeing his guest covered in flour and looking somewhat disheveled from her efforts.

"Mr. Sweetooth, I am happiest in the cooking area and am having more fun than you could ever imagine with these wonderful appliances! I may never leave!" answered Annie.

"She is a magician, Monsieur Denny!" said Pierre, "Even I, the great Pierre, have learned some secrets from this amazing lady. Annie, this has been some of the best food to come out of this kitchen in a long time!"

Soon, Denny, Pierre and Annie were working side by side putting out several batches of cookies among the elves to raves and compliments. All three were enjoying themselves immensely.

Denny said to Annie, "I truly hate to leave this happy scene, but you and I must leave to meet with the Council again."

"Do I have time to clean myself up and make myself presentable?" asked Annie.

"I think you look marvelous, but of course we have a few minutes. Pierre and I will clean up here and you can run along to your room," he answered.

"Pierre, this has been a true joy to work with you and I thank you for teaching me about your incredible innovations," she had said to Pierre.

"Mrs. Annie the pleasure has been all mine," Pierre replied in French with a deep bow.

Annie smiled and left for the room.

At a different area of the North Pole Frederick was saying something similar to Kris. It was time to end the tour for the time being and head back to the large hall where the Council met.

They had explored the other manufacturing areas and had long discussions over what could be brought to the children and how it might be transported to the various countries. Frederick said it would be possible to move the products overland to some of the warehouses, and more could be created as the need arose. From there the elves might be able to distribute the toys to the towns.

Kris said how much the children would enjoy playing with the wonderful products he saw produced this day. The wonderful candies and fruit tarts and other foods would turn any frown to a huge smile across the lands.

Kris was shown amazing ways to transport even food across immense distances. He was beginning to agree with Frederick that the word 'impossible' did not seem to exist here.

They were heading toward the inn to collect Annie and head off to the hall together. As they arrived at the inn, Ann Marie was just descending the last stairs with Denny. Kris asked how her day of relaxation was and she and Denny burst into laughter.

She said to Kris, "Here dear, have some cookies, I am sure you could use some nourishment after your toils," she said as she winked at Denny.

Kris and Frederick each took a handful they moved to the door to head to the Great Hall.

Before they all took their places, the Council again asked if the Kringles would excuse them for a few moments while they discussed some things among each other. The Kringles remained in the outer hall trying to guess what the Council was deliberating about.

The wait was not nearly as long this time, Whitey came out to the hall and collected Kris and Annie and invited them back to the main hall.

Again it was Frederick that addressed the Kringles with the following information. "Kris and Annie, I have the distinct pleasure to make the following invitation and offer to you both:

We find you both imminently enjoyable and good hearted, and however you respond to our proposal, we want you to know that it is truly our pleasure and joy to have had the opportunity to spend this time with you."

Kris and Annie beamed and made a similar statement back to the elves.

Frederick continued, "We have discussed this between ourselves and with some others of our village. We would like to put the full resources of the North Pole at your disposal and have you distribute toys and gifts to the children throughout the world. We will provide you all the presents and will help you move the massive amount that would be required to accomplish this task.

The only request that we have is that at least during this period in time and until decided otherwise, that you keep our location and the fact of the origin of these presents secret from your civilization. We will help you load and move packs, but we wish to be kept dark from the eyes of the world."

Frederick looked at Mrs. Kringle and said, "We wish to build you a grand home and workshop in our village that will be for your sole use. You are welcome to live here as long as you wish, which we hope would be a very long time indeed."

"Not unlike you, our ancestors, including myself, try not to call much attention to the passing out of gifts, and most often as you saw in Tilburg, I prefer to do this task late in the evening so children would not know it was me, and might attribute it to God as the giver," explained Kris.

"And how is that working out for you?" asked Frieda. The other elves chuckled at her comment.

"Apparently, not as well as I would hope," he shrugged.

"What you need is an alias, a nom de plume as it were," said Carrow, "Might I suggest you adopt the one that has already been given you?"

"I agree with Carrow," said Denny, "You should travel under the name of Santa Claus, rather than Kringle. It has become what many countries already have named you, and it would be a good way to keep your true identity suppressed from others."

"I think before we start renaming the Kringles and asking them to change their lives at our suggestion, that we first ask them their thoughts on the whole idea first," said Frederick to the rest of the Council, "Our apologies," he continued, "as you may tell, we are a little excited over this prospect and are already making plans without your consent or consultation. If I may ask on behalf of this Council, would you remain with us and what are your thoughts and feelings about our proposal?"

Kris and Annie looked at each other and Annie

shrugged with a smirk to her husband. Kris turned to the Council and said, "We would be honored to represent all the people of the North Pole. I swear that I will keep your secrets and give all of my strength and being to accomplish this massive undertaking you have asked me to perform."

With a collective sigh, the Council sat back in their seats.

"I would imagine," continued Kris, "that even with all your resources, it may take a while to piece together all the elements and essentials of putting such a plan into action. Where would you like us to stay while all the planning and schematics of such an operation is mapped out?"

Ella, who hadn't spoke once during the meetings, broke the silence first, "The dissemination of information and the planning of each warehouse alone will take several weeks to work out."

Ulzana looked at Carrow and then back to the Kringles and said, "If you are comfortable at the inn for the time being you are welcome to stay there, otherwise Carrow and I have room for you."

Carrow choked, saying "Oh! Uhh...Well...If we must...I'm sure the Kringles would rather not..."

The other elves began laughing at Carrow and his reaction to Ulzana's invitation.

Kris held up a hand and said with a smile, "Relax Mr. Chekitwice, the inn will be quite comfortable for now."

Jackson said, "We will make you as comfortable as possible and see to your needs for undertaking this endeavor with us."

Denny laughed and said, "I have a feeling that Annie will be taking as good a care of us as we will of her, after seeing her skills in the kitchen today!"

Annie smiled brightly and said, "As long as Pierre allows me to."

Denny retorted, "Let him just try and keep you out!"

With that the other elves had a good laugh.

The final decision was that in a couple days there would be a huge feast in the North Pole where Santa and Mrs. Claus would be formally introduced to the residents of the North Pole and their mission made known to all.

Chapter Five

...for us physicists believe the separation between past, present, and future is only an illusion, although a convincing one.

- Albert Einstein

Compromises

The banquet in honor of Santa and Mrs. Claus, as they were introduced, was held that Friday, and the Kringles were welcomed warmly and with awe. Gone were the debates, discussions and worries about tallfolk taking over the North Pole.

Word had spread about the kindness and big-hearted nature of their new residents, and how the Council had voted unanimously to accept the couple. Even old Crabby Carrow had given his whole-hearted approval.

Work already had begun on a new building that would also house a large workshop, as it was told that Santa liked to "tinker" with toys and build things as well. Also, they needed an area large enough for the elves to introduce the couple to all the innovations, discoveries and plans of things the village was working on, now and into the future.

Activity was also stepped up as the mission for Santa would soon begin bringing toys, food, clothing and all else for the children. Soon everything could be finalized and put into motion for the delivery. Shipments on large sleighs and vehicles were already being moved south to the coastal areas.

Santa was also busy at this time making plans with Carrow, Frederick, and other elves over how many toys and other things they thought they might need. Everything was pretty much a guess at this point as few accurate records concerning populations or the sizes of towns were kept. Plus Kris said he wanted to make sure he had enough to try and give something to the more rural farms and ranches along the roads he traveled.

Most of the discussion, however involved delivery and transportation. Kris said it would be unbelievably difficult (he wouldn't say impossible anymore) to tend the needs of every Christian child on earth. Even then, he had made the elves agree that the children that believed in Christmas would be the only benefactors, unless the elves delivered to the other nations themselves.

Not because Kris loved those children any less, but it came down to a matter of effort and ability.

Kris was concerned about how much time it might take to deliver all the gifts. He wanted to deliver them towards the end of the year when everyone would at least be mindful that the Christ child's birth was coming. This was his ancestors plan and wish, and he wanted to try and fulfill his destiny to the same cause.

There were many discussions and some of them heated, about how he could limit his deliveries to around Christmas and still cover the globe as the elves had wanted. Many times Kris asked if he could use the vehicles, saying he would only travel at night and would keep them out of sight during the day.

The Council voted down his suggestions time and again saying the risk was too great, and that people were not yet ready to find faster ways to move their cannons and men at arms around the countryside. Kris was allowed to use, and would even be escorted, to areas of inhabitants with their machines, but once against the shores of other countries he had to use the modes of transportation that were available to the region.

He said it would take him months and possibly the entire year to accomplish what they wanted him to do. It was during one of these discussions between Kris and Frederick that finally a very young elf named Ariel suggested to Frederick that Santa talk with Aeon Millennium. Frederick slapped his head and yelled out, "Of course! I should have thought of that before! Thank you, Ariel!"

Frederick took Santa to an area that was deep in the elves forest. It was still amazing to Santa that the elves brought and raised so many trees of every variety, and created a horticultural forest under the dome. Here they continually harvested and replanted whatever type of wood they would need or want.

Just about the time Kris thought they had come to end of the forest, he saw a thatch roofed house. It was a good size with log siding around and it looked very old indeed. Frederick knocked on the door and was greeted by an elf who had a wild look to his eyes and crazy hair going every direction. His clothes were rumpled and he looked older than most, but not quite Carrow or Ulzana's age.

"Frederick?" said the elf, "You need me again so soon?"

"Uh, Aeon, it has been 5 years," said Frederick, "and yes, I need your help again." He introduced Kris to the wild looking elf. Kris hesitantly offered his hand as if he thought Aeon might take a bite out of it.

"How do you do young man? If I am not mistaken you are a tallfolk, are you not?" asked Aeon.

"You are quite correct sir, I am," Santa answered as pleasantly as he could.

"Surprising. Well do come in," said Aeon, "We may get around to the reason for your visit faster if you do, heh, heh."

As they walked into the house, Kris saw formulations written on every wall and piece of paper throughout the house. Everything was strewn around and the house was a shambles.

Frederick looked around and chuckled saying, "Yes, just as I left you last time."

"Not at all!" snapped Aeon, "I have worked out many more ideas and formulations since you were last here. In fact I have gone back and forth so often you are lucky to catch me here at all. I was just gathering notes, as it is time for me to go before the Council again with more discoveries I brought back."

"Really?" This caught the interest of Frederick as he looked at the old man, "Tell me!"

"Now you know I like to tell the whole Council at once. Saves me the trouble of explaining it multiple times," said Aeon.

"Please Professor, just a couple hints?" Frederick egged him on.

"Now you know the rules, just as we have determined that tallfolk are not yet ready for many of our innovations and discoveries, so too, I am the only one sanctioned to give that information to our society when I deem it appropriate or necessary."

Frederick looked deflated, "Not even one morsel?"

"Well...okay, you know I always had a soft spot for you Fred," mused Aeon, "What if I was to tell you that many of the machines we now use are long obsolete into the future. So too is our information circuitry. In fact, implants will be installed in our minds that will access every known piece of information on the planet at the speed of thought. And this antiquated barter system using metals and paper will finally cease to exist, and everyone will be credited for their knowledge and usefulness to society."

"When? When will this all take place?" an excited Frederick asked.

"I'm afraid not in our lifetime, Fred" Aeon said dejected, "At least not as we know it. It is centuries off, and as with all other advancements will happen after many more violent episodes in history, or rather the future, well you know what I mean."

"Excuse me sir," said a confused Kris, "but I have no idea what you mean."

"The professor here is a time traveler," said Frederick, "He moves in and out of time as he wishes. Professor this is the one you told us about."

"Of course, I should have recognized him immediately! Rosy cheeks, white beard and hair, not as fat as they often depict you, but it is you!" Aeon said excitedly.

"Again my apologies, sir, but I am...what?" asked Kris.

"You are Santa Claus! You bring joy and hope throughout the world!" exclaimed Aeon.

"You know this? I mean you have seen this?" Santa was getting excited now, "How do I accomplish this feat?"

"Well I can't tell you that now, at least not everything, it would interrupt the continuum." Aeon shook his head and then looked at Frederick, "So Fred, that's why you are here, you want him to be able to use the continuum. I should have known."

"He doesn't need it all, he only needs to control and stop current events so he can do everything in a short period of time," pleaded Frederick.

"Uh, I had heard something about controlling time, but I thought you were referring to the magnetic properties of the North Pole and not time itself!" said Santa.

"What if I told you that I could make time stop everywhere at the same instant and keep it there indefinitely?" asked Aeon to Santa.

"I would say that would be an unrealistic boast," scoffed Kris.

"Really?" questioned Aeon, "It has already happened, let's step outside." He led them to his garden in the back. There the stream by the house had ceased moving. He then pointed to a bird in mid-wing going from one tree to another but frozen in the air.

Kris asked, "How is it possible that we are still moving but everything else is frozen in time?"

"Since I am controlling the time, I can determine who and what is affected and set the continuum for that range. The rest remains in one place until I reset the continuum," said the wild haired professor.

"So can you teach him?" asked Frederick.

"I owe you a huge apology, Professor Millennium," said Santa, "Ignorance prevented me from accepting what you said as sincere speech."

"Apology accepted, and it is your destiny to know this any how," Aeon said and turned to Frederick, "You actually did find him, or at least the first one of them."

"I'm sorry the first…" Santa began.

Aeon began waving his hands and said, "Never mind, you cannot know too much about the future, it will affect the outcomes, we have enough work to do. You must come with me."

As Kris followed his teacher he asked, "So I will really be able to do all I have been charged to do in a couple months?"

"Ha!" laughed Aeon, "No…one night."

Mrs. Claus, as she was known through the village, was also keeping very busy. She had begun taking charge of the types and kinds of the products that Santa would take with him. She would consult with Stacey Buttons on the type and styles of dolls, Smokey Crackenbush about bringing pine trees to help decorate the interior of the homes, Frieda Cutinglass and Priscilla Huffenpuff about ornaments and decorations, Denny about treats for the children, and others throughout the establishment that would contribute different items for the trip.

The elves sensed natural leadership ability in this strong woman and they found themselves listening more and more intently to her suggestions and wishes.

Today, she was working with the builders overseeing some of the more important details to their new house. She and Kris were flabbergasted at the generosity and adornments the elves were putting into the home as well as the overall size. The elves were building a castle for the Kringles, complete with turrets and huge rooms.

They had tried to scale this down when the elves had presented the initial plans, but the elves would hear none of it. They said tall people need a big home with lots of room and that is what they would get.

Today was an important day for Annie; she was getting her appliances for the kitchen. The ovens (there were two) were massive and could easily hold the largest cut of meat or several trays of cookies. She also had what was called a refrigeration system that held a similar amount.

She had already become quite used to the indoor plumbing and was thrilled with the size and depth of the containment system...oh what did the elves call it? Oh yes, a sink. It was made from that same special metal alloy that had incredible properties that made it easy to remain shiny and clean.

Yes, Ann Marie Kringle was settling in nicely to her new environs. She was always good natured and felt blessed in her life, but she had never felt happier than she had since arriving to the North Pole. The time spent at the inn would soon be coming to a close, and their first permanent home since she married Kris was about to become reality.

She knew Kris was concerned about what the elves wanted him to accomplish, but she knew if any man could do this incredible task, it was her husband. She had never known a man with a stronger resolve. It was just part of his makeup.

She had met him when he was in Italy, She ran across him one day in a small village just south of Naples in Portici. He was talking and laughing with the children who were scattered around him like flowers. He was playing with them and giving out several gifts and having the time of his life.

When he looked up at her he just stopped. He smiled broadly and said in perfect Italian, "Hello little girl, can I interest you in a toy to play with?"

She had laughed and said that she was too old for toys, to which he replied that no one was too old for toys, but if such was the case, how about an espresso instead?

They spent the next couple days meeting up in various places around the village they were in. Annie had lost both her parents when she was younger and did not have any siblings. She lived with an aunt on her mother's side that had taken Ann Marie in when the aunt's sister had passed away. Kris had come along just in time. It was the right age for Ann Marie to move on with her own life, and she was ready and wanted to settle down with the right man.

Kris too, thought that he needed a partner and was ready for romance in his life. They married a month later and even though they never traveled extensively and never laid roots in one area for long.

Annie and Kris had a full life, but she would have liked children. For whatever reason, she was never able to get pregnant and the two substituted the children they gave presents to for children of their own.

She was thinking about that single regret to their lives when the elves brought in the next large square appliance which Annie had not seen previously. She inquired as to its purpose. The taller of the two elves said, "It's something that will clean your dishes and cooking utensils for you. It is meant to help take the place of a servant. You put them in and turn this dial and it will wash and dry everything for you."

"Unbelievable," Annie said.

"You need to try harder," Aeon said in a frustrated voice, "Put all your thought into it. Don't pay attention to your surroundings, just concentrate. Now stare into the disk and try again."

Kris held the circular medallion-like object that Aeon referred to in the flat of his palm and stared into it with all his might. A few moments later his eyes began to tear up from the effort but nothing seemed to be happening. "I don't think this works for me," he said in a dejected voice.

"Nonsense, it works for anybody. I have used it with countless elves," replied Aeon.

"Maybe it is because I am not an elf?" asked Kris.

"Or maybe it's because you do not believe that you can do it in the first place, or disbelieve the principle of it. People never look at time as a place. They think of it as a two dimensional concept, when it is very three dimensional. Just as you can travel through London, you can travel through time. Try thinking of it as a destination. And you only want to walk through the door. We won't attempt to travel beyond that, as my guess you wouldn't be ready anyway."

Aeon walked closer to Kris and stared into his eyes saying, "You are the gift bringer, you are the light for children throughout the world. Eventually more children than you will ever imagine will look to you for hope and wishes every year. You need to master this to fulfill your destiny, now do it again and this time KNOW you can do it."

Kris closed his eyes this time instead of staring at the disk and brought all his surroundings into his mind. He focused on the moment, hearing the water outside, the sound of the breathing of Aeon and Fred, and his own deep breath. He concentrated on all these things and the disk.

Aeon whispered, "Now open your eyes."

Kris saw that he and Aeon were still moving but that Frederick in the corner had seemed frozen.

He could also tell the water had stopped flowing and that no other sound could be heard.

"I told you anyone could do it. Now shift your concentration like you would a torch allowing light in other places and allow other things like our friend over there to move and become fluid with you."

Kris moved his gaze toward Frederick and he suddenly began moving as if he had been animated the whole time. Kris commented more to himself, "This is amazing, is everything else frozen in time?"

"All other things in the world are being held in suspended animation until you release them. You may hold them as such for as long as you care to, although I would strongly suggest that you do not hold this state indefinitely as I do not know what the outcome might be," answered Aeon.

"He's done it!" exclaimed Frederick, "I can see it, see Kris, I told you that you could."

With that, the spell was broken and the water outside began flowing again. "I lost it," Kris said in a deflated tone.

"The point is you did it and you can do it again, and pretty soon you will be able to turn time on and off like a light switch," grinned Aeon.

"A what?" asked Santa.

"Oh never mind, you will know that soon enough, the point is you can control time, so now you can do everything you want with time being your friend instead of your enemy,' cackled Aeon.

"What if I lose the medallion?" questioned Kris.

Aeon and Frederick both started laughing and Frederick told Aeon to let Santa in on the joke.

Joe Moore

Aeon turned to Kris and said, "What if you do, it has no meaning, I just gave it to you to make you think that the object would help you achieve your goal. You will notice that when you actually achieved the continuum you were not staring at the medallion, but actually had your eyes closed. People just think they need some sort of talisman to accomplish things."

Kris shook his head and muttered, "Unbelievable."

"Well you can believe it. And that is enough for now. You must return everyday this week so we can practice this until you can do it whenever you wish and include or stop things with only your mind wishing it," ordered Aeon.

"Won't the others get tired of being stopped and started again all the time?" questioned Kris.

"They will be unaware that it has happened," stated Aeon, "Just as you have been unaware when it has happened to you. And while you can change events or happenings to others while they are suspended, it is advisable not to do so as it could have ramifications for the future. However, you will be able to focus and allow those you wish to move through time with you no matter where they are."

They talked a little longer and then Frederick said it was time to leave and suggested Kris pay attention to their route as he would return tomorrow by himself.

On the way back Kris asked his new friend, "Can any of the elves do the time continuum and travel?"

Frederick replied, "Only those that we allow the study of it. We can't have too many people stopping time or jumping back and forth through history, and most have to clear the reasons with the Council before proceeding. Of course we would have no sure way of knowing if they didn't, but that is one of those rules that is unmistakable in its enforcement if we were to learn later."

"This power is so great, imagine the problems that could ensue if misused," contemplated Santa.

"That's why we control it," sighed Frederick, "So much good could be done if we could only trust others to do the right thing instead of knowing for certain they would not."

"Now let me ask you, once I learn from Aeon how to control the continuum, do you think it might be possible to use your machines to help me complete the task more quickly?" Kris asked eagerly.

"You tallfolk, once you get fixated on a problem, you never look for another solution," chuckled Frederick, "We will figure something out before it is time for your journey, a solution will present itself in due time."

"That phrase has taken on an entirely new meaning to me, now. 'in due time' indeed," Kris laughed, "But nonetheless I hope it is soon. I am impatient for that solution to present itself."

"One thing at a time my impatient friend, this morning you were all a flutter as to how you could possibly do this in a reasonable time, and we have solved that problem for you. And we will solve the transport problem as well," said Frederick.

"My apologies, you are quite right," answered Kris, "God and my good elves will answer the question when it is time to be asked in earnest."

Kris visited Aeon nearly every day over the next couple weeks and had spent at least a couple hours (or so it would seem to any one else) practicing learning how to use and control the time continuum.

It was unnerving to his wife when occasionally she would be moving and everyone and everything else around her was frozen. It never seemed convenient when it happened, and she would have to wait a seemingly long periods of time before things could get on to normal. At one point, she asked Kris to please find another subject to practice on as she would rather remain frozen with the others.

Annie had become even more involved with the goings on in the village and soon she was being sought out by the other elves to ask her opinion on particular issues they were wrestling with. Carrow, Denny and other elf leaders had noticed and were pleased with this new change of events.

They found in Ann Marie Kringle a very capable and knowledgeable woman with a good grasp on organization and a natural business acumen. This also relieved some of the burden from the Council. Many elves were seeking out Mrs. Claus instead of waiting for the Council to reconvene at its once a week proceeding to resolve their concerns.

Everyone found Annie easy to consult with and as wise as any elf. This, plus the fascination of being the first tallfolk to ever be allowed at the North Pole, and the wife of their new gift-bringer, all made her somewhat of an attraction. Annie took it all in stride, and felt proud that she was indeed becoming a critical part of village life at the North Pole. The whole idea pleased her immensely.

There always seemed to be so much to do, and an abundance of things going on everywhere in the village. From baking breads, pies and tarts, to the horticulture area where they grew anything from Pine trees to Poinsettia's and from Strawberries to Apples. The greenhouses that were erected were massive and made from the same dome substance that protected the North Pole, which meant they could be similarly controlled with their climate. This made it easy to reconstruct ideal growing seasons regardless the time of year.

The elves, because of their knowledge of indoor and outdoor plumbing, were able to control the irrigation. Since the North Pole was basically surrounded with water, they had all the moisture to grow whatever crops they chose.

Annie was soon scheduling the choices based on growth cycles, yield, harvest difficulty and storage. She also began having more and more say with regard to the manufacturing center. Her thoughts on what products to produce and in what order to produce them raised the eyes and admiration of the Council and those working on the lines.

It was Britney Clearwater the elf in charge of irrigation that actually created a new title for Mrs. Claus. After watching and talking to her about where to put the various irrigation hoses with the other elves she said, "Why Mrs. Claus, you are a genuine chief elf organizer!" The title stuck and after a time she was just referred to as the CEO of the North Pole.

As the end of that first year began to approach, it was Forrest Hedemup and Sky Globetrotter who made the next exciting advancement in the first trip of Santa Claus.

While Kris had mastered the time continuum after much effort, he was still upset that a method to travel across continents and oceans hadn't been resolved. While he could virtually stop time for an eternity if he needed to, he couldn't find a way to travel fast enough over the lands without our machines.

Forrest came up with the first part a solution. He said he had given the matter great thought and after watching a drift of hogs get into that feed that makes them float around for hours and sometimes days afterward, he got an idea.

He put their fastest horse onto the feed, and after a day the horse was bounding off and flying through the air with Forrest on his back. Forrest then tried taking the horse on long runs guiding him hither and yon, and found the beast had incredible stamina and speed even when taken outside the North Pole. Further, the horse was even able to fly above the clouds.

Forrest then took his findings to Sky Globetrotter, the navigational elf that worked on the charts for the boats and flying machines. She began charting a possible course based on the Earth's revolutions and allowing for the International dateline and the rotation of the Earth around the sun.

It could be done easily when the principles of the time continuum were applied along with flight and a few navigational tricks. They showed Santa how he could achieve the goal he sought. A second horse was prepared for flight, so that Forrest could teach both the horse and Santa how to fly. While Kris was an accomplished horseman, he had to learn to take the horse from linear runs to three dimensional flight, which went well beyond the side to side and front and back movements to up and down, and even diagonally.

Both the horse and rider were unsteady at first, and a couple close calls ensued where Kris almost lost control and fell. But soon he was learning the movements and the horse was gaining confidence. Afterward, Santa Claus and Forrest Hedemup were going on long jaunts and testing their endurance and speed.

Santa had said that he was already known for riding a large white horse throughout Europe similar to the one Forrest was riding. he had done so for years, and this would not be an unusual sight to the villagers. When he was away from the village, they could take to the sky and even stay above the clouds until the next village approached.

The gifts he would deliver, were already being staged at one of the local warehouses. Special carts would be constructed that could be pulled behind the horse while Santa was on the ground. Once Santa was done with that location he could detach the cart, leave it for one of the farmers as another gift, and fly off to the next area.

When they presented their findings, suggestions and trials to the Council of Elves, it was agreed upon unanimously. The only stipulation being that Santa continues to travel at night to try to prevent detection and keep accidental sightings to a minimum. Santa Claus agreed with the Council and the plan was set.

He would do his first trip on Christmas Eve.

Chapter Six

There will always be a way to accomplish a great task if we give sufficient thought to the problem and not rush a solution.

- Forrest Hedemup

Flying High

We all gathered for Santa Claus' first trip that Christmas Eve. The entire Council of Elves was in attendance. Each one wished him great success and thanked him for taking on such a monumental task.

Upon kissing Annie goodbye, he mounted the great white steed named Amerigo and the two began galloping off at first on the ground, and then soon into the air until he was out of sight.

Santa and Amerigo followed the charts that Sky Globetrotter had laid out for him that took into effect the ellipses of the earth and its various jet streams.

His first area was where this whole adventure began, in the Netherlands starting with Friesland and moving across Groningen, then south into the rest of Europe than across Asia. The first couple stops seemed to take forever with the elves sorting and packing all the presents and Kris had to keep going over the list he had. He vowed that in the future he would check the list ahead of time and then check it twice when he reached the warehouse. As planned, as the horse and rider reached every new territory, Carrow set up a warehouse that seemed just large enough for Santa Claus to restock and gather the intelligence of the area.

In some places he was told that people were very suspicious of newcomers, especially if they had a large sack on their back, as he was using. It was suggested he might want to be careful and have Amerigo land on the roof instead of right outside the door. They said most fireplaces were easily accessible, and by this time, most of the coals had gone out so he could jump down and jump back out before anyone would know he was there, especially while using his time continuum.

Since he was flying with Amerigo more than he was riding, he thought this may also make his journey less tedious. And so on they went in house after house, country after country. Sometimes he left the gifts in plain sight, other times he put them in stockings drying by the fireplace as his ancestor had done, and sometimes even in the children's shoes if they were laying about.

That next Christmas morning, tens of thousands of children awoke to find gifts of food, clothes and toys along with ornaments and occasionally a pine tree or sprigs of greenery to remind them that soon the promise of spring would return.

The following year went more smoothly. They had corrected many mistakes and made the assembly of filling the sacks much more streamlined, and in real time Kris was able to accomplish as much in half the time. Kris was having a marvelous journey. While this was more work than he could have imagined, his adrenaline kept him going, and knowing the smiles that would grace the children's faces upon the discovery of the gifts bolstered him even more.

In many towns he actually rode Amerigo through the streets and was seen a few times. He did this not because he wanted recognition, but because he wanted to test the attitudes of the people he was visiting. He also was curious to hear what they were saying about their mysterious night visitor.

As the years began to progress he also noticed that more stockings were being hung each year and more shoes being placed by the fireplaces. Some were even placing their shoes outside the door, not risking being missed by Santa Claus.

And so the trend continued for many years. Every year they added more warehouses and tried to get larger sacks for the presents. And each year the world seemed to get a little bigger and the night a little longer. He sensed poor Amerigo felt it, too. The horse was having a tougher time getting through the entire night without frequent rests. It seemed crossing oceans were putting a heavy burden on him, and Kris wondered if maybe he shouldn't reduce the length of the trip or spread it over more nights.

Another interesting thing began taking place. After a couple yearly trips he started finding notes and letters left for him asking for a particular item for the following year. Santa made a note about where the house was and the item requested. After a time he had quite a list that also grew longer each year. It was becoming quite an endeavor and more difficult to track each year.

While he could stop time, he knew that it was becoming harder and harder for Amerigo to make the endless night trip. Also even with a cart behind him, it was increasingly difficult to pull so much for each region and there was only so much you could load onto a horse.

We discussed this with the Council and expressed his concerns for Amerigo. Many discussions were held with the Council, and with Willie Movinmuch, the transportation expert that Kris had first met on the journey to the North Pole. He also brought Forrest Hedemup the animal trainer and handler for the North Pole, as he was as concerned as Kris about the strain on Amerigo.

The Council was still unwilling to have Santa use more advanced forms of transportation saying that even though Amerigo could fly, he was after all, still a horse, and could be more easily explained and not used for ill-purposes. The problem with using more than one horse was the width. One horse could adequately fit on a roof, but two or more was just too wide and would slide to one side or the other on many roofs. They tried doing practice runs using different configurations but all to no avail. For one reason or another it just wasn't practical.

One day, while Kris was doing one of these practice trials with two horses, he flew over a great herd of reindeer that were migrating, and remembering that reindeer were often used in Lapland and some of the other Nordic countries, he immediately banked the horses back to the North Pole.

"We have the wrong animal," he said in an excited voice to both Forrest and Willie.

"How do you mean?" asked Forrest, "What's wrong with Amerigo?"

"Nothing," grinned Santa, "But it is not a horse that we need. We need to try using reindeer."

Willie looked pensive and said, "They would have to be pretty small to fit on the roof. Almost tiny, but then we'd need enough for pulling the sleigh I am designing to handle all the gifts for each region."

"How many do you think we could fit on a roof?" asked Forrest.

"With a little practice, I'll bet I could fit 4 or even 6 on a roof at once," replied Santa.

"Four tiny reindeer pulling one big sleigh, you and all those toys?" stammered Willie, "I will really have to check the possibilities."

"You know you may be onto something," Forrest's eyes became large, "The antlers might help with the slip stream and really give a boost to speed. And if you had six or more they probably wouldn't tire as easily." He was obviously beginning to see the possibilities.

"Of course we would have to have trials to make sure it would work," stated Willie, still working the concept in his head. "I think we need to bring Sky into this and see what she says about how reindeer would fit into the equation of the jet streams and other factors."

The others agreed and there was an element of great excitement between them as the three of them went off to find Sky.

They found her in her home mapping out new charts, She laughed saying, "The way these Americans keep spreading out, not to mention you keep adding new areas in and around England and other parts of Europe and such, I am having to change my charts almost daily, Santa."

Forrest said, "Well we have a new challenge for you Miss Sky, we are thinking of changing the type of animal for Santa from a horse to reindeer, and we were wondering how that might effect Santa's travel?"

Sky immediately began her calculations and began asking Forrest about the type and configurations of the antlers, the size of the deer, the approximate height in hands and width of the animals." She poured over the charts and was writing feverishly going back and forth to her various maps.

After a time she looked up and said, "It may very well boost the speed of the journey and allow Santa to reduce the amount of actual time it takes to traverse the various oceans. Santa, do you think you could handle the great deal of additional speed that might be gained from the number of animals you are asking for, and accounting for the slipstream of their antlers?"

Santa responded, "I am sure, unless you are talking some unholy speed, I could probably adjust well as long as I don't overshoot my mark."

Sky smiled as she reviewed her calculations and looked up at Santa saying, "How about traveling faster than sound?"

Kris just stared at her with his mouth agape and finally said, "Excuse me?"

"This is just amazing," she said to everyone in the room while looking over her figures, "It seems that between the weightlessness of the reindeer and the jet stream it might be possible to travel faster than sound itself!"

Kris suddenly seemed less sure about his previous statement. He looked at the three of them and said, "That couldn't be practical, and how can a person travel faster than they could talk? What would happen when I tried to give commands to the team? They wouldn't be able to hear me as we would be moving faster than my speech!"

"Well I expect that you are talking in absolutes, which as we know is never a good idea," answered Frederick, "I suspect it is time to return to the Professor and talk to him about the prospect, but either way, you obviously could travel much faster than you have in the past."

Sky said that she would bring her calculations and have them checked with Aeon as well. After she reviewed them again she said, "I wouldn't mind getting his opinion on these, though I am pretty sure I am right."

Forrest then said, "Well, I suppose I should begin looking for some tiny reindeer and do some calculating of my own. I have only ever used them to haul carts and lighter loads around the village, and only when one of the other vehicles was impractical for some reason or other. I don't even think I have a harness I could come up with for four or six reindeer." He was scratching and shaking his head as he said the last comment.

They agreed to get together the next morning and all four of them would visit Aeon Millennium together.

Santa returned to find Annie full of her own issues. She was going over the production schedules with Carrow and me. I had stopped to talk with Carrow about our latest issue and walked with him to the Claus' home. The two were talking about how it may be time to put an additional shift on the line.

"Problems?" asked Kris.

"You might say that," said a concerned Annie, "It seems you are becoming quite popular and we are getting more and more requests for presents from more and more locations."

"Requests? How are we getting requests?" a perplexed Santa inquired.

"Well," answered Carrow, "New letters are finding their way to our village all the time because somehow people have figured that you live with us elves."

I said to Kris, "We have elves down south being

handed letters from tallfolk saying they know we are your 'helpers' and that they could get the message to you somehow. Further, the elves are seeing lots of letters being discarded from the postal centers and are picking them up and having them brought up here with our other correspondence"

"Well I'm not saying anything, how did they figure this one out?" a flustered Santa asked.

I replied, "People aren't stupid, just not as advanced as our culture. Even after you release time, they can see you flying off on Amerigo. And they probably watch you ride north as you go. Stories are growing out of every country that you visit.

"But how are the letters getting here?" Santa asked.

"Dearest, we have elves everywhere, remember?" said Annie, "They had begun delivering letters before, that we had received. And some of the more industrious elves told the postal stations that they will take care of any of these letters they get."

"Yes," said Carrow, "Stamp Packanletter said he has been getting letters in each shipment from the south. He's been trying to place them in one area but they are getting to be quite a number of them and all addressed to you."

"So now, dear husband, we are having to produce items based on what is being asked for, and we are having a heck of a time figuring out which line should produce what," claimed Mrs. Claus.

"Ho, ho, HO, so I am doing my job too well?" laughed Santa.

"Not at all, we just need to make adjustments to our plans," stated Carrow, "We are nowhere near total capacity, especially since we were forewarned by Aeon that this would eventually happen. And according to him, we haven't seen anything yet. That is why we built three plants and have five more in the design stages."

"What? Five more!" exclaimed Santa Claus, "How could I possibly deliver that many gifts?"

"Well, according to Aeon you will be able to do this every year, and your descendants as well," said Carrow in a matter of fact tone.

"Descendants? What descendants." snarled Kris, "We have no children or descendants to do this."

For a brief moment Annie looked sad as she also knew there would be no direct descendants, but she did not want to say anything to disappoint the elves.

Carrow answered Kris, "Don't think of it now. Something may present itself, and I shouldn't discuss the future."

"Well Kris, it seems you will do all the things your ancestor hoped to accomplish and more than he ever dreamed!" said an excited Annie.

"Well since you mention it, I might as well let you in on what several of us are working on to go along with what you are saying..." and Kris began to explain about the reindeer and the possibility of going faster than sound.

The following morning Frederick, Sky, Willie, Forrest and Santa Claus headed off to the forest and Aeon's dwelling. Aeon opened the door and Frederick said he was surprised to find the professor in.

Aeon smiled and said, "Oh I have been waiting for this meeting for a while, and you will find me very prepared for our discussion."

And so the rest of the day passed with Aeon verifying Sky's calculations, explaining to Santa how while in the vortex as he travels, he will not have difficulty ordering his team or making himself heard to his reindeer, or anyone accompanying him which he will soon have. He said he had already developed an envelope which will protect him, the sleigh, reindeer and packages from the damage of friction at the high rate of velocity that he will be traveling at.

He then turned his attention to Forrest and Willie explaining to them exactly how to create the harness and gear that will be needed. While he was describing the process, Santa Claus cleared his throat for attention.

"I suppose this is very selfish on my part, but I would like to ask a favor if I may," he looked down and said more to the floor, "May I have sleigh bells?"

Forrest and the others looked at him, Frederick laughed saying, "What, you don't bring enough attention to yourself?"

Still staring at the floor, Santa answered, "I have always loved bells, especially sleigh bells. They just sound so bright and joyful. Most people wouldn't hear them since I need to enact the time continuum when I arrive to an area, but since I now know I'll be able to hear, I would like to hear sleigh bells."

Forrest laughed hard enough to startle the others in the room, "Santa Claus if you want sleigh bells, then by God you will have sleigh bells. I'll make sure every mount we have has a full array of them on their harness. We will hear you for miles if you are not in "stealth" mode!"

As Forrest, Willie, Frederick and Sky went over some other details, Aeon asked Santa Claus to join him outside. Once out of hearing of the others Aeon turned to Kris and said, "Now that this is in the works, there is something else I need to teach you to help you complete your task. Now you already know how to stop time, but you can also use time as a destination."

"You mean as a physical place?" asked Santa.

"Precisely," explained Aeon, "I can not only control when I appear in time but where. For instance I can leave the here and now, and pop into the south of France, if I so decide. But it has its limits, I can't take my household or more than one or two beings with me. Here let me demonstrate with you, take my arm."

Santa did as instructed and without a sound found himself and Aeon standing in the middle of Philadelphia in the new United States.

"That's amazing," he said as he looked around, "What year is it?"

Aeon answered, "Same year, even the same time, day and month. This is just for demonstration purposes. Let's go again." and Santa quickly grabbed Aeon's cloak. They then appeared on the outskirts of London.

"Incredible," said Kris, "So you can go not only into any time, but also any place you want with a thought?"

"Pretty much, and with few restrictions. Such as I cannot travel beyond the earth, and if I cannot imagine the place in my mind, I would have difficulty transporting to the location and might end up somewhere I didn't plan, which can be dangerous," said Aeon. "Okay now it's your turn, take us back to our time and place with the others."

Santa just looked at the ancient elf, "I can't! I do not know how!"

Aeon shook his head and said, "Okay just as before, picture it in your mind and remember how I showed you how to stop time. I don't have a talisman handy, like the one I gave you before, so you'll just need to do without, alright now, let's do this. When you think you can sufficiently concentrate, just pinch yourself or something."

"If I pinch myself I may lose my concentration, and

I don't want to wind up somewhere or sometime I didn't plan to be," said a concerned Santa.

"Oh alright," said an exasperated Aeon, "Then just touch your finger to the side of your nose and blink."

Santa thought that might be fun and took his first stab at it. Sure enough he did as he was told and went...nowhere.

"You will have to do a good deal better than that. That was pitiful," Aeon said, "I didn't even feel a shutter from that. Let's try this in steps. First let's freeze time."

Santa concentrated and watched as everyone and everything including birds in mid-wing came to an abrupt halt except Aeon and him. Aeon nodded and said, "Good, okay it is a similar principle except now I need you to expand your concentration to the place and time we are aiming for. And don't forget to touch your nose, as that will convince yourself you are ready to proceed."

Kris closed his eyes and tried again. This time they traveled back to the right place, but the wrong time. They wound up inside Aeon's cabin at the same time as Kris and Frederick were walking up to the cabin on Kris' first visit.

Quickly, Aeon grabbed Kris' arm and propelled them away from there. They reappeared outside the cabin and Santa could hear the voices of the other elves inside. "That was close!" said Aeon, "Well I guess it was too much to hope you would get it right the very second time. I couldn't myself and I completely understand the laws and principles of time travel."

"What happened?" asked Santa.

"We almost got caught in a time warp, and that would not have been a good thing," explained Aeon, "You brought us back to the first time we met. You almost met yourself in time, and you want to avoid that, especially before you knew time travel existed, as you could drive yourself mad. But at least you got the 'where' part right and that is not a horrible start. The when may be more difficult, and the reason I am showing you how to do this is so you can land on a roof and appear inside the home without using the fireplace or door."

"That would be a huge help," exclaimed Santa, "Annie is constantly on me asking me to be more careful as I keep singeing my suit and making it filthy from the ash and soot. Plus sometimes I make a terrible mess if the fireplace hasn't been cleaned for a while. Not to mention some of those chimneys have a long drop."

"You will be able to pop in and out of homes by imagining the fireplace and the room it's in. You will be able to bring the presents and up to two persons if you so decide with you," finished Aeon.

"So why do I need reindeer, sleighs or anything else? Why not just load up and jump from here to there?" asked Santa.

"Could you imagine trying to do that tens of thousands of times? And remember there is only so much you can include with you when you travel so making multiple trips at once would be out of the question," answered his tutor.

"So I need to use this in combination with everything else, okay I understand," replied Santa.

"Ready to try again?" asked Aeon.

Santa looked to the cabin inhabitants, "Won't the others start to get suspicious?"

"Why would they? In their eyes, we just walked out the door," replied Aeon, "I'll take us to the first leg and you bring us back." with that Aeon held out his arm.

As Annie was talking to one of the line foreman at the Manufacturing Center she was approached by Ulzana Stitchnsew.

"Well hello, Ulzana, what brings you way over here?" asked Annie.

"I have been asked to see if I could find you along with a couple other Council members. We have a special request to discuss with you and Kris and we would like you to meet with the Council later this afternoon," Ulzana said.

"Is this about the amount of products we are producing, or Kris planning to use reindeer?" asked a concerned Annie.

"Not in the way you think, everything is fine, we

just have a question and another favor to ask you of your busy lives," Ulzana chuckled, "If you give my husband a small measure he will soon expect the world, and he has whipped up the Council into bothering you for more." She said while she shook her head.

"With everything you and the rest of the Council have done for us, you may ask anything of either of us, and we would be very hard pressed to ever turn any request away," answered Annie.

"Fine." Ulzana smiled, "How about 3:00 this afternoon?"

Annie nodded and just wondered to herself, *What could they want of us?* She had a couple hours to find out and wondered where Kris was about now.

At about that same time Kris was getting a similar message from Jackson Kilowatt at Aeon's cabin. Kris gave a similar answer and promised to be there at 3:00. He returned to his the lesson with Aeon.

"Now this will be a simple one," said Aeon, "Just put us inside the cabin instead of outside. Since you managed getting us from Italy to here last time, this should be easy."

Kris pictured the inside of the cabin, and putting a

finger to his nose he blinked and they both disappeared from outside and reappeared on the inside by the fireplace. As if they had never left, Frederick looked up and asked Aeon if the drawing before him looked about right. Aeon, without missing a beat said, "Except you will have to give a little more angle to the front of it so it doesn't cause wind resistance."

Forrest answered, "Yeah, I see what you mean, make it more aerodynamic."

Willie said, "I'll work on this to get the best design."

After a few more minutes Frederick said it was time to head back to the village.

When they were walking back, Kris asked Frederick if he knew what the Council wanted to talk about with him and Annie.

Frederick said, "Well I know, but I would rather not discuss it with you, but it is nothing to be concerned about. We have a couple questions for you, and the whole Council wants to put it before the both of you."

Santa knew better than to push the issue and since it was less than an hour away, he figured he could wait until the meeting.

Kris and Annie were reunited heading back towards the village, her coming from the Manufacturing area, and him from the Woodlands.

Annie smiled and said to Frederick, "So do you know what the Council wants to see us about?"

Santa laughed as Frederick said, "I swear you both are the most curious tallfolk there could ever be!"

Santa said, "Forget it dear, I already tried and he's as tight as a clam."

A little while later both Santa and Mrs. Claus stood before the entire Council. Everyone was smiling, which caused the Kringle's to smile as well.

"We have discussed and deliberated much, and we have a couple questions for you both, and hope that you will agree to them," said Carrow.

"May I?" asked Frederick.

"Well, I suppose since it was your idea in the first place, though I daresay we were all thinking along the same lines, anyway. Go ahead, Frederick," responded Carrow.

Frederick beamed and said, "The Council of Elves has unanimously decided to ask if you would both sit on the Council with us. Further, we would like Mrs. Claus to be formally recognized as Chief Elf Organizer of the North Pole, and we ask Santa Claus to be President of the Council."

The Kringles were floored, they couldn't believe that not only did the elves want tallfolk to sit on the Council, but to lead it, and the village, as well.

Santa Claus stammered for a moment, and then with head lowered, said, "The honor you have offered is without measure. If I accept, I would ask as my only condition that on any issue, my vote would only be used as a tie breaker, and that I would not have any undue influence over the Council. As for Annie, my wife may speak for herself."

He looked over to Annie and she curtsied to Kris and then the Council. "It would be my great honor and with pride that I accept the title you wish to bestow on me. I will tell you that I will perform my duties to the Council, the village and the elves of the world to the best of my abilities."

Santa looked at his wife and said, "How long have you practiced that acceptance speech?"

Annie blushed and said, "Since the first day I came to hope that one day they might ask me."

Everyone laughed at her response and Britney said to the other Council members, "See what I told you, she thinks as fast as anyone of us." She turned to Annie and said, "You will do everyone in this village proud in your "official" position, especially since it has been in our hearts for quite some time already."

Frieda practically yelled to the rest, "This is cause for celebration, I motion that we have another feast and make a formal announcement to the village."

"Yes," said Whitey, "and we will help Ella Communicado get the word to all elves outside the village, so that they may attend as well. We haven't added another Council member in over a hundred plus years!"

Santa laughed and said, "Now is there room up there on the dais or do we need to remain on the Council floor?"

With that two larger chairs were brought in and placed in the center of the Council members. This time Denny blushed as he spoke and said, "We were kinda anticipating that you would agree so we had these chairs specially designed for you both."

After a brief swearing in ceremony, Santa and Mrs. Claus took their place as the newly appointed leaders of the North Pole.

The next morning Forrest knocked on Santa and Annie's door. Santa opened it and Forrest said, "Got something to show you, if you can come with me."

Santa kissed Annie goodbye and walked off with Forrest. They came to the stable area and Forrest asked Santa to wait by the corral. He came back a few minutes later leading an entire team of reindeer.

"This seems to be the best of the bunch. Not only are they strong for their small size, but they are the smartest of the one's we have currently. The two in the back are the biggest, and they are Donner and Blitzen, the two in front of them are Ginger and Cinnamon, the front two are Flame and Flash," he said while petting Flame.

"They look beautiful, do you think they could do

the job?" inquired Santa. They seemed much smaller than most reindeer to him and he wondered if a big sleigh filled with presents and his bulk would be too much for the reindeer.

"As soon as I can get the reins put together and get them on the weightless alfalfa we can do some test runs," he answered, "Then we will know if this has all been conjecture, or if we really have a working plan."

Santa spent the next half hour looking over each reindeer trying to familiarize each one in his mind. "You know I have seen them work and they are a hardy stock from the little I know of them, as I was always raised around horses. It will be fun working with a different kind of animal. Most of the time I have seen them, there have only been one or two together. Do you think six could ever function as one?"

Forrest said, "Hard to say, we also have only used two at the most for one cart. Though I will say if you have two hardy reindeer they can be as strong and as fast as any horse team, though I would never say so around Amerigo and the others. And the splayed hooves give them better purchase and less slip in the snow."

Suddenly Santa noticed a red light emanating from the stable. "What's going on in there?" he asked as he pointed to the barn.

"Oh that? It's the darnedest thing you ever saw," chuckled Forrest, "It seems that one of the reindeer was born with a very unusual feature. Instead of being born with fur on his nose like the other reindeer, he has a pigment that glows red. Sometimes when he is excited he can get that thing going like a beacon."

"Mind if I take a look?" asked Santa.

"Be my guest," Forrest showed Santa to the barn, "We call him Torch because he kinda lights the way when we have him out."

Santa stood before the beautiful reindeer with the bright red nose and asked, "What do you think causes this?"

"We believe it is a pigment that he had when he was born. Kind of like a firefly. Near as I can figure out, it is something deeply recessed in this young guy's heritage. Just as you are tall and I have green eyes," shrugged Forrest, "Probably comes along once every several generations. Kinda like the albino we have in the next barn. Pure white with pink eyes, looks strange and beautiful at the same time, just like this fella."

Santa smiled and said, "You know perhaps you could make two harness sets, one for six reindeer and one to include this little guy in the front. I have a strong sense that using him on some particularly bad Christmas Eves might help me out."

"Well he is still pretty young," stated Forrest, "It might be a year or two before he could keep up with the others."

"If this works out, as I expect it will with the reindeer, then perhaps we could devise some exercises to help build strength and stamina," suggested Santa.

"You know, most of these guys love to romp around," thought Forrest out loud, "Maybe I could devise some games for them so that they wouldn't even realize it was a workout, but we could see how they interacted and which ones got along well and which didn't. You know we have an almost endless supply of these animals running around right outside the dome. That's how we got some of these guys."

"You mean these aren't from Lapland and the Netherlands? I thought they were brought in with the other livestock or were born here," puzzled Santa.

"Some were and we have had a few good years for fawns and calves, but some were picked up wandering around the North Pole. This guy's parents are both. Dad was a domesticated bull, but Mom was a wild cow, and we have no idea which side contributed the bright bulb on the end of his face," explained Forrest.

"Too bad," pondered Santa, "I would hope we could get a couple more just like him."

The two men walked back toward the pen and Forrest said, "We have dozens of reindeer and if some reindeer in this group don't work out, I have my eye on some others."

"Well, we will know soon enough," said Santa, "As soon as you get those harnesses completed we will test them out."

"I should have a practice set done by tomorrow, I

have several leather-smiths working on it right now," answered Forrest.

Santa nodded his head, thanked Forrest and said he had to get going.

From there Kris headed into the woodlands again to visit with Aeon. They had been working on his entering and exiting homes by only using his concentration, and what he understood about time travel, which really wasn't much compared to Aeon.

He knocked on Aeon's door and received no response. He knew Aeon was expecting him, so he knocked a second time and after receiving no response went to the elf's garden behind the house. After sitting for a few minutes, he began trying to do some lessons himself. He jumped from the garden to his own home in the village and back again. He tried it again and when he returned, he heard himself knock on the front door.

He quickly went back to the house and sighed. *Got to work on that timing issue*, he thought. He concentrated again and returned to a quiet garden. He then heard what sounded like moaning. Santa ran around to the front and opened the door. He saw the ancient elf lying on the floor all cut up and bleeding, and ran to his aid.

"What happened Aeon?" he asked as he grabbed a cloth and started dabbing the cuts.

With labored breath, Aeon said, "I traveled right into the path of a car that I didn't expect." He looked at Kris through the blood on his face and chuckled saying, "I told you time travel was dangerous. Just a little off the mark and wham."

Santa carefully gathered the elf up and took him as quickly as possible to the physician center where several doctors immediately began working on him.

Several other elves who heard of the accident began gathering at the clinic including many of the Council and Annie, their new CEO.

After a time, one of the doctors came out. He looked tired but carried a half smile. He wiped his forehead with a cloth he had been carrying and said to the group, "He is out of danger. He has some internal bleeding and he will need much rest. Even for up here he is ancient by our standards, and I think his time travel days are behind him." The doctor laughed at the irony of his last statement.

"May he have visitors?" inquired Annie.

"Actually," responded the doctor, "He is sleeping comfortably right now so I would prefer we hold off the welcoming committee for another time. You know, if it wasn't for many of the medical advancements he brought us, he might not have made it. In a way he saved his own life. I will miss learning about new medical advancements from him." The doctor returned to the surgery area shaking his head.

While they were waiting, Kris inquired if there were other elves that could help him with his lessons on the time and space continuum.

Carrow answered, "He wasn't very forthcoming on his lessons. That's why he moved to Woodlands. The Council asked him to train a few apprentices, but he always said that the less who knew how to do this the better."

Frederick said, "I guess I was as close to a friend as anyone in the village, and he never showed me anything more than to freeze time, and I had to beg him for that. There were a few sticky situations when I traveled south that tallfolk would try to hurt or rob me, thinking I was an easy mark. If I hadn't known at least that, I might have wound up where he is now, or much worse. But even after relaying my harrowing experiences, he didn't offer any more information, saying I knew enough to get out of harms way."

Denny said with a smile, "We all thought it was amazing and wonderful that he began training you. Some villagers were sour about him teaching a tallfolk at first, instead of one of their own, but now everyone sees the wisdom of it."

Frederick said, "Yes, I was totally surprised at first until he related events into the future..." he held up his hand at the next statement, "which I am not going to disclose so don't ask, curious tallfolk. But I understood why he had begun to show you much more than us."

"I'm afraid that you now hold the most knowledge in the village outside of Professor Millennium," said Whitey, "I don't mean that in a bad way, it is just I can't think of anyone who knows even as much as you do."

"Guess that now makes you our resident expert," said Carrow.

"He's not dead, just banged up a bit," protested Kris, "He will be back and good as new in a few days."

"You heard the doctor, he thinks Aeon's time travel days are over, as they probably should be, considering..." reflected Frederick.

"We shall see what we shall see," said Denny, "But I for one would not want to risk whatever days the Professor has left for our own selfish purposes. Perhaps Santa, you know enough to do what you need without pushing things beyond this point?"

"After all," Jackson jumped in, "If this could happen to Aeon a few times, we surely don't want to see it happen to our gift bringer, no matter the cost to our advancements toward the future."

"A few times?" questioned Santa.

"Oh, yes," responded Carrow, "We have had to carry him in here a few times as he would just pop into the middle of a Council meeting all broken and bloody like this. Time travel is certainly not without its hazards."

"One time he appeared in the middle of a major battle, with 'bullets flying all around him' he said. He caught one in the shoulder and it nearly killed him. A little further south and it would have hit his heart or a major artery," Frederick was white even now as he relayed the incident.

"What you may wish to consider is that perhaps this was as much as he planned to show you, and you should carefully practice only what you have learned," said Whitey. "And if at some time you decide to teach others some, or all, of what you know, the Council will leave that decision to you."

The others nodded in agreement. Without a formal vote, it was decided that Aeon would retire from time travel, Santa would be the keeper of the secrets, and that any who would ask to learn would be at his sole decision whether or not to teach.

Santa also decided at that same time that unless specifically required to, he would stay within the time frame and location he was at, so his fate would not end up like Aeon's.

The following morning Kris and Annie learned from the doctor that Aeon had a tough night, but was now resting more comfortably. The Council had asked the doctor to keep Santa informed of Aeon's medical condition for reasons of being both the new President of the Council, and the new resident Time Consultant for the village.

Santa had several elves spread the word to the other members of the Council and to anyone that had come to check Aeon's progress. He then headed back to the stables to check Forrest's progress.

As he came into view, Forrest yelled out to him, "Excellent, I was just going to send someone to fetch you. We finished the practice reins and we have a makeshift sleigh to attach it to. Also I had the reindeer on the alfalfa since we spoke yesterday, and while they can't go around the world, we should be able to learn enough about whether or not this will work."

Santa came up to the corral, and another elf he knew only as Pepper brought out the team of deer. Forrest motioned him over to the front of a beautifully made sleigh for two. It was jet black with red piping and bright red runners. It had beautiful curves in the front and a comfortable looking red bench seat.

"Is that the new sleigh?" asked an astonished Santa Claus.

"What that old thing?" Forrest chuckled, "No that was just something we use around here if we feel like getting around a little more leisurely. We built several for the Americas and we kept a few of them down here. But for our purposes, it should tell us what we need to know. We have Randy Woodturner, who you met when you first arrived, working on the big sleigh."

Forrest and Pepper hooked the team to the sleigh and as Forrest entered the sleigh he looked to Santa and asked, "Ready?"

Santa shrugged and said, "Whether or not, we

better find out."

Santa jumped into the sleigh and started laughing at his own thoughts. When Forrest asked him what was so funny, Santa said, "I really hope this works, I had saddle sores for a month after Christmas, and I would guess this would be much more comfortable, even if it is more exercise."

Forrest smiled and with a crack of the reins the reindeer began to charge off. He led them around the corral a few times and then with a mighty pull Forrest forced the reindeer to veer upward and begin to leave the ground. At first the animals began to try to go every different direction, as they realized they were not on solid footing anymore. Forrest had to pull the reins this way, then that way, to try and straighten them out.

Santa was paying close attention to how each reindeer was acting and whether it was working at all with the others or if they were just not cooperating. Some of the deer seemed to work well after a while, but the front pair were just not pulling with the others and kept disrupting the rhythm of the team.

Forrest asked if he should try and push the team for speed or maneuverability, but Santa said, "I am not convinced we have the right team. I think we should wait until we at least have a set of deer that runs together."

Forrest nodded his head and tried some simple banking maneuvers. The back four consisting of Blitzen and Donner and Ginger and Cinnamon were doing fine, but the front two of Flash and Flame seemed out of control. As Forrest tried to rein the team in, Santa commented, "Well, I think we have four, but the front set needs to be switched."

They brought the team to the ground and Forrest said, "I have a few more in the barn that I began on the alfalfa yesterday, along with these six. Let me take two of them."

So they unhitched Flame and Flash from the harnesses and brought out a few more to see which looked to be a good pair.

They tried the next set which seemed to work better, but Santa said if they were planning on approaching the speeds they were discussing, that the team needs to function as one.

Forrest said he could try a couple more reindeer and as long as they now knew that the theory worked, it was just a matter of the logistics of the team.

To this Santa gave his thanks and said that he really wanted to see how Aeon was fairing. He left Forrest wishing him good luck and proceeded over to the clinic.

As he entered the clinic, Santa thought about how this was another great mystery that had fascinated Annie and him. Unlike other parts of the world suffering from everything from dysentery to the common cold and other ailments besides, no one ever got sick in the North Pole. The only reason that the clinic and its medical staff were needed was for occasional accidents and mending broken limbs. The last death here had taken place when Kris and Annie first arrived to the Pole. That elf had put Carrow and Aeon to shame living almost 50 years more than either of them.

No one ever became ill at the Pole. Not even a stomachache as far as he knew. The same was mostly true with the animals. Amerigo should have passed on years ago. But the horse, while tired and showing signs of age, would still put horses less than half his age to shame.

Even the bears, reindeer and other animals lived excessively long lives. There were dogs that were over 40 years old still pulling sleds! The magnetism of the North Pole was astounding.

When Kris arrived, there almost seemed a glee in the clinic as though everyone was celebrating having someone to care for. In fact, Aeon was the only person in the clinic not actually working there. Kris opened the door to Aeon's room and saw him sitting at an angle and looking far better than when Kris brought him in.

"Well you are looking fit," Santa exaggerated, "Nice to see you up."

"Thanks in large part to you for getting me here in time. I don't know what I was thinking. I guess I could only focus on my home so that's where I landed," said Aeon weakly.

"You were probably in shock from the accident. By the way, what is a 'car', I think you called it?" asked Santa.

With a weak wave of his hand he said, "It's like some of the vehicles we have around here only they go even faster and hit even harder." To the last part he gave a weak chuckle, "Ooh, that hurts to laugh."

"It seems you are lucky to be talking at all," a concerned Kris stared at his teacher and said, "The doctor says your traveling days are over."

"They told me that before. But if it is true, I know the place and time I wish to end up in," said Aeon wistfully.

"Not here?" questioned Kris.

"Not even remotely, too many busybodies and they would never leave me alone. Let's face it you and I both know I am not the most social elf in the village," scowled Aeon.

That brought a laugh from Santa saying, "That's for certain, every time I am with you, I feel like I am intruding."

Aeon looked seriously at Kris and said, "I never felt that way about you! I am sorry if I acted that way, as I truly never had a problem being around you. In fact, I looked forward to our visits."

Kris waved it away and said, "I got over it long ago. I figured that was just your way. Kind of like

Carrow."

"Harrumph, don't compare me to that crotchety old goat!" he said sneering. "I am the persona of charm compared to that crabapple."

Santa apologized, but then said, "His bark is much more severe than his bite, and I think you would find a great deal more in common than you might guess. But let's put that aside, I have some questions that I wish you to answer."

Aeon looked at him quizzically, and said, "As long as you are not going to ask me to go off on some insane trip with you. I don't think I have it in me."

Again Santa laughed and said, "Perish the thought! No, but I want to talk to you about what I know and what I do not. For instance, I believe I know enough to accomplish my mission for the children and the North Pole, but I do not wish to jump forward and backward in time as you have done."

Aeon's eyes softened and the corners of his mouth curled up into a small smile, "I am pleased to hear this. I thought about showing you more if you truly wanted to learn, but on the caveat that you not teach anyone else, ever."

Santa looked directly into the old Professor's eyes and said, "It may seem selfish of me, but I have no wish to further my education in that field."

"Selfish how?" Aeon looked puzzled.

"Well if I do not jump forward into time, I cannot

bring back advancements and knowledge of the future, as you have done. I would only be using it for the here and now and to finish what I began with the children. The Council will be unable to know or produce more things based on the information you brought. The doctor even said if it hadn't been for your advanced knowledge they might not have been able to save you. Surely this is a selfish act on my part," explained Kris.

"The Council has enough advances and many more will be discovered and perfected without too much more help from me," said Aeon softly, "Your mission to the world is very different from mine. I could not, nor would I try, to do what you do in a single night. I have provided you tools that you will need now and into the future, as will your descendants, to accomplish these tasks. You will only need to show them how to do what I have taught you, along with what you, yourself will learn, and nothing more. As I have said before, there are many things that are better not known. For instance, I have never looked forward into my own life, as I have never wanted the knowledge of what will or will not happen to me. Having that ignorance has helped me never fear the future or what it brings, but accept the things that I can control."

Aeon looked up at the ceiling and said he was tired.

Kris apologized for straining the old elf, and said he would take his leave. Aeon looked at Kris, gave a half smile and said, "Just so you know, you have been my favorite student and I have great admiration for you." With that Aeon closed his eyes and laid back into the pillow.

As preparations for the feast were made, the news had spread about the Claus' and their positions on the Council. Especially when the Council met a couple days after the swearing in, and both were in their new places in the dais. Everyone who came before the Council for various purposes applauded the news and were excited for the upcoming feast.

Annie had already taken her role as CEO quite seriously. She was beginning to map out more and more presents and ideas. She had almost daily meetings with Stacy Buttons and went over doll lines and ideas, and with Orwin Ironwood, who was the master woodcarver of the North Pole and worked on many of the pull toys that he designed and were carved by elves.

Toys were still the smallest part of the presents that Santa brought. Most children didn't play much, as their chores ate up the entire day. But the new clothes and foodstuffs were always in great demand, especially the sweets, which children hardly ever got as a normal course.

So Annie and Denny worked everyday to increase the amount and variety of sweets. One day Denny came to Annie with a great grin and said, "I think I have something you may really like."

He pulled from his apron a piece of candy in the shape of a shepherds crook and said, "Here, try this."

Annie took the treat and placed it in her mouth, "Ooh, peppermint, my favorite! Wow, that is really good, and it's harder than some of our other treats."

Denny said, "I can have these made in great batches and they wouldn't soften or melt, they travel pretty well and the crook lets Santa leave them in the top of the stocking for children to see."

Mrs. Claus looked at the white piece of candy and said, "It is missing something, though." as she looked at the crook her eyes got big and she said excitedly, "I know...it needs a stripe running around it. A big red stripe!"

Denny caught her enthusiasm and said, "Exactly right! And then these candy "canes" will really stand out. Great idea Miss Annie!"

Mrs. Annie Kringle who went by almost as many names as Santa Claus down south was counting her every blessing. As a woman she had achieved heights that would have been impossible in her own world. She was not only married to a wonderful and loving man who was beloved throughout the world, but she was in charge of everything made at the North Pole, and most of the other activities that were affected up here. She had a large and beautiful home, was in great health and had all the comforts she could reasonably ask. She was a member of a Council that was the political system for the entire elf world, and she loved, and was loved, by all around her. If heaven was better than this, she couldn't imagine how.

Forrest had once again requested Santa join him at the stables. It seemed he had finally worked out a team that he thought Santa Claus would like.

"This time I would like you to take the reins. You control this not much differently than a bridle, or more exactly like a carriage or other cart, with the exception you pull up for lift and ease off the reins for descent," explained Forrest.

"So who do we have here?" Santa asked as he examined the new deer.

"The last four are the same Ginger and Cinnamon, and Blitzen and Donner except I reversed them so it is now Donner to your left and Blitzen to your right. Now the front two are Dasher on your left as I think he may be good, especially with Dancer there on your right." Forrest pointed as he spoke.

"Okay got it," said Santa, "Hop in and let's see what they can do." Forrest hopped into the sleigh and with a crack of the reins yelled out, "On Dasher, on Dancer, now Ginger and Cinnamon, away Donner, on Blitzen!"

As if the reindeer loved hearing their names they gained speed quickly and were in the air almost immediately.

"Wow, that didn't happen before!" exclaimed Forrest, "I think they like you."

As they climbed out through the dome and into the air they increased speed until they were high above the clouds. Santa banked the team to the left calling out their names again, they instantly responded and Santa brought them around in a tight circle. Forrest just nodded his appreciation of the skilled sleigh driver. "You've done this before, haven't you?"

Santa ho, ho, ho'd his laugh and said, "I used to drive a cart around Europe and into the Netherlands. It was how we used to get our goods and belongings around. I was practically born with reins in my hands."

After several tests of maneuverability they aimed back to the dome and the village. Santa was extremely pleased and said that this would be the team to take on Christmas Eve.

"Now I've got some more just in case of a mishap," said Forrest, "I think their antlers match up very well and each is about the same size except the twins in the back, who are obviously bigger." Santa nodded as Forrest spoke, "I think Sky will be right about the antlers, that they may effect the speed of the team, so we will want to keep them as even in all six spots as possible."

"Seven," said Santa, "Don't forget little Torch, I

would really like to use him."

Forrest just shook his head and chuckled, "Seven."

Several days later Santa Claus returned to the stable area, again at the behest of Forrest. He came down the path and turned to the paddock where he found a most amazing sight, and one he would never tire of.

There stood the whole team including Torch in a harness set filled with bells and beautiful leather-works from front to back. And it was all attached to one of the most beautiful pieces of construction he had ever seen. A stunning red and gold sleigh of amazing proportions and extraordinary detail. It was obviously crafted by a master. Large enough to comfortably seat three tallfolk up front, and a cavernous back for holding gifts. While it seemed very large and roomy, it also was angled so that the footprint of the sleigh itself was actually smaller than a sleigh half its size.

Kris whistled and said, "Please give my deepest appreciation to Randy for the beautiful sleigh and of course all the elves who worked on the harness. This is just breathtaking!"

It had a series of buttons and levers on the dash of the sleigh. Santa began to look more closely on the inside and Forrest called out saying, "Be careful there! Wait until I have had a chance to tell you what each of those do!"

"Forrest, this is amazing! Everything is incredible. I wish I was leaving tonight to try it out!" exclaimed Kris.

"Better wait until you know all of its little tricks and how to fly it. This will be a little bit different than before," stated Forrest.

"How do you mean 'fly it'?" asked Santa, "This doesn't work on the same principle as those winged people movers, do they?"

"Not entirely," answered Forrest scratching his beard, "But Willie designed vertical lift and boosters for when you may need greater speed for ascent or a standing lift. Also there is a hidden seat that will appear when you need to carry more passengers than cargo." Forrest pointed to a green button on the dash.

"So can we try it out?" Kris asked with all the eagerness of a boy with a new favorite toy.

"I kinda expected you may want to make a trial run with it, so the deer are all ready to go and everything is hooked and secured," said the elf, "But let's review some of the buttons first and then we can get going."

Forrest showed Santa the various functions of the sleigh and explained how to work them in tandem with the reindeer before him. Finally he said, "Well I think that covers everything. Now it may feel a little strange because the sleigh isn't nearly as heavy as it looks, as Randy and I used all composite materials that are unknown to the outside world as yet."

Santa laughed, "Let me guess, something Aeon introduced you to?"

Forrest beamed, "He said these would come in very handy when he gave me the formulations."

Santa shook his head and chuckled to himself, "I sure do miss that elf."

About two weeks after Aeon returned from his accident and left the clinic, he came before the Council of Elves and made a startling announcement. He had decided he would leave the village, never to return. Even Carrow was surprised at the news and asked in a soft voice if there was any way the Council could change his mind?

"I feel I have done all I can, or am willing to do, and I am going to a special place and time that I have prepared for myself to 'retire'," answered Aeon, "Santa knows everything he needs, and I am getting too old to keep popping back and forth from hither to yon."

"Can't you quietly live out your days here?" asked Frederick.

Santa already knew the answer before Aeon said it. "It would be better for all concerned if I could take my leave of this village, so I could not be coerced or tempted into jumping back and forth into the future."

Denny looked at Aeon and asked, "When would you be leaving us dear friend?"

Aeon gave a rather large grin and said, "I will think of you all often, and I hope you will remember me fondly.

Kris and Annie, you both have begun a legacy that you will be very proud of. I would wish you and your descendants' great success, but I already know you will have it. Good luck and God bless you all." With that he disappeared before their eyes and into his retirement.

Santa missed him greatly and often wondered where he might have gone to. He also wished Aeon would have shared a little more about his own future, but knew that Aeon would not have been forthcoming with the information, anyway.

Santa snapped the new reins and was delighted to hear a chorus of sleigh bells as the reindeer sprung to life. He gently pulled the knob Forrest showed him how to acquire lift for the sleigh and, along with the reindeer, everything began to lift off the ground.

At first Kris had a little difficulty keeping at the same altitude as the reindeer but quickly got the hang of keeping both the sleigh and deer balanced. He saw Torch had a little problem at first matching the other reindeer, but he worked mightily to keep ahead of the pack. Soon he was holding his own ahead of Dasher and Dancer.

Santa again put them through a series of maneuvers and lifts and descents trying different patterns. The bells rang out gaily through the air and seemed to give even more lift to both his and the reindeer's spirits, as they twisted and turned over the North Pole and around the massive dome.

Santa finally decided it was time to test the speed

of the rig. He climbed until he could feel the jet stream in the atmosphere and snapped the reins giving and getting a burst of speed that was exhilarating. While he did not have the benefit of Sky Globetrotter's maps and charts, he knew he could ride the jet stream all around the world if he so desired. And at the speed they were traveling now, that wouldn't take long at all, even without using the time continuum.

As Aeon had promised he was enveloped into a type of cocoon that protected the team, its possessions and occupants. This allowed him to easily give commands without shouting at the top of his voice and the team responded instantly.

He took his team out of the stream and lowered the sleigh just enough to get his bearings. As he had traveled the world many times he could recognize landmarks that many would miss. "Amazing," he said to himself out loud when he realized how far he had traveled.

He returned in almost no time and placed the team in the same paddock he left from. He realized he was grinning from ear to ear when Forrest chuckled and said, "I assume from your look you found this satisfactory?"

"Incredible," answered Santa, "It is amazing how far and fast we can travel, just as Sky had anticipated."

"And that's without training or fully grown antlers," replied Forrest, "I intend to start them on a series of games that will build their strength and stamina, especially your little guy up front."

"Yes," agreed Santa, "I noticed he was having difficulties at first, but he was able to manage his own."

"Well, a couple months of extensive workouts and he'll be able to do a good deal more than that!" chuckled Forrest.

Santa Claus felt that he was ready to go and that time would be slow going until this Christmas.

A few days later, the banquet was held with thousands of elves from the village and making the trek from the other parts of the world. Every elf wanted to meet the new leaders of the North Pole and wish them well.
The crowd was staggering and even Denny, Pierre and their assistants were put to the test providing enough food and drink for the masses. They had made it look easy, however, and everyone received their fill and then some.

There were many speeches from the Council and roaring ovations followed each. Mostly they involved the pilgrimage of the Kringles to the North Pole and the wonderful accomplishments they had added to the mission of the North Pole along with their leadership. The Kringles just blushed at the comments made about them and Annie kept wiping her eyes after each speaker.

Finally the Kringles rose to speak and the crowd

cheered wildly for a full five minutes before finally calming down. Kris was humbled by the show of affection and acceptance, and spoke of a life more rewarding than any other on this earth, because of the elves and their choice to include them in their desire to bring joy to all around them.

Annie spoke about how they had achieved so much, and that there would be many more miracles they would accomplish going forward. She also spoke of the legacy that had been started and wondered aloud about how much more would soon come.

Willie then followed and discussed the new reindeer and how Santa would be traveling this Christmas Eve in an entirely new rig. He explained to the elves living outside the Pole in particular what to expect.

As he finished talking about the new concept everyone heard bells and began cheering as Forrest brought the full rig, including Torch and the other six reindeer and sleigh, to the front of the dais.

It was a glorious way to finish the remarks and everyone crowded around the new transportation devise to get a good look.

The feasting, congratulating, and cheering continued for three days until the Kringles had a chance to meet every elf that had been in attendance. At the end they were exhausted and spent an equal number of days trying to recuperate from the festivities and well-wishers.

It wasn't as long as Kris expected until they were looking at Christmas Eve. But when the time finally came, there was again a tremendous fervor around the Pole as Kris mounted his team for the first time officially. A crowd had gathered from all points of the North Pole, and with Ella Communacado's help, everyone outside the Pole was standing ready as well.

With a mighty wave Santa Claus gave his first commands to the team of reindeer, "Ready Torch? Now Dasher, now Dancer, on Ginger, on Cinnamon, away Donner, away Blitzen, we have many children to visit tonight and history to make!"

Everyone watched in awe as the reindeer gathered speed and the sleigh helped boost them into the air. A moment later and they were through the dome and out of sight.

With a few exceptions, Santa found the whole trip effortless, and with command of the time continuum, and the speed and agility of his reindeer and sleigh, this was one of the smoothest deliveries he had accomplished thus far.

He loved listening to the bells as they strode through the air. And for a while people could hear the bells approaching, and then leaving, not knowing they had been frozen in time as Santa arrived, delivered his presents and disappeared as quickly as he came. But even so, the word spread once more of the magical gift bringer and his team.

And even though many only caught a glimpse, on the late evening of Christmas Eve in 1799, the first sightings of Santa Claus and his sleigh were made. As the new millennium was about to unfold, so was a whole new chapter in the life and times of Santa Claus and the North Pole. The legacy of Santa and his flight was soon to become known worldwide.

Chapter Seven

The way in which the world is expanding makes one think that there was a race to populate it.

- Sky Globetrotter

Expansions

Each year the months went by quicker than Kris and Annie thought possible. Annie was busy all the time setting up more production lines and overseeing the work needing to be done. Kris had gotten into preparing his lists and reading all the letters that were now coming in by the sack full.

He continued to achieve successful runs, and each year his fame, and his list, continued to spread farther and longer.

"Do you really think we will be able to fill all these wishes?" he asked his wife one evening.

"We will do everything possible to take care of as many as we can. But yes...I think we will be able to do it. The question is should we?" responded Annie.

"How do you mean?" a surprised Kris asked.

"Well some of those children may not be the most well behaved and I worry we will be rewarding poor behavior as much as good." Annie stated.

"How could we ever know? It would be impossible to keep track of who is bad and who is not." protested Kris.

"Maybe this year, but I think I am going to put some people on it and see if we can't determine this in the future. I have been told that we will be getting millions of requests every year in the not too distant future, and I think we need to know." Annie said matter-of-factly.

"MILLIONS?" coughed Kris, "How can we deliver millions of toys? Even with everything we are working toward, I can't imagine visiting millions of homes!"

Annie smiled and said calmly, "You will, just wait and see."

It was during a year when he saw hundreds of thousands of products being shipped to various distribution centers around the world that he thought of Annie's prediction and just shook his head. As he planned his route with Sky, he talked about how much more area he could cover.

Sky said, "The world is definitely getting bigger. Look how much more land the Americans have settled this · year alone."

The year was 1803 and she pointed to the area acquired by the United States from France. Kris said the biggest problem was that everyone was so spread out.

"Well they won't be for long. People seem to be populating every corner of the world and much of the world is adopting Christianity as you had hoped they would." Sky laughed at the last statement and chortled, "Be careful what you wish for, because it may come true!"

"Well at least I will be known, and not feared, if I

am caught in their house!" Kris rebutted, "Heaven forbid we return to the days when they thought I was a thief instead."

Together they poured over how best to begin and end the journey. Looking at the potential jet streams and which way they might change was bad enough, but trying to figure how to effectively cover an entire area in a very short period without putting the whole world in a perpetual state of suspended animation was puzzling Kris considerably.

"You know you could still do this over several days, instead of one night," suggested Sky.

"How could I when they are all expecting me on Christmas Eve?" Santa said as he shook his head.

"Not everyone," Sky commented. "According to some legends, many people now put out shoes on the feast day of your ancestor – December 6th, or more precisely on the eve of that day, December 5th. You could take them their presents and treats on that day and leave the rest for the 24th like usual."

Kris knew that special celebrations were being held around the day the original St. Nicholas had passed away, but did not know children were hoping to receive gifts then. "Perhaps I could try it out this year and see what kind of reception I get. It seems silly to hitch up all the reindeer for a handful of countries, though," Santa mused.

"Why not just take Amerigo as you have in the past? Chances are he could handle that well enough, and it would save the strength of the reindeer for later that month," advised Sky.

"That's a good idea, Sky. I think I will talk to Forrest regarding that, and I need to put it to the Council, and my wife," he said with a mighty "Ho, ho, ho."

After clearing everything through the Council (and asking his wife beforehand) he loaded his trusty steed once more, and left for the European and Nordic countries that celebrated the Feast of St. Nicholas.

In order to further save Amerigo's energy he asked, and received, permission from the Council to take one of the fast boats to Spain, and begin his journey there. For many decades afterward this tradition would continue.

In consideration of Annie's concern, he also decided to bring along a stern looking elf from the North Pole that had a remarkable characteristic. By just being around a person, he could tell if that person had evil intent, or was of a "blackheart", as he called it. Annie said it wouldn't be perfect, but perhaps if children were found to be of 'bad quality' that perhaps to leave them a switch would be better than treats.

Kris was concerned about what kind of message he would be sending parents and children if they were to be punished rather than given gifts on the feast day. Annie had the Council put the idea to a vote, and it carried with a majority, especially since Kris was unable to vote except in ties.

However it was amended that Zwarte Piet, or Black

Peter as he became known, would only visit children prior to the Feast of St. Nicholas, and not around or at Christmas, which was a time of forgiveness for all men, especially children. Anywhere he left a switch would announce to Santa Claus that the child there was not to receive a present or treats.

Black Peter was called by many names, mostly Krampas or Grampas in Europe and was often drawn as a grotesque monster, which he laughed about. He was actually from Holland, but carried a dark complexion and walked with a large staff. He was taller than most elves and was quite gaunt when compared to Kris. An imposing figure to children, he sensed most children as good hearted, but wasn't afraid to leave a few switches when he felt otherwise.

In the end, it did make it easier for Santa Claus to distribute many of his gifts and treats to children there, and it allowed Amerigo to continue enjoying his celebrity status as St. Nicholas' horse throughout Europe.

This change in delivery further allowed Kris to take care of many countries prior to the Christmas Eve run. The other continent that was growing as fast as the North American land mass was Australia.

Australia had officially celebrated its first Christmas on December 25, 1788. It had taken a few years to catch on, but once it truly began, it spread like a wildfire. Soon Santa Claus and Sky were mapping out an entire new route for the Southern Hemisphere.

Like the Americas, the area to the south was gaining more and more people. Originally starting out as a penal colony from the British, Australia attracted other citizens as the other new world, America, to colonize it. The seasonality of this area was in complete opposite of Great Britain and the rest of Europe, with summer being in the latter half of the year and winter being in June, July and the surrounding months.

One especially good thing for Kris, is that by being at the opposite end of the world, they were a full day ahead of the rest. Meaning that their Christmas Eve was actually December 23rd in the other parts of the world he frequented. So he could actually do his visits a full day ahead of the remainder of the world.

Kris had contemplated using Amerigo for that trip as well, and had discussed it at length with Forrest.

"I don't know, Santa. Amerigo is getting pretty old to be taking on yet another journey," said a concerned Forrest, "Is there a particular reason you do not want to use the reindeer?"

"For the same reason I worry about using my horse," Santa replied, "I really don't want to wear out my reindeer either. The rest of the continents are growing so fast and I am thinking that a full two day run may exhaust the team."

"Why don't we add a couple more reindeer instead?" questioned Forrest.

"Bring the team up to nine?' Santa scratched his

head, "I am not sure they would all fit on many of the roofs."

"Why not give it a try, as you do not seem to be having too much trouble with seven. Besides if a roof isn't long enough you could just set the team on the ground, as you do on occasion and pop in and out, like you usually do," said Forrest.

"I finally just got the hang of making seven run as one. Who would you add?" Santa asked curiously.

Forrest thought for a moment, "As you know we have begun switching several of the deer each year, I would just add a couple more of the ones you like, and since they are already seasoned, it probably wouldn't be much of an adjustment. Besides, you don't always use Torch, so it would be eight instead of nine. On those trips you would have the same length as when you have seven."

Forrest looked toward the barn, "Besides ever since you came up with this brainchild of yours, we have been adding more reindeer and running them through the reindeer games to see what other deer we might put on that team of yours. I have a great one that I have been anxious to try, but the darn thing keeps getting pregnant every year just before Christmas. We changed her name to Vixen because she attracts males to her like 'flies to honey'."

"Seems we have that problem with Cinnamon, too," Santa laughed.

"Yeah, that's another one, look how often we have had to switch out her for Comet. And Ginger, while not as

often, we had to use Pocatello for her many times, too."
Forrest said shaking his head. "And if they are not
pregnant, they are losing their antlers early."

"Yes, but even with all that, you can't beat the
speed and strength of the team. Okay, we'll try eight and
hope the weather holds this Christmas. But you better have
a ninth halter just in case, said Santa.

"You already know I will," laughed Forrest.

The world was expanding rapidly. Every year Santa
and his team went out, they had to cover more homes,
more families, and more land. Santa Claus was given a
miracle every year in that he never seemed to tire. He kept
going in and out of every house and would pick up more
letters and notes and would leave more treats.

Something began happening that really picked up
his spirits. Often he would pop into a home and not only
see the stockings hung, but a plate of treats left for him.
Often accompanied by a glass of milk or cream and a note
thanking him for the presents.

In America often it was cookies, sometimes it was
sherry and mince pies in Britain and Australia, in Sweden
children left rice porridge. After a time they began leaving
carrots for his team also. Forrest often complained about
the smell of the stables for days after Christmas as the
carrots didn't always agree with their digestion, even if the
reindeer were anxious to eat them.

In Ireland they had begun leaving Guinness and
mince pies or cookies. Santa often had to take several

breaks after leaving Ireland to empty his overly full bladder. Another miracle was he never became inebriated, no matter how much he drank that night. But no matter the offering, he appreciated their gifts and always ate and drank as much as they left him.

He was really getting into a routine every year. Just before the eve of St. Nicholas he would send Peter on his way to identify the bad children, then he and Amerigo would follow up with his goodies for their shoes.

On Christmas Eve, he always began in the Australian continental area now on the 23rd and left his presents with them. While there wasn't nearly the settlement increases like in the U.S., Kris knew he might as well get used to this part of the world because it wouldn't be long until Australia became a heavily settled and populated country. He'd then cross the International Date Line and begin the Northern Hemisphere starting with the Netherlands and circumventing the globe a few times until he finished his rounds.

Another tradition was beginning in the Latin American countries especially in Central and South America. There they would await their gifts for the Epiphany which took place on the twelfth day of Christmas or January 6th. While they celebrated Christmas, it was kept as a strictly religious holiday with the twelfth day or "Three Kings Day" reserved for gifting and celebrations.

This gave Kris a chance to once more rest his

teams and to bring presents on another day other than Christmas, while still keeping the Christmas meaning of the presents intact.

So now Kris was traveling several times from the North Pole in an effort to meet the variety of celebrations. By the second week of January he was exhausted, and while the adrenaline rush kept him going, he was ready for a couple quiet weeks when he finished.

Annie had finally suggested that he take an assistant with him to help with his duties.

"I already have Peter running all over Europe, what else do you suggest?" he asked.

"I mean a helper with you. Someone who would travel with you during the Christmas runs," argued Annie.

"I suppose, but who would I pick? Whoever I chose would seem like favoritism over the other elves. And I can think of dozens of elves I wouldn't mind accompanying me on the trek. I can't take them all," said Santa.

"Don't pick one, let it be decided by vote from the other elves," replied his wife.

"Absolutely! We could have a voting throughout the North Pole, with one elf chosen to represent the entire elven community! That's brilliant, my dear!" Santa was exhilarated at the thought. "It might be especially nice to have some company on the long Christmas Eve trip."

"This way you could have someone to work with and prepare your next visit while you did your current one and that might help speed things along," grinned Annie.

"Yes, and he or she could assist when we get to the distribution centers and allow me to have some rest in between. I think this is a great idea. We will let the Council hold the balloting and elections and we will announce the winner the day before I leave. We could make a big event of it." Kris was smiling from ear to ear over the prospect. He had been contemplating a similar notion but it took Annie to spur him into action.

A few years later the United States and Great Britain were once more at war with each other, as was France and Russia. It was a difficult time for all nations, and blessedly the Treaty of Ghent was signed on Christmas Eve of 1814. Santa and Annie had been praying for peace and it finally came, albeit uneasily.

Again the American economy was in ruin from the war. It had been especially difficult on the New England area and Washington, itself, was left burned and in ruins. The requests for help including clothing and other necessities were staggering. Kris thought he would never be able to supply enough of everything needed.

Several years afterward, the Spanish left the Florida's, and other parts of the continent, to the U.S.

further increasing the size and population centers of the United States. Quickly the country was in expansion mode once more.

Kris could see another dark cloud on the horizon in this young country, and was fearful of the problems it would eventually cause.

Often the elves of the North Pole would become disgusted and discouraged over the continuous warring among nations, but Kris assured them that there were many more people who wished for peace than war. And because of the unending conflicts, people needed Santa more every year.

Then came a series of events that changed the course for Kris, Annie and the North Pole considerably.

Chapter Eight

A baby is God's opinion that the world should go on.

- Carl Sandburg

A Whole New Life

Annie was going over the new production facility one morning when it happened. She had been feeling poorly most of the morning, something that hadn't happened since her arrival to the North Pole. She had a pale look instead of her usually rosy complexion. She was with Carrow, who was now in charge of all the production centers at the North Pole.

As they were going through the new facility and discussing which lines might be set up first, Annie suddenly fainted. She dropped to the ground like a load of rumpled laundry.

Carrow called for help, but there wasn't anyone near enough to the new facility to hear him. So he took off as fast as his ancient legs would carry him to another building that was occupied. Several elves ran with him back to where he left Mrs. Claus.

Annie had regained consciousness but was still feeling a little sick. The elves brought over one of the hovering cargo movers called a "squibble". They helped her up and then the elves took the squibble from the manufacturing area down to the medical clinic.

One of the elves was dispatched to let Santa know something had happened to his wife. He had arrived at about the same time as the elves and Annie. The doctor came out at once and ushered Annie back to an examining room. He asked Kris to wait a moment or two while he did a preliminary examination.

A few more elves had come in as soon as they had heard about the incident. The grave looks on their faces did nothing to console Kris who was now very worried and thinking horrible thoughts to himself. *I thought we were in great health, as I for one haven't had any aches or chronic pains, not even a cold, he said in his mind.* He had hoped that they might live as long as the elves. Now in truth he knew that they were ancient by normal tallfolk standards. As it was now 1854, this was his 114th year on this earth, which was unheard of in regions outside the North Pole. He thought that perhaps life was running its final course, all be it slower, when compared to the rest of the world.

But Annie had always seemed to be in the best of health like Kris. She was a few years younger than him chronologically, and had never complained about a single ailment. Was the stress of running the North Pole too much for her? Had she over-taxed herself and worn herself right into the ground? His mind bounced from one problem to the next and from one worry to another.

It seemed forever before the doctor entered the room again. Everyone gathered around pressing Kris until he felt he wouldn't be able to breathe. The doctor assured

Kris and the others that Mrs. Claus was just fine. "Although I am going to turn her over to the care of Dr. Goodlife," he said. A couple of the elves started giggling right then, while Kris looked confused.

"Dr. Goodlife? Is he a specialist?" Kris asked.

"She. And yes, she is responsible for bringing nearly all the babies we have into the world here," he smiled.

"Excuse me?" said Kris.

"Congratulations Santa, you are going to be a Papa!" the doctor laughed.

It was inconceivable. They were both over 100 years old. How, when they were unable to have a child when they were younger and in their prime, could they be having a baby now?

Dr. Hope Goodlife smiled and looked at the couple. She said, "As you already know there are some strange properties taking place at the Pole. It is possible that whatever prevented you from having a child in your younger years is no longer an issue now."

"Will it be safe for Annie to have this child in her advanced years?" asked Kris with a strained look.

Annie gave him a hard look.

"How do you feel right now, Anne Marie?"

questioned the doctor. "Too be perfectly honest except for the morning sickness, I have never felt better," she admitted.

"Well then," continued Hope, "you seem to be in excellent health, and I don't see why there would be any cause for alarm other than the usual concerns during pregnancy. I do not even recommend that you change your usual lifestyle until the last trimester. Possibly go a little easier running all over the Pole, so you don't faint or feel light-headed again. We will keep things closely monitored and I would like to see you every two weeks for now."

Annie laughed and said that would be fine, as they had much to accomplish before this new life would change many things for them both.

"And in wonderful ways," laughed the doctor.

As they left the doctors office Annie snuggled up to Kris and said, "Imagine, the one thing that I thought would make our life complete, but gave up hoping for, a child."

Santa shook his head and said, "I thought we were busy before. I can't even fathom what this will do to all the other things we were trying to accomplish."

Annie gave him a concerned look, "Do you not want this baby?"

Kris looked horrified, "Of course I do! You misunderstand me! I was just saying that we were so busy before, and had such full plates...I guess I am just trying to conceptualize how with all we were doing, how to fit all the activities a baby will require into the mix as well."

Annie laughed and said, "Like every other set of parents do! I am sure nearly every couple starting a family wonders how they will do everything they need to when a baby comes along. We are no different than any other parents."

"With one exception," said Kris.

"Yes we are older, but then who has more experience around children than we do? Think of the thousands of children you are meeting every year now," said Mrs. Claus.

It was true. Kris was now leaving the Pole several times and traveling among children to see how they were behaving. Often he would meet up with other elves and they would observe children at play or doing their chores and make notes.

And several came to him to thank him for their gifts or to give him ideas on what they might like to see for that year. Sometimes he brought Annie just so she could see the results of her operations running the North Pole. She always enjoyed meeting the children as much as Kris.

While Zwarte Piet would still go through Europe checking on children, Santa was trying to determine how other children were behaving. He and some other elves had been working on a way to monitor children's activities, but for the now this was the only way. Besides, he enjoyed meeting them and getting hugs and kisses from them.

Suddenly Kris laughed and said, "Yes, but we have always been able to give them back if they acted up, or when they started asking too much from us, now we will have to keep this one! Ho, Ho, Ho!"

"Well, we will just make sure that we will never want to give this one back as it grows." and she gave her husband's arm a squeeze.

And so as the year got longer, Annie became rounder. But slowing down was not in her nature, and she kept a full agenda of activities for herself and the rest of the Pole. She finally allowed the Council to convince her to take help from some of the volunteers that were offering to do laundry and cleaning around their home, and even allowed some of the elves to bring meals occasionally.

"You know it is tradition in the Pole that whenever one of our own is pregnant, that everyone chips in to assist. They only want to do what they would do for others up here," Ella Communicado stated to the couple during one Council meeting.

"It's not me," protested Kris, "I have been telling her the same thing. I keep asking her to slow down and she just keeps charging forward as if the house was on fire."

"Oh, alright," Annie finally said with a resigned voice, "I just feel that while I have the strength, I should be getting these things done. But I guess letting others help out will do us both good."

But she still was charging around the Pole working on the plans for Christmas for that year. Even Dr. Goodlife had asked her to slow down just a little.

One morning, there was a knock on the door about

the time Annie usually left to begin her rounds. She opened the door to a small congregation of elves each grinning from ear to ear.

"Good morning, Miss Annie, your chariot awaits," chuckled Frederick Salsbury. He motioned to a smaller than usual dogsled with four pretty Huskies anxiously awaiting their passenger. "I spoke with Hope and she said she wished that you could at least be transported on your various rounds by something other than your own feet. So here are your own sled and driver, Hans Hindquarter, to assist you each day."

A young man with a narrow face and bright blue eyes smiled at Annie and said, "It will be my pleasure to work with you Mrs. Claus. I am at your disposal everyday." and he gave her a little bow.

Annie just shook her head and laughed. "Seems there is a conspiracy against me doing much of anything," she chortled. "Oh very well, I'll be out in just one moment. And Hans, please call me Annie or Miss Annie if you must. If we are to spend much time together at all, I prefer less formal titles."

The young man smiled even broader and bowed again.

She told Kris about the latest delegation, to which Kris said, "Bless you, Hope. Annie, these people have your welfare at heart, and you should thank your lucky stars for it."

She kissed Kris goodbye and just chuckled as she

left.

Boarding the dogsled, she actually felt quite comfortable while Hans expertly maneuvered the team through the village to the destinations Annie requested. After a short time, she wondered why she hadn't thought of this herself, except she thought it might be presumptuous to ask to be taxied around the North Pole all day long.

But bigger things were in store as Frieda Cutinglas and Britney Clearwater were in charge of yet another delegation. As both of these women had raised families of their own, they were collecting items on behalf of the new baby's arrival. A stroller, carriage, furniture, clothing, toys, a high chair, bassinet, bathing needs, and all those necessities that would be needed once the child was born was being assembled by the two women. Many of the things were new as they expected a tallfolk's child would be larger than their own elven children. And whether new or used previously, each was a work of art in its own right. As everyone knew this was for the Giftgiver and their CEO, it had to be the best ever created.

Between the exceptional care given by Hope Goodlife, and the help of the other elves, the time for the blessed event went smoothly and quickly. Around the beginning of September as the Council convened for the first time that month, Annie announced she had come to a decision.

"It is time for me to stay at home and await the arrival of our child," she stated as the meeting was called to order. "This will be my last official act until sometime after the arrival of the baby. I can, of course, be sought out anytime to make suggestions or offer advice, as the need arises."

Everyone knew the time was coming, so this was no surprise. They all wished her a good rest and said they would be checking on her needs.

Then Frieda stood before the rest of the board and stated, "As this is Mrs. Claus' last board meeting before the birth, I think we need to send her home properly prepared." As if that was the cue, suddenly elven men and women came down the central corridor and through both sides wheeling, carrying, and pushing a full array of baby items.

Britney beamed at the Clauses and said, "We expect everything you may need for the arrival of your baby is here. We will set these things up later, but we already have people working on painting and decorating your nursery right now. Hopefully, they will be finished by the time you return today.

The rest of the afternoon, Kris and Annie marveled at all the wonderful gifts that were bestowed on them like so many jewels, and thanked each of the elves in turn for their treasures.

When they returned home they found a beautiful nursery with all manner of furniture and more gifts to make the necessities of raising a baby as comfortable as possible. The room was done in brightly colored murals of the North Pole and its residents, right down to Annie and Kris pushing a baby carriage and stroller through various parts of the village. A note was left on the new baby's dresser. It stated:

For the couple who does so much for elves and tallfolk alike, may you always know how beloved you are by all.

It may have taken nearly one hundred years, but the couple was completely ready for the birth of their child. Annie wept with joy.

About the middle of the month, Annie once more seemed like she was on a mission. She was racing throughout the North Pole again, checking on the production lines and comparing Santa's lists and letters against what was being produced. She was still being taxied around in her custom-made dog sled, but she was a sight walking around the various places with her now very bulging tummy.

While Annie was busy, Hope Goodlife had also been hopping that week. She had delivered five babies to various elves. Each elven child weighed in between four and five pounds, with the five pound, 1 ounce child, delivered to one of teachers at the Elf Trade School being an unusually large baby.

The baby room was filled with many small cribs, except for one that looked twice the size of the rest. In the corner by the window it sat empty, waiting for the Clauses baby. There were a few more elves expecting, but none were due that week.

It was when Annie was being sped from one of the production centers toward the greenhouse when she felt a stabbing pain followed by a gush of water. She lifted her hand, which was Hans' signal to stop. Then she was racked with another spasm and cried out. Hans went white. While he knew it was certainly a possibility that this could happen, he really had hoped it would take place while she was at home.

He looked at Mrs. Claus and said, "Miss Annie, do I need to veer over to the clinic?"

A slightly out of breath Annie just nodded her head and said, "Yes, I believe it is time."

Hans steered the sled as quickly, though gently, through the snow as he possibly could. He also pushed a red button on the bar which immediately set off a blinking red light at the clinic, the Clauses home, the Council chambers and a small box on Kris' belt. It was to alert everyone that the baby was imminent and that Kris needed to get to the clinic quickly.

For September 16, 1854 this invention was unheard

of outside the North Pole, and Jackson Kilowatt was very proud of it. He had it installed when the idea of the sleigh was presented to him. As his own red light kicked on, Jackson signaled the other elves.

Annie went in at 2:15 pm and Nicholas Kristopher Kringle was born at 5:38 pm.

The entire area of the clinic was packed with well wishers and excited guests awaiting the news. When Kris came out and announced it was a boy, the cheers and roars of approval could be heard throughout the Pole.

An heir to the Giftgiver had been born! This was a truly joyous occasion and one that would need to be celebrated. A week later when Annie was feeling better and up and around, the North Pole threw a feast and party, as had not been seen since the banquet for the Kringles as the leaders of the Pole, but now it was in honor of the birth of Nicholas. It rivaled almost anything that had taken place with the tallfolk for Nicholas' descendant, St. Nicholas in December.

Annie was enjoying being a mother with all her heart. She was having the time of her life feeding, clothing and spending every waking moment with her newborn. Kris walked around the North Pole with his chest puffed out all the time regaling the latest looks and movements of his newborn son.

Every day different elves would come by to assist and give Annie a little rest or a nap while they cared for the first, and only, tallfolk born to the North Pole. One thing the Kringles knew without question is that Nicholas would be provided for in all his needs, and would receive quite a good deal of attention from all the residents of the North Pole.

Chapter Nine

His eyes, how they twinkled! His dimples how merry! His cheeks were like roses, his nose like a cherry! His droll little mouth was drawn up like a bow, and the beard of his chin was as white as the snow. He had a broad face and a little round belly, that shook, when he laughed like a bowl full of jelly.

- Clement Clarke Moore

The Legend Continues

Mary was a sick little girl. Her father, despite being a learned academician, could do little for her except bring one doctor after another to their mansion named "Chelsea". One evening while sitting by his daughter's side he asked if there was anything in particular that she wanted that Christmas.

"Could you write me a story, father?" she asked.

"What kind of story my dear?" he inquired.

Mary shrugged her shoulders and said a nice story would suit her just fine.

Mary's father was actually a rather stodgy man. As a professor of classics at the General Theological Seminary in New York City, his most notable literary work to date had been a two-volume tome entitled *A Compendious Lexicon of the Hebrew Language*.

Later that week the man was out riding in a sleigh doing some Christmas shopping and a thought came into his head. He began scribbling notes as soon as he got home. Soon after, he had finished his daughter's story.

The year was 1822 and he gave the poem to his cherished young lady. The following year Mary Clarke

Moore made a miraculous recovery and was fine after that. Professor Moore also gave several copies to friends following Mary's recovery. One friend passed it on to the editor at the *Troy, New York Sentinel* which published the poem on December 23, 1823.

It took Professor Clement Clarke Moore fifteen years to finally admit to his authorship for penning the piece he called "a trifle". But it set the wheels in motion as one of the largest publicity pieces for all time with Santa Claus.

Kris remembered the home, and knew he had even received letters from some of the Moore children (there were six in total). He had no recollection of ever meeting Moore himself, but thought it was possible. Sometimes he was a little careless and ran into a couple inhabitants of the houses he visited, especially when he thought time was actually on his side.

Several times he would arrive at a home and then invoke the time continuum. So the sighting of the sleigh and reindeer was certainly a possibility. The fact that Santa didn't use chimneys anymore was probably taken from lore about his earlier visits.

But soon there it was for the world to see. A story about his visit, and while Kris felt Moore had overstated his stocky build, he supposed the suit made him look fatter than he really was. His face and story spread as fast as any news he could remember, and soon a new tradition of reading "A Visit From St. Nicholas" on Christmas Eve was begun in countless homes. Later the poem would be better known as "The Night Before Christmas", but regardless of its title, it was a wildfire that was moving through the United States and other parts of the world with incredible speed.

After the birth of his son, and later that same century, another man was having fun showing Kris off to the masses. It became especially popular to draw cartoons of Kris as an inspiration of hope, especially as the United States was being ripped apart by a civil war.

Several times Kris looked at the scorched landscapes during the 1860's as he flew over many battles, raging fires and mass graves, and the poor inhabitants on both sides of the war left him sad and shaking his head.

In spite of all the bloodshed and tragedies that had raged for years, Santa Claus welcomed giving the people a respite from the bad news and instilling hope to the people each year.

While it was tough to receive letters asking the safe and healthy return of loved ones, it was also fun to hear about what the children were doing to prepare for his visit and some of the things they requested. Many were of a simple nature still, like clothes and candy, some were more involved and more heart-wrenching, such as the young man who requested that no one come and take the scarce harvest his family was able to secure. Regardless the subject, Kris used to delight in reading many of the letters to Nicholas who was growing rapidly.

In January of 1863, a cartoonist by the name of Thomas Nast had another one of his cartoons published on the cover of *Harper's Weekly*. The cartoon showed Santa Claus meeting with the Union troops at Christmas. Interestingly, the suit he depicted Kris in for that cartoon also later became the standard for Uncle Sam, which he drew in later years.

Later that year on December 26, 1863, Nast introduced Santa's famous bag and he drew him a few more times up through 1865.

Kris' likeness and his fame were growing in ways he couldn't fathom. After the end of the Civil War, around the 1880's, in New York they had begun giving Christmas presents to one another on an unprecedented scale. And in 1890, a compilation of Nast's works was released and Santa Claus was again put forth to the morass of people now celebrating Christmas.

But it wasn't only Kris that was suddenly being portrayed and discussed. Just prior to the Civil War, the famed author Louisa May Alcott completed, but never published a book entitled *Christmas Elves*. Now for the first time the rest of the North Pole was being spotlighted, even if not publicly.

A few years later in 1873 in *Godey's Lady's Book*, Santa's elves were depicted whilst at work. With the front cover illustration for its 1873 Christmas Issue showing Santa surrounded by toys and elves with the caption, "Here we have an idea of the preparations that are made to supply the young folks with toys at Christmas time." Additional recognition was given Edward Eggleston who authored the *Godey's Lady's Book*, and also an 1876 work "The House of Santa Claus, a Christmas Fairy Show for Sunday Schools".

While it wasn't as accurate as it could have been, it brought forth the whole concept of the North Pole being behind Santa's good works. The Council of Elves was not exactly happy about it when Kris showed it to them, but they had already resigned themselves to the idea that they would not be able to keep secret forever.

This was especially true since a different elf accompanied Santa each year, as was suggested by Annie. Each year the Council took ballots from all the elves in the North Pole and elsewhere to determine who would accompany Santa Claus each year. An elf could only be chosen once in their lifetime, as there were many elves that wanted to receive this prestigious honor.

As a result, even with the time continuum being used, eventually people would spot the elves just as they had with Amerigo, the reindeer and sleigh.

While the civil war in the United States had partially slowed the steady expansion in that country, more people were settling in Australia and New Zealand and South America. Kris' route was still growing larger each year.

Kris had been using the eight and nine reindeer teams ever since Forrest suggested it. They still switched the reindeer out each year and used various teams depending on how large their antlers grew during the year. It was a carefully balanced plan and many times changes had to be made the week of the trip.

The year he made the trip that Clement Moore made famous, he did indeed have Dasher, Dancer, Prancer, Vixen, Comet, Cupid, Donner and Blitzen. The following year Vixen was pregnant and Prancer lost his antlers, so he used Ginger and Cinnamon again, and the year prior to the poem, both Dasher and Dancer had lost one of their antlers and he used Blaze and Fireball with Torch leading the way that year.

Mostly due to the rigorous training that Forrest had developed, many of the reindeer like Blaze, who wasn't able to do the first run with Santa, became stronger and more coordinated. Santa was pleased with the results and knew that he now had a stable of nearly 30 reindeer awaiting the chance to pull the sleigh Christmas Eve.

By the close of the century, another idea that would soon become a tradition repeated in thousands of places across the United States and later, the world, had sprung up. This was also based on the drawings of Thomas Nast from the 1860's.

In 1890, James Edgar a merchant in Brockton, Massachusetts dressed up as Nast's Santa Claus to entertain the children at his department store. The result became something that for many decades Kris would have mixed feelings about. The commercialization of Santa

Claus and Christmas. Edgar became the father of the Santa Claus at the department store, and later in history, Edgar's idea would be repeated in the malls.

Once again the speed at which something caught on baffled Kris. His likeness was soon popping up all over the world. While some of the legends and lore were off the mark or culturally changed to make sense in one particular country or another, many of his movements were correctly mimicked and he began wondering if people were beginning to see him even through the time continuum.

Even Annie started appearing in stories and was popularized by James Rees from Philadelphia who wrote about Mrs. Claus, although he gave her different first names. He had penned her into his short story "A Christmas Legend" in 1849.

But it was a later poem by Katherine Lee Bates in 1889 entitled "Goody Santa Claus on a Sleigh Ride" that brought her front and center. Goody is short for Good Wife, as in Mrs. Santa. In the poem she finally has her say, and travels with Santa Claus as recompense for all the work she does at the North Pole.

In truth, Kris asked Annie to accompany him more times than not, but she never wanted to go saying it was far more important to the other elves, and she was quite content to rest on Christmas Eve and prepare the Christmas feast instead.

There seemed to be a "Santamania" developing across the country and spreading across the oceans. It was as if everyone was trying to learn, or put forth their own theories, about Santa, Mrs. Claus, the elves, reindeer, Amerigo and the other elements of the North Pole.

Santa just laughed his now patented "Ho, ho, ho" and brought the stories to the Pole to share with his wife, son and friends.

In fact, only Nicholas seemed invisible to the outside world, which was just fine with everyone at the Pole, including Nicholas. He grew fine and strong and attended all the schools that the other elf children went to. He was very bright and the teachers were pleased that he seemed as smart as the top elves. He had a stocky build like his father, with a full head of brown hair, though red streaks would appear when he would turn his head a certain way in the light.

He loved hearing about his father and seeing the cartoons and drawings. He laughed particularly hard when his father introduced him to "The Night Before Christmas" at the part about the "bowl full of jelly" describing his father's waistline.

Nicholas loved the North Pole and all its residents. He had requested taking a Christmas Eve trip with his father on a few occasions, but was told he would have to wait a little while longer for that to happen.

As the new century came around, Nicholas had reached his mid-forties and had taken on a good deal of his mother's authority and work with the production lines. He had become a fine looking man, though he still waited patiently for his father's invitation to come on the Christmas Eve run.

Chapter Ten

If men would ever learn the true meaning of the word "respect", wars would cease to exist.

- Nicholas Kringle

A Very Different World

From the beginning the 1900's had a tumultuous start, starting with the assassination of King Umberto I of Italy. The next year brought the death of Queen Victoria and later President William McKinley was gunned down and later died.

But also in that first decade, the Wright Brothers flew, the first message made it around the world, the first silent movie (The Great Train Robbery) was released, and the world saw the first World Series and later pitched in to help San Francisco through its monstrous earthquake in 1908.

The world was already beginning to get smaller as tallfolk had learned to harness things like electricity, communications, and flight. Ships were crossing the Atlantic in record numbers and they kept getting bigger and grander.

Santa was truly visiting places nearly all over the world. The U.S. was still expanding and by 1900 was up to 45 states, the Commonwealth of Australia was officially recognized in 1901 and Santa was even making trips to China as Britain, France, Russia, Japan and Germany controlled parts of China and much of its economy. So with all the Christians and Christian converts, China had become as much a part of the Christmas Eve journey as the rest of the world.

Much of Africa was being ruled by other empires as well, mostly British and French. Now that the Suez Canal had been opened, the British had a stronghold in North Africa. They wrote letters to Santa almost as often as the populace in Britain itself.

Santa Claus was beginning to feel his age, now 160, and knew that it would not be many more years before he would have to turn the reins over.

Nicholas has become a strong and intelligent man and had (for the most part) taken over the manufacturing process from Annie and Carrow. Carrow would still match him step for step and would actually initiate any new changes himself. Nicholas had the good sense not to step on Carrow's pointed shoes and let him remain "in charge" of the production and manufacturing areas.

He would also spend a good deal of time around the stables, the trade schools and some days just would walk for hours around the vastness that was the North Pole taking in all its wonders. His parent's house was so large, he never felt the need for his own quarters and often he would be in the home never knowing if his parents were there or not. They did try to have dinner together every evening and would talk openly about the outside world and its problems.

"It's a whole different world than the one before," Kris told Nicholas and Annie, "Try as we did to keep a lot of the inventions we have up here out of the hands of tallfolk, they have managed to figure out a great many of them on their own."

"Well father, while the elves are quite brilliant and have 'borrowed' ideas and processes from the future, everyone knew it would just be a matter of time until everyone else on earth found ways to create many of the same products," said Nicholas, "There has to be a few other extremely intelligent people out there, and I believe this century will see advancements on an unprecedented level as one invention will lead to another."

Annie said, "And wouldn't it be marvelous if they began using these improvements to help others instead of destroying each other."

Kris shook his head saying, "If only. I am afraid that for some strange reason they all feel the need to butt into the affairs of other peoples, which of course causes many conflicts. I have an uneasy feeling that we will see many new wars along with these new advancements. I just hope they do not become too serious."

Then the topic switched back to production events at the North Pole, new composites that had been created and the like. Suddenly Kris looked up at Nicholas and began laughing.

"What's so humorous?" asked Nicholas.

"Your hair! I just noticed you have a bunch of gray streaks starting in your hair!" laughed Kris.

"I told you he was very observant about some

things and not at all about others," chuckled Annie.

"Father, I have had that for a few years now, and yes it seems to be getting whiter by the day. I also am having trouble keeping stubble off my face for even a day as it seems to be growing at an alarming rate," Nicholas answered.

"Why not just let it grow?" questioned Kris, "Seems that I had a beard and mustache before I was 40."

Nicholas shrugged, "Perhaps. And you were doing deliveries before you were 40 as well. Of course if I grow a beard, I may wind up looking even more like you, and the elves may pack the sleigh for me instead!"

Kris laughed and said, "The day is coming soon, my son. I expect that before the end of this century that will happen, but I have much to teach you before then. You still have difficulty driving the mail sleigh, and that never leaves the ground."

Nicholas retorted, "Perhaps if you could take some time and begin working with me then I could start learning what I need."

"I agree, and we will start this year, so long as you don't try to push too hard and only do what I am willing to teach you," Kris stared at his son.

"Agreed." answered Nicholas.

Kris had a bad feeling about what was ahead of them in this new century. He had already seen some political moves that he thought might put the world on very shaky ground. He certainly did not want HIS son flying around while countries were shooting at each other.

Heads of state were being assassinated, powers were shifting, revolts and revolutions were taking place, and Kris thought this was just the beginning. He had even thought on more than one occasion about using the time continuum to see how bad things might get. He decided that whatever was coming he would deal with at its own time. One thing was certain, he knew that it was going to be bad. It wouldn't take too many years before he realized how right he was.

But no matter how bad things got in the world, there were still the children. He realized that their innocence was the one bright spot in a dark world. They knew nothing of conquest, of political strife, and while they were sometimes caught up in the troubles of the world, more often than not, they managed to keep their childlike qualities intact and could smile at a stocking full of candy canes and a simple toy to play with.

The future was as bright as their eyes. If Kris could only keep the light of kindness in them, they may remember that kindness when they were older. Was he being naive? Possibly, but if no one did this, then he felt the world might truly doom itself in the future. As long as he could inspire hope and love, he would visit every child who asked for him. He was already concerned that he was missing far too many children as it was. In spite of the thousands, no tens of thousands, of letters he received each year, he still knew that many couldn't read or write well enough to send a letter. And even if they all did, could he truly fill every request for all the children of the world? It was a daunting thought.

He thought about these problems often and they consumed a great deal of his time and concern. He had discussed them with some of the elves as well, like Denny and Frederick, who would listen with sympathetic ears, but had no practical advice.

Frederick asked Kris if Aeon had offered any more ideas on bending or manipulating time, to which Kris shook his head.

"If he knew more than he told me, he kept it to himself and assumed I would eventually figure it out," replied Kris.

"Well when the time is right you will find the answer," Frederick said with a shrug, "Aeon had more faith in you than he did with others of his own kind. There was something in you that he truly liked."

Nicholas was also vexing on these problems and was out walking with Jackson Kilowatt discussing the new electric lights that were beginning to take serious foothold in nearly every advanced country, he brought up how to reach all the children of the world the way electricity was beginning to.

"It seems to me the answer to that riddle is in all your impersonators." Jackson mused, "If there was a way to harness all the requests going to them instead of you, then perhaps you would learn who every child is, and what they wanted for Christmas."

Nicholas' eyes got very large as he looked at Jackson, "That's it! I could work something out where, as they meet the children, the requests could somehow be transmitted to us here! And while we are at it, perhaps we could somehow tap into the hospitals to records the births as they happen, so we could at least be aware of their existence."

Jackson looked at Nicholas and said, "This could take years to implement, but I could see the possibilities, especially since tallfolk are catching up with electric current. We could devise a system and just tap into the information for our own uses. Someone told me we have a couple very bright elves that are doing some wonderful things with machines that produce what they call "data". Apparently, they can keep tabulations on an infinite variety and mass amounts of information. Perhaps you should talk to them?"

"Indeed, who are they?" Nicholas seemed genuinely animated at this new turn of events.

"I know one of them," Jackson continued, "His name is Macintosh Gelfeeney, the other who I haven't met yet, is Ion Crosswire, his cousin. You can usually find them hanging around together near the Trade School up on

Mount Elvish. They spend long hours working on their machines."

"Hmm, I guess I will have to take a walk up to the trade school later," smiled Nicholas.

"Probably a good place to start," replied Jackson.

In the year 1914 the world boiled over into the "Great War" as it was being called. Many nations were fighting, and it was almost impossible for Santa Claus to go anywhere and not see destruction and the wounds of combat from nation upon nation everywhere. The one exception was that America was still neutral and was scarcely aware that year of the raging battles taking place across the oceans.

Kris wished he could skip the European theater all together, but remembered all the children who were desperately hoping for his visit. And he would not disappoint them by not showing up with their requests, regardless of the peril.

So he dutifully filled every request he had received during the year. Most were simple enough, but requests for Daddies to come home were a tougher lot. He had left notes that he and the elves had written explaining that this was in God's hands, and he would say a prayer for their safe return, which he and Annie did every night of the year.

But even through the tumultuous problems in Europe, there was a tremendous bright spot that happened one fateful year. It happened while he was in New York City that Christmas Eve. That was the night he made one of his greatest discoveries.

While he was in a large estate, he had just begun to fill the stockings at the fireplace, when he looked to his left. There was a full length mirror reflecting his entire image. As the occupants must have wanted to enhance the size of the already massive room, there was a duplicate mirror on the opposite wall, which reflected the image in the first. Kris was fascinated looking at the image in the mirrors being reflected time and again, back and forth, between the two mirrors.

As he stared, a thought formed in his head.

He soon realized right then and there, that time would never again be an issue. The last puzzle piece of the time continuum had presented itself in that reflection. He was anxious to try his theory, but would wait and practice during the year, rather than possibly make an error on this important night.

But he knew instinctively that he was right.

The next year brought forth some major discoveries

and implementations that would forever change the future of the North Pole and would set the stage for all Christmas deliveries to come.

Nicholas did indeed meet with Macintosh and Ion regarding the problem of reaching all the children who believed in Santa Claus and the North Pole. They presented several concepts and plans having to do with tapping into the information at hospitals and birthing units. The elves also suggested that every time a letter was received in the Pole, that as much information as possible be gleaned from it and put into what they called a "database".

"Just consider it a massive list of information that can be sorted and manipulated in several ways," beamed Macintosh, "I foresee some year these machines will be everywhere and people will use all the information they can hold in many different applications."

Nicholas rubbed his newly bearded chin and said, "Well before that takes place, I hope we can get the maximum use out of it before the tallfolk get it."

"Spoken like a true elf," Ion snickered, "You are sounding just like your father and the rest of the Council. Information will someday be the most important thing in our world, and when that happens, perhaps tallfolk will quit beating each other up and share things better."

Nicholas asked, "So how do we harness all this information for our own use?"

Macintosh said that first they need some

communication equipment ideas from Ella and then they would need to develop a set-up for each potential "Santa Claus" that would record a child's request and transmit the information without wires to the North Pole to a receiving station so it could be entered into the information holding machine.

"Without wires?" Nicholas asked, "How can you do this without the impersonator not being attached to something?"

Ion laughed and said, "You know, calling them 'an impersonator' may not be the best choice of words. It may be difficult enough in soliciting their help without insulting them."

Nicholas chuckled, "I guess you are right. Perhaps since they would be representing Santa Claus and the North Pole, a better title might be ambassador."

"Certainly sounds more official and important." agreed Macintosh, "But back to the issue, we already have one and two-way radio devices that can transmit information and recordings over a great distance. Similar, but far more advanced than the radiotelegraphy being experimented with in the South."

Ion interjected, "But it is important that they are beginning to place radio sending and receiving stations around the earth that we can use as well, to broadcast the signal here."

"Will this advance tallfolk's society using our technology?" asked Nicholas, "If so, we will have to run this past my father and the Council, and I am not sure how open they will be to the idea."

"We are only talking a short time gap here, perhaps six months to a year or so," answered Ion, "They seem to be making rapid advancements in communications with the telephone, telegraph and radio. So we wouldn't be providing anything they won't have themselves shortly."

"Besides we have far more advanced products that they will not see for several decades such as we have already begun sending out images and building data transmitters that can be shared throughout the North Pole," said Macintosh, "Pretty soon we will be coming to your home and installing all manner of machines for your work and enjoyment."

Nicholas just laughed to himself.

We are also working with Henri Muzak and Carol Joynote to put a system in place where soon music will be everywhere throughout the North Pole, so you can enjoy it as you are moving from one place to another," grinned Ion.

Nicholas said how wonderful he thought that would be for everyone, "Now, let's get back to how we capture this vast amount of information, and how will we sort and use it once we have it?"

Nicholas and the two elves talked many more hours about how to implement the system and how they might initiate the first "Ambassadors" for the North Pole. Nicholas would have to go before the Council and talk about how much and what kind of information would be shared from the Pole in order to gain the necessary cooperation for the program.

It too was going to be a very long discussion for a much later date.

Meanwhile, Kris was anxious to try his new theories. It involved using and practicing with the time continuum. Kris had decided the best place to begin putting his theories into practice was the very place he learned of the time continuum.

The house was vine covered and showing signs of abandonment, but the gardens were still pristine, and Kris wondered if old Aeon might come back secretly from time to time to tend them. He still wished he would catch the elf back in his home, but a quick survey showed he hadn't been there since he left the Pole, now many years ago.

Kris did a little clean up of the inside and decided it was good enough for his purposes. He took a deep breath and began concentrating. Soon he vanished from the cottage. When he returned it was only for a moment and then he disappeared again.

When he returned the second time, he had a big grin on his face. *Okay,* he thought to himself, *let's see how many overlaps we can do, and how, and if, they effect each other.*

Kris spent much of the day at the woodland cottage, though he wasn't there physically very long at all.

He returned later to Annie and explained the exciting new breakthrough he came upon. Annie gave him a broad grin and said, "I told you that you would eventually figure out how to continue doing more and more to fulfill your legacy!"

Kris shook his head and wondered out loud why Aeon never told him.

"Perhaps he knew you would figure it out all on your own," said Annie, "I know you said he knew a good deal about your future travels, perhaps he had seen this in one of them and left you to discover it yourself."

"You know I still get the feeling I will see him again?" said Kris softly, "I feel like he is just out there somewhere in the shadows. He said so much and so little at the same time. I still feel he has a significant part to play in all this."

"Speaking of, you had made a promise to your son about beginning his training this year," Annie reminded Kris.

"Annie, my love, it is such a dangerous world, I dread the idea of something happening to Nicholas. We waited more than a century to finally have a child of our own and I am so proud of him, what if he was injured, or worse?"

"Kris, did you believe what Aeon told you about your descendants?" asked Annie, to which Kris just nodded, "Then you know this is his destiny and he will be safe. Besides not one person, including all the elves, has said it is too dangerous for you to go. If I have to, I will put it before the Council to make certain he is trained by them and you if necessary."

"Believe me the elves down south look concerned enough when I make my run, but you are right, and there is no reason to bring this before the Council, yet," Kris sighed, "I will begin his training. But I must ask you why are you so anxious to put him in harms way?"

Annie look disgusted, "You know I am just as concerned as you are, and I hate to be indelicate, but just as you had recently noticed your son turning white, have you looked at your own face in the mirror, lately?"

"What do you mean?" asked Kris.

"My husband, you are looking tired and a bit worn out. I have had to give over a good portion of my duties to Nicholas, but you have given none. You have been able to accomplish so much more than can be explained, and it is getting time to let another give you some much needed rest."

Kris nodded and admitted more to himself, "Yes, I have been feeling it lately. Each night gets longer, and there seems so much more to be done. But I think you're right. It is time I seriously contemplate giving the reins over. But even so, it may take a while to complete his training."

"Then the sooner you begin, the sooner you can retire and enjoy more of my company!" laughed Annie.

Kris smiled, "Well I guess that should give me plenty of incentive, Ho, ho, HO!"

That year Kris had asked the Council to do a moratorium on the elves contest in order to allow him to take Nicholas with him instead.

Ulzana Stitchinsew said it was about time he had asked that, and volunteered to make several suits for Nicholas that would match Kris' outfits. She said she would come by later to measure him.

Almost nothing else was said about the issue, and Kris was surprised to realize that the Council had been patiently waiting for him to make this suggestion. *They must have realized, like Annie that my flying days are soon coming to an end.* He thought to himself.

When Ulzana came by to measure Nicholas, he made a request to her. "A good many of my father's suits are cut with a long robe. I would like to ask the coat be made shorter to where it just falls below my caboose."

Ulzana cackled and said, "Whatever our prince

requests, but won't your legs get too cold?"

Nicholas thought for a moment, "Not if the pants are made of a heavier material. Besides things are popping up on roofs and they might snag longer robes and could rip them."

"Will rip them," said Ulzana flatly, "I spend quite a bit of time mending your father's robes because of it. Very well, we will bring you more 'up to style' and give you more maneuverability."

Nicholas was well aware of the dangers of the world after listening to his father and visiting several places himself, but he was excited to finally begin what he knew God had put him on this earth for.

So while the world was trying to blow itself to bits, Kris and Nicholas tried to hold it together with faith, hope, reindeer and a sleigh full of toys and gifts, to convince all who lived during this time that better days were coming.

Nicholas was learning the control of the sleigh, and was working on the time continuum, but was having a trouble mastering all its secrets.

Kris on the other hand had perfected the last part of the continuum, and was able to bring the "multi-destination continuum" as he called it into play.

One Christmas Eve in 1944, he had popped into a home without using the 'stop-time' continuum and was approached by the dad. The young man explained he was a soldier home on leave, and that his two children had asked how Santa was able to accomplish so much in just one night.

Kris who was having trouble getting this concept through to Nicholas thought that this might be good practice, and put the soldier and him into the stop time continuum. Santa Claus said while it may be difficult for him to understand, it worked as follows:

"The first thing is you need to think of time as a destination and stop thinking of it as a thing. Imagine a place you want to visit and then imagine yourself there. But even more important than that, imagine yourself in many places at the same time."

The soldier looked confused and said, "Different places at the same time?"

Santa nodded, "How I discovered it was like this, if you put two mirrors facing each other and put yourself between them you see yourself endlessly reflected in them, right?"

The soldier nodded.

"Now, imagine that each of those reflections was actually a different place even though it remained in the same time. It would allow you to fold many different actions and layer them within the same time frame. So you could actually visit many different houses and leave different gifts, and yet, still maintain the same amount of time doing it."

The soldier just pulled a hand through his wavy hair and said, "I can almost understand it, but I just can't imagine it."

Santa chuckled and said, "Well as I keep telling my son, when you can understand it AND imagine it, then you will be able to accomplish it!"

"Huh, a son...I never imagined that either. Aren't you eternal?" the soldier questioned.

"HO, Ho, Ho! No I am actually the tenth Santa Claus and my name is Kris Kringle. And soon I hope to retire and have my son, Nicholas, who will be Nicholas the eleventh, after our ancestor St. Nicholas, take over. Although I have been around quite a long time," stated Kris.

"Well Santa, I have a special Christmas wish to ask of you," the soldier blushed as he spoke, "I want to be around to see my children grow up. Can you help end this damn war...sorry, this war?"

Santa Claus looked solemnly into the young father's eyes, "My friend, my powers and abilities are limited, especially against what seems to be a destiny man has against his neighbors. I can only pray that you and your family will someday see the peace you seek. In the meantime, make sure you give your children, Becky and Robert all the love you can and teach them to be respectful of others. If you do this for your children, than perhaps you can effect a change in future generations. I have been Santa Claus for almost two hundred years, and unfortunately too few of those years haven't consisted of war being waged somewhere."

With that Kris announced that it was time for him

to leave. The father thanked Santa for taking time to talk with him, and promised he would do everything he could to find peace in their lifetime.

Santa smiled and shook the young man's hand. "I wish you a very Merry Christmas and pray for a safe New Year for you."

And just as quickly as he came, Santa Claus disappeared from sight with only the gifts and full stockings left behind to show he had been there at all.

When Kris returned to the sleigh, Nicholas noticed a tear in his eye and asked if his father was alright.

"These wars do so much harm to so many, and most of the people that get harmed or killed in them have no wish to be involved. Maybe if all the soldiers would just stay home, then there would be peace. Let the people wanting to wage the war fight it out themselves, that might change their black hearts," Santa wiped his face with his fur lined cuff and snapped the reins.

Nicholas knew when to speak, and when not to, around his father. This was a time for silence.

The number of people being visited by Santa Claus near the mid 20th century was staggering. And while Kris would occasionally have Nicholas pop in and distribute the gifts, he said that until he could master all the secrets of the time continuum, he could not officially take over the reins from him.

Kris suggested that the following year they would spend a good deal of time in Aeon's old cottage.

Chapter Eleven

Time is a destination, not a thing, and any person is its agent when properly instructed.

- Aeon Millennium

A New Reign

Almost as soon as they finished their Latin American trip and returned to the North Pole, Nicholas wanted them to start working on the lessons for the time continuum. It took Kris a good deal of arguing with his son to wait until they both had gotten some rest.

Nicholas acquiesced even if not quietly. He spent several days going over the last trip with Carrow, Frederick, and other members of the Council and discussing some new ideas that Nicholas had been forming in his head.

Kris had allowed Nicholas to take over the "Santa List" project as it was called. He was working with Ella, Macintosh, Ion and other elves to devise and implement the communications between the "Ambassadors" as they were called and the North Pole. However when the second world war broke out, Nicholas explained that before they implement anything, it might be better to wait until that conflict resolved itself.

Even so, they had figured out a way to hide a transmitter into the pompom of the long hat that Santa usually wore. As the children would speak their requests, each one would be transmitted to a new database that was being created. A whole new wing was built to hold the machinery that collected the data. They decided to call the new machines after their inventor, Macintosh.

The Macintosh would align the request with as much other information about the child as they had collected from other sources including previous letters, geographic locations, birth records, etc. and create a file on that child. Other data was entered on whether the child seemed naughty or was well behaved, if they had siblings, and how they behaved in school.

Nicholas was pleased about how much they were able to learn about the children. But he was very disenchanted with the other side of the equation.

Nicholas learned from some of his visits, that many of the men who dressed as Santa were only doing so to bring money to their pockets, with no care for the children or their needs. Most had fake beards. The time when men wore beards with regularity had fallen out of fashion ever since the Civil War era, and now all but a few men were clean shaven.

Nicholas would often just shake his head at the large number and poor style of beards they used. He told his parents one evening at dinner, "They might as well throw mops on their heads for as much realism as what they have on their faces."

Many of the Santa's just frightened the children and many more knew nothing about his father or his ancestors, let alone the North Pole and what happened there. But a few, a very few, had a genuine love for children and were trying hard to portray a true representation of Santa Claus and his kindness.

He had asked the Council of Elves if it might be possible to bring these exceptional ambassadors to the North Pole to get a better understanding of what took place and to learn the history of Santa Claus.

He was summarily turned down for his request and reminded again of the importance of keeping the North Pole secret from the tallfolk. Especially now while the whole world seemed to be in conflict.

He talked to his father about the impasse he was at, wanting to train the ambassadors, but not being able to bring them to the North Pole.

"This seems to be a situation of 'If the mountain can't come to you...you must go to the mountain'," said Kris to his son, "You know there are many places that you could train them. Why not hold a school somewhere centralized, but remote enough to bring some reindeer, elves and I may even pop in for a talk or two."

Nicholas said to himself as much as his father, "How ridiculously simple! Of course, then we could show them exactly what they need to know, and not have to worry about revealing too many secrets. Who do think should teach them?"

Kris thought for a moment, "Seems that I would choose someone who knows about as much of the North

Pole and the job of Santa Claus as possible, someone who has actually performed the job and understands the inner workings of the Pole itself."

Nicholas chuckled, "Okay, I get it. Add one more thing to my fairly substantial schedule."

"Well, you would only have to do it a couple weeks out of the year, as I don't think you have too many ambassadors to keep this thing going full time," said Kris

"Guess I will start thinking of some sites where I might do this. Thank you," said Nicholas and began to head off.

"Just a moment, Nicholas," Kris stopped him, "I was thinking tomorrow might be a good time for us to take a walk together to the woodlands area if you are game?"

Nicholas brightened and said, "I would be very pleased with that!"

"Then we will head off after breakfast, and you may want to clear your schedule for the next couple days," smiled Kris.

With that Nicholas waved goodbye and simply said, "Will do!"

The next morning the father and son had begun their trek to the woodlands. As they passed many of the

elves, the elves would giggle or point to the two tallfolk, who now resembled each other greatly. Nicholas had quit shaving as his father suggested, and was sporting thick salt and pepper colored beard and his hair was nearly entirely white even if not quite as long as his fathers. They were about the same size and build and looked like bookends coming down the road.

They reached the cottage and Kris warned that the interior might be a little dusty. As they opened the door the cobwebs had taken hold of much of the cottage. Kris himself hadn't returned since his previous practice session, and he hadn't done too much to be rid of the excess dust even then.

"Wow," Nicholas exclaimed and coughed, "Maybe we should find somewhere else."

"It just needs a little sweeping up and some fresh air," stated Kris.

Nicholas shrugged. When his father came up with a plan he was pretty gung ho about it, and wouldn't sway too far from it. So he began looking around for something to sweep up the dust and cobwebs.

He found a broom in a corner of the dwelling and began pushing the dust toward the door. Kris found a cloth and started cleaning away the cobwebs from the rafters and corners.

After getting much of the dust from the flat surfaces, Nicholas said tomorrow he would bring something more suitable to clean the books and other items

around the place. They stepped out to the garden in the
back for some fresh air. The garden was immaculate. Not a
weed or wild flower growing where it shouldn't. Nicholas
looked at his father and asked, "How is this possible?"

"Beats me," his father replied, "I certainly have not
been tending this. I wonder if one of the other elves uses
this as a retreat of their own?"

"It seems improbable that the garden would tend
itself," Nicholas mused, "You are probably right, maybe
Frederick takes care of it as a favor to Aeon."

After a few more moments, they returned inside
and to their straightening.

Kris was pleased that his son was trying to put
things right in the cottage, and while he teased Nicholas
that Aeon may have thought it much ado about nothing, he
thought the old elf would appreciate the gesture
nonetheless.

Once a little more serviceable, Nicholas said,
"Well, that is the best I think we can do without proper
supplies. Tomorrow I will get this looking better."

Kris began the lessons with Nicholas. Nicholas had
already grasped the stop time part of the continuum, but
was still having problems with the moving through time
and wasn't able to understand the multi-destination portion
of the continuum at all.

Kris thought he should begin with the basics again
and once more explained how time works as a place. He
thought Nicholas' biggest problem was that he still thought

of time as a thing. This was why he could stop time, but couldn't travel in and through it.

He had Nicholas concentrate on a place he wanted to visit, just as Aeon had taken Kris to multiple places when teaching him. Nicholas concentrated on a place he had seen from the sleigh and thought would be wonderful to visit. He held the image tightly in his mind, but the two men stayed where they started.

Kris said, "Perhaps I should do it the way Aeon did it with me. I will take us somewhere and you bring us back." Nicholas took his father's arm and the two disappeared from the cottage to an area with a running stream in the middle of a forest that looked to be in a mountain area.

"Where are we?" Nicolas asked.

"In the Great Smoky Mountains. It is a newly inaugurated National Park from 1940. I want to take your mother here sometime, and if you ever learn how to do this, perhaps I will be able to," Kris teased.

"Okay, message received. This is really beautiful. I wouldn't mind spending some time here myself," whispered Nicholas.

"First things first," admonished Kris, "Now picture Aeon's cottage in your mind, when you have it pictured soundly, think about this moment and take us back there."

Nicholas closed his eyes for a moment and then opened them again to see his father and him surrounded by the dingy surroundings of Aeon's cottage.

"Very good," said Kris, "That's a good start. Now let's try a place of your choosing. This time stop time first so that we don't advance beyond the moment."

Again Nicholas closed his eyes and the two men appeared on a bustling city street. "Where are we?" asked Nicholas.

"Shouldn't you know?" questioned Kris, "I thought you picked the place."

"I had picked a farm we visited last Christmas Eve outside of Chicago that I thought looked charming," answered Nicholas.

"Well you aren't close, this looks more like San Francisco. Though at least you stopped time effectively. I will get us back and you can try again," said Kris. Kris touched the side of his nose as was still his custom and they popped back to Aeon's home again.

"How could I be so far off?" asked Nicholas.

"You just need to concentrate harder, somehow you must have pictured San Francisco in your head," commented Kris.

Nicholas laughed and pointed to a postcard on Aeon's shelf, "That might have done it."

Kris looked at the card and said, "Yup, even down to the street. I was right San Francisco. This is why using the time continuum can be so dangerous. Any little thought could throw you completely off course."

Nicholas said, "Try it again?"

Kris just nodded his head and said, "And this time

concentrate. You better stop time again as we don't want to be mowed over by a train or shot on a battlefield like Aeon once was."

"Really? You'll have to tell me more about Aeon, I wish I could have met him before he left, or that he would return from wherever he went," sighed Nicholas.

"Who knows if we practice enough, we may even run into him somewhere," laughed Kris.

Nicholas took his father's arm and they vanished from the cottage again.

After a full day of popping from one place to another Nicholas was getting the hang of moving from one place to another. For his last test, Kris had chosen several places himself and told Nicholas to take them there. After five consecutive correctly transported attempts, Kris said it was time to return and rest.

When they arrived back Nicholas had returned them to their home, instead of the cottage.

Kris asked, "Was this intended?"

"Absolutely, I'm tired and I thought we'd skip the long walk back," said Nicholas, "If you want we can skip the walk and I will just take us to Aeon's tomorrow along with cleaning supplies as a bonus!"

Kris thought tomorrow might prove to be an interesting day indeed.

Nicholas was ravenous the next morning and ate four eggs, sausage, potatoes and some fruit. His father laughed and said, "You know you will get to eat again, no matter where we end up!"

"I don't understand why I am so hungry this morning, except to feel that I am going to expend a great deal of energy today and think I need to be prepared," Nicholas chuckled.

When Nicholas finally ate his fill, he kissed his mother and gathered the cleaning rags and such that he had pulled together the night before. He turned to his father and said, "Ready?"

Kris just nodded and moved to his son and rested his hand on his shoulder. Instantly they left home and reappeared in the dusty cabin.

"Well, first things first. Let's see if we can't make this place a little more comfortable," said Nicholas as he began to pull rags from the bucket he carried.

His father said, "I'll fill the bucket with some soap and water," and took the bucket from Nicholas. "You know I am still not sure why we have to be so particular about cleaning this place. I almost feel like I am intruding on Aeon's life."

Nicholas answered, "I don't think he would mind in the least, and besides if we are going to be spending some long days practicing, it might feel better returning to an orderly home."

Kris knew Nicholas had always had a "cleaning

bug" in him and most times he left him to it. Nicholas was very organized like his mother and was uncomfortable if things were not very neat and tidy. Kris on the other hand could step out of the dirtiest fireplace covered in ashes and soot and just laugh about it.

Annie was far happier that Nicholas took after her than his father. All the years growing up he had been particularly neat as a child and even as a toddler seemed bothered if he made a mess. Annie knew she was spoiled in that regard, but figured after a hundred plus years with a man who cared little what type of mess he made, she deserved a neat son.

Nicholas started on the bookcases and was dusting off the books and wiping down anything on the top. He stacked the books on the little table Aeon used for everything from map making to eating. Apparently Aeon had the sense to clean up the table and little kitchen before "going into retirement" as everyone in the Pole called it.

Most of the cleaning consisted of dusting things off and sweeping the floor. As Nicholas started on the second bookcase, Kris had taken a damp cloth to dirtier pieces and placed them back where they were originally removed as if he did not want Aeon to know he moved his stuff.

As Nicholas began the other bookcase he began to dust off the books and had pulled out a rather sizable volume. As he cleared the layer of dust off it he froze.

"Uh, Dad," he just said to his father. Kris came over to his son and looked at the book he was holding.

Nicholas' hands began trembling. His father soothed him and had his son set the book on the table. Kris said, "Apparently you were expected. Well, you should see what Aeon has to say."

The book was entitled, *To Nicholas Kristopher Kringle, The Next Santa Claus.*

As Nicholas opened the book he read aloud what Aeon had written at the beginning:

To my young Nicholas,

Though you and I haven't had the pleasure of physically meeting, I have had the pleasure of catching glimpses of you growing up, developing to manhood and assuming the mantle of Santa Claus.

Let me first say that you will make a wonderful Santa Claus and will be every bit as proficient as your father has been. While he has created the legend, you will further it and serve even more children and families than he has.

Now for the reason of this book. Your father had the advantage of my personal tutelage at the North Pole, which you shall not. Some day we will meet, as I have made certain to do so with you, but as to whether or not I am still in existence then I cannot say. So we will say for now that you will meet my ghost as it were, and leave it at that.

In the meantime there are things that I feel you will need to know and events that I would like to forewarn you about so you are better prepared.

Kris scoffed and said, "Why that dirty old scoundrel would never tell me much of anything about the future saying it was best I didn't know too much. He never even told me about you!"

"Perhaps it was because he knew if it was really important he would be around to explain the events or the results of those events," Nicholas shrugged, "I don't know, but perhaps we should learn more about what he has to say before we judge him too harshly."

He could see his father was clearly agitated because Aeon had not even left him a letter or note when he left. Nicholas continued to read but now did so to himself.

You have had a little difficulty learning everything your father knows now, but you will not only master these accomplishments, but exceed them. You need to do this quickly, because since the next World War has come to an end, an explosion of the population never before seen is occurring. Also, many more technical advancements across the world will come in waves, and you will even help be the instrument to many of these accomplishments.

While this may not seem likely, or even possible, trust me that it will happen. But before then, this book will help you become proficient in the use of the time continuum and give you some other tools to help you accomplish all that you shall need to for your job as Santa Claus.

By now your father has learned, and put into use, the multiple dimension timeline continuum that allows him to visit many places while remaining in the same period of time. This is extremely important, but as you will learn, you may also lay several timelines atop one another so that you may accomplish an exponential number of visits in one moment rather than just several places in one time.

I am certain that you will have many questions at the end of this, and I will tell you right here that most of these will go unanswered. As I had told your father often times, it is best that you do not know too much about your future. However that said, there are some key elements in your future that I will not leave to chance, as they are too important to your future *and those you affect. We will get to those later in this book, but please do not rush ahead. You need to look at this book the way I have written it. Things will make much more sense if you do.*

This book is for you and you, alone. This contains secrets and knowledge that is not to be shared lightly. Not even with your family, though many of its lessons will be passed onto your heir some day. But I implore you to keep this secret and safe from prying eyes.

Again, I wish I could be there to instruct you personally as I did with your father, but I thought this would be the next best thing. So let us begin with a discussion of the time continuum, both as you understand it now, and as I will explain its other subtleties to you. Your lessons begin now -

Nicholas looked at his father who was still cleaning up around the cottage, now with a broom in his hand sweeping a cloud of dust toward the door. Nicholas bit his lip, not quite knowing how to proceed.

Should he dismiss his father and tell him that Aeon would teach him everything he needed from this treasure he uncovered? Or should he hold its secrets until later. He could work with his father today, so as not to further hurt his dad's feelings and possibly make him resentful of

Aeon's teachings?

He decided on the latter. Now, how to make the book seem like less of a big deal and get back to the more affable time when they arrived. Nicholas closed the book, as difficult as that was, and said to his father, "Well we better begin with the lessons if I am going to accomplish anything today."

Kris swept the last of the dust outside and turned toward Nicholas, "What, you still want to work with me after your find?" questioned Kris.

"Of course, this says it may help me into the future a little bit. Though he gave me the same warning as you, that it was never a good thing to know much about my future, so I presume this will come in handy for later, but I need you to teach me the basics," stated Nicholas.

Kris scoffed, "Still up to his old ways, even in written form?" He then smirked and said that they better get started and hoped his son had gotten his cleaning bug out of himself.

"I'm all yours to be taught and to learn," smiled Nicholas, as much to himself as to his father.

"Okay, let's pick up where we left yesterday," said Kris, "Pick a place in your mind and concentrate on the here and now..."

And so began the travels of the present and future Santa Claus as they moved across continents and later time intervals, though never moving far from the present.

The following day Nicholas popped into the old cabin and went right to the book that he replaced on the bookcase. He opened it up and started to read where he left off the day before. So began his tutelage with Aeon.

While Nicholas expected to find the highly technical information difficult to disseminate, Aeon has used a good many common sense examples and relational stories that helped Nicholas see exactly the principles involved.

He tried a couple of theories and explanations that Aeon had laid out and along with what his father had already taught him, found them easier to do than he expected. He had trouble grasping the multi-dimensional time layer that his father was trying to explain. But coupled with Aeon's examples and less complex instructions he could now do what he couldn't grasp with his father.

So in accordance with Aeon's instructions, Nicholas performed several multi-dimensional time continuum jumps and returned successfully after each.

After a while Nicholas decided to take a break and look through the next part of the book. The first thing he read shook him to his very core. Aeon had wrote:

The first thing you will need to know is that within fifty years of taking the reins as Santa Claus, the world population will swell from 2.5 billion people to over 6 billion with nearly a third of these people being Christian. This means that in one form or another they will celebrate your annual return as well. Even if you cut this in half, this means you will probably be delivering more than one billion presents each year. So now you understand why it is so important for you to have complete and total control over the time continuum.

You will also need to know how to reduce the size of the gifts, so that many more may fit into your sleigh than do currently. As the world gets more crowded you will have less room to cover larger areas. One of my gifts to you are the sheets that is in the back of this book. When I request it, please take these to your most advanced elves in technology. I believe I know who they will be, but in the event things change, I leave this up to you.

Only after the elves had a chance to look over the schematics, and agree it is practical, should you go to the Council with the concept and advise them that it is in the works. They will see my hand in this, and that is okay, but no sense letting 'the cat out of the bag' until it can become a reality.

The next thing you need to do very soon is to meet your future wife, and this is too important to leave to chance. While I am fairly certain this will happen as it should, I wish to insure these events. You are to take Rory Mattle to California, where you will meet with a company that has recently formed there. You need to set up a meeting between you, Rory, Ruth and Elliot Handler, also Harold "Matt" Matson. Rory will become part of their company and will assist them in becoming the largest toy company in the world. When you go, you need to fly commercially and arrive in Los Angeles, where you will be met by one of their employees who will take you to your meeting. Her name is Mary Theresa Atwater. Get to know her, and let nature take its course.

Let Rory do most of the talking at the meeting and you just offer your support and suggest that soon their toys will soon be sought all over the world.

There are many more things I could tell you, but once more, to know too much is a dangerous thing. However I will tell you, that along with the Mattel company, you will need to create and align with many more corporations in order to create enough toys to perform your function and to supply enough materials to the Pole for all you hope to accomplish.

For this you must rely even more heavily on Frederick Salsbury and others. You will need to establish a complete global network utilizing elves as best you can, but also learning to trust more tallfolk in order to fill in the gaps. You must devise a way to integrate them into the North Pole, and convince the elders that it is finally time to allow tallfolk to visit the North Pole. There are some truly brilliant tallfolk within the world, and it would be a terrible waste if we were unable to utilize their talents because of distrust. If you are to truly be global, than you must reach out globally.

You will have many exhausting years as the world expands greatly and you have much to change and much to grow. As you are already aware, television sets have begun to take root in America and soon no household will be without at least one and many homes will eventually have several. But the broadcasting of information will soon skyrocket and even as the world increases, it will become smaller, figuratively.

All of this will have multiple effects on you, and you will need to deal with these as best you can. But my advice is to learn how to use this technology to your best advantage rather than work against it. And even as fast as technology will increase among the tallfolk, the elves will still surpass them and keep ahead of the rest of the world.

Everything I have placed in this book will assist in guaranteeing this advancement. Some of the schematics are to be held until the year written on the upper margin of the schematic, so it will be up to you to keep this information safe and only release it when appropriate. I always did this with the Council, and they knew it. So they won't be too surprised when you do the same, if they even catch on.

I was pleased that your father had the good sense to use the time continuum for his purpose and not for time travel. I am hoping that you will do the same. Time travel is not safe in the best circumstances, and while I have used it often, this will be one of those instances where I ask that you do what I say, and not as I do. I have made notes on the pages before each of the schematics with a little hint of what is coming, in part to help quell your curiosity, but more importantly to make certain that you do not feel compelled to discover events out of time as I have, and to keep you safe. This is my personal request and I ask you to honor it.

Now I will ask you to continue your time continuum studies and then take the first set of schematics to the elves as requested.

Nicholas sat back on his chair and rubbed his graying hair. So much. An unbelievable amount of information, a wife and a BILLION souls to deliver to – every year. Is it all truly possible? Obviously, since Aeon had said it would, he must have witnessed it, himself.

"He did say that we would meet up some time and that I would have the chance to talk with him. I wonder what year that will be?" Nicholas wondered out loud.

He looked at the schematics and noted the year in the margin. 1948. How could he know? He felt an eerie cringe, as if being watched, and then dismissed it. Aeon obviously had been keeping closer tabs than anyone knew or suspected. He then thought about Aeon's 'retirement' and wondered how someone that had seen history and the future – backwards and forwards – would suddenly find life on a quiet stretch of sand so interesting? Answer: he couldn't.

I'll bet he has been hanging around and checking on us from time to time, Nicholas thought, *That is probably why the garden looked so good, even though the rest of the cottage was a shambles.*

"Well if you are hanging around, you old spy, then

I tell you, you have my promise to uphold all that you ask me the very best way that I can," he announced. Then Nicholas smiled to himself. The time continuum, maybe he would never know all its secrets, but he bet Aeon did.

Nicholas rolled up the pages on the first set of instructions and closed the book. *Now, where to hide this from 'prying eyes',* he wondered to himself. As far as he knew he and his father were the only two souls in the North Pole that knew of its existence. But he couldn't guarantee that would always be the case, especially once he took the drawings to his little band of elves working on "the Santa Project" and other new ideas Nicholas would come up with.

He looked around but only saw widely accessible areas that wouldn't conceal a book so large. The other cabinets and drawers were too small. He went out into the garden and saw an area by the fountain that had large stones. He went to move a few of the larger stones and soon discovered that Aeon had prepared a hiding place himself for stowing away secrets, and it was just large enough to hide the book. But before stuffing it into its hiding place, Nicholas went back inside and carefully covered the book in plastic to protect it from any elements.

After he squirreled the book away, he grabbed the plans and began walking toward the main village. As he walked, his thoughts turned to some of the ideas he already was working on with several of the elves. He didn't tell his parents about the ideas. Instead, he decided to "test the waters" to see if any of his ideas would float or if more importantly, if they could be implemented.

Besides the Santa Project, he was also working with Keeney Eagleye on a more sophisticated and less intrusive way to determine when children had been particularly, or continuously, naughty.

Keeney was working on a set of scanners that they could test out to see the level of kindness or lack thereof in people as they would pass by them.

He also knew Aeon was right and sooner or later the North Pole would need to be more involved with tallfolk to accomplish all that they would need to in coming years. Now he, himself, was certain of it.

Nicholas decided to try persuading his father about the prospect of bringing the Santas to the Pole. As expected, he was shot down as soon as he brought up the subject. He was prepared for that, and backed down quickly. But Nicholas knew it was only a matter of time until the outside world would play a considerably larger role in the goings on of the Pole. He thought that time was the here and now.

He had another idea based on his father's complaints about so many tallfolk not honoring the true spirit and reason of Christmas. On several occasions he remarked how disappointed his ancestor, St. Nicholas, would be if he traveled the world today.

It seemed the older his father was, the more cynical he became. Nicholas wasn't sure if he truly believed what he said, or was just wearing out. But he felt his father's retirement was long overdue. Many heated discussions ensued when Nicholas countered his father's rants with the fact that there are as many good people as bad, and there are some wonderful souls that uphold all the importance, beauty and ideals of Christmas, that he only needed to look a little harder.

In response, his father had basically told Nicholas to prove it, which is precisely what Nicholas was attempting to do, again with Keeney. Unbeknownst to the Council in particular, Macintosh Gelfeeney, Ion Crosswire, Keeney and Nicholas, along with a several others, were all working to develop a rating system to determine how good or bad people are, and this would work in tandem with the scanner system.

The first set of scanners would be a broad range system of colors, while the "pinpoint array", as it was termed, would be more precise and give an actual base number to let the Pole know just how good or how bad people were based on their actions, kindness, and a host of other factors assigning a positive (good) or negative (bad) number to that person.

Once Nicholas could prove that the system would work, he had a plan to take an area of the North Pole that was being utilized for shops within the elfin community and redesign it into a "Visitor Center" for tallfolk. He planned to change some of the shops to stores where visitors could shop and see some of the masterful ways and items the elves made.

Since they had already put in a railroad system to bring materials and food to the North Pole and transport toys and goods to the distribution centers down south, they could just add a passenger train that could bring the people to and from Fairbanks, Alaska, the closest town to the North Pole. Especially since there was already talk about making Alaska the 49th state, it meant that soon it would fall under the purview of the United States.

As they were making the passenger train, they would build a grand inn for the visitors to stay. It would have every comfort and each guest would be well attended to. While most of the advances the Council was concerned about would be kept from prying eyes, some things that the tallfolk were already close to could be shared.

But most importantly, the spirit of Christmas would be demonstrated and observed in everything that the visitors would see, bringing home the true meaning once more of why the North Pole (and all others) celebrate Christmas in the first place.

Nicholas knew he had an uphill battle to convince the Council of this idea, but he had been working on certain members quietly and putting thoughts in their heads about working with tallfolk. Interestingly, his toughest critic to date, had been his own father. But he knew that if he could sway the majority of the Council, then his father couldn't interfere. His father's vote only occurred in a tie, and he was unable to sway the votes of the Council because of his own feelings.

He could see the village through the last of the trees and veered toward the right to where he would walk by Keeney's lookout retreat. He headed further up the road until he entered the elves trade school. He went to the dormitories he had visited many times before and found first Ion Crosswire and then Macintosh Gelfeeney.

"So what's the latest to report?" he asked knowing they would be bursting at the seams to tell him.

"Well it appears that we have solved the data problem and that we can now retrieve and store as much data as we will need for the next couple decades," Ion spoke first.

"Yes and we have just finished hardwiring into the last of the hospitals and birthing centers in the Christian world," Macintosh jumped in, "Did you know they had recorded like 6,000 births in the first four hours we were patched in?"

"It is going to be very interesting to see how you keep up with the world literally exploding with new babies," sighed Ion.

"And we have developed small scanner modules that can be hidden virtually anywhere in the world, and record all the data you would want on whether a person is good or bad," said Macintosh.

Nicholas smiled and said, "That is all excellent news, and I will soon have the program I want to lay out to the Council. As far as the increase in population, I may have a way to assist with that challenge, too. Is there somewhere private that we can talk, I have something to show you."

Both elves looked puzzled and excited that Nicholas wanted their help on another project, they both thoroughly enjoyed the ideas he was coming up with. Not to mention he always challenged them to work beyond the next level.

Macintosh said, "Why don't we go into one of the classrooms that aren't occupied? We would probably have as much time as we need there."

Ion asked, "Is there anyone else we need to join us? Many of the elves are out of class by now."

Nicholas whispered conspiratorially, "Not at this time, I think it is best we keep this among the three of us."

So the three of them checked the various classrooms and found not only one room empty, but the rooms on either side were also vacant so they wouldn't be overheard.

As they sat around one of the longer tables used for woodcarving, Nicholas pulled out Aeon's plans and laid them before the two elves.

"What is it?" asked Ion.

"I was hoping you could tell me," replied Nicholas.

Macintosh stared at the plans for a while and after a time he gave a low whistle and his eyes got very big and round. "Where did you get this?" he asked.

Nicholas had decided that for the time being he

would keep secret the book and the other schematics hidden inside. "I really can't tell you at present as I am sworn to secrecy," he answered.

"Well I can tell you these didn't come from any elf around here. These drawing are much more advanced than anything we have now," said Macintosh.

As if a light bulb suddenly went off in Ion's head he exclaimed, "Oh my heavens, it's a miniaturization machine!"

Both Macintosh and Nicholas shushed him into a quieter voice. "I had guessed that was the premise of this when I looked at it," said Nicholas knowing all along its purpose.

"You mean you really didn't know?" an amazed Ion questioned, "Then who or how did you come up with these?"

"As I said, I really can't divulge my source right now. The person I got these from just told me to take it to the brightest elves in the North Pole, so I immediately thought of you two," Nicholas smiled.

"This will take some time to figure out, and a good deal more time to build. Not to mention it would occupy a very large structure," said Macintosh.

"Just how big are we talking, Mac?" asked Nicholas.

"According to the dimensions here, probably about two thirds the size of one of our manufacturing buildings, or about half the size of one of the warehouses,"

Macintosh replied.

"Not to mention the raw materials are going to be substantial, we won't be able to build this out of spare parts as we did the scanners and data machines," added Ion.

Nicholas hadn't thought of that. So far they were able to keep some of the projects from the Council until they were closer to putting on a full scale demonstration, and this also allowed time to run some of the ideas and gain support from his best allies on the Council, his mother being one of them.

But this could present a whole new problem. He was hoping that he could present the idea once the concept was at least proven sound, but they couldn't do that without a working model. *Wait*, Nicholas thought, *that's it! We make a miniature of the miniaturization machine!*

"What if we created a scale model?" he asked the elves, "It could just be big enough to take before the Council and demonstrate it."

"Why not just take these plans before the Council and ask them to construct the full size thing?" asked Macintosh, "It is bound to make everyone's life easier both up here and at the distribution centers. I can't imagine they wouldn't approve it."

"I really do not wish to make my source for this public to the Council at this time," Nicholas sighed, "If you could at least build a model, than it would look like this was your idea."

Ion barked, "I won't take credit for someone else's

work! That's not at all ethical!"

"Relax, Ion, my source has no problem with that, and unless I miss my guess, the elf in question had some help from others that we will never know about," chuckled Nicholas.

"Can we keep these and look them over for a day or so?" asked Macintosh.

"Just keep them secret and safe and you may keep them as long as you like," said Nicholas, "After all, it's not as if I am going to start construction on it." and he laughed with a perfect copy of his father's laugh.

"I swear you are more like him everyday," Macintosh said shaking his head.

Ion rolled up the papers and they all agreed to meet in a couple days to discuss what they thought could be done and what could not.

Nicholas returned to his home and saw his father sitting in the living room. Kris looked at his son and asked, "Where have you been all day?"

"Mostly practicing the time continuum and visiting some of the elves working on various projects," Nicholas answered.

"How are you coming along with your jumps?"

questioned Kris. 'Jumps' was the term that Nicholas and Kris decided to call the more bulky time continuum wording.

"Actually quite well!" Nicholas said in an animated voice, "I really have the multi-dimensional thing down cold now. I'll be happy to show you whenever you'd like."

"Was Aeon a help on that?" queried Kris.

"Actually, it was more what you said," Nicholas exaggerated, "You told me that once I was able to get the concept down even once, then it would fall pretty much into place. And that's what happened." The last part was certainly true.

"Well good, I was hoping you would catch on," Kris hesitated and stared off into space.

"What's the matter, Dad?" Nicholas looked into his fathers old eyes with concern.

"It seems your mother and a couple Council members want me to pass the reins over to you as early as this year. Apparently they think I have traveled the globe enough for one, or maybe even a few lifetimes," Kris shook his head.

Nicholas held his jubilation in check and asked in the most concerned voice he could muster, "And how do you feel about the idea?"

"I won't deny I have thought about this for a very long time, and while some years are easier than others, most are becoming more exhausting each year. And after all you are approaching nearly a century yourself. I guess I should have started with your training earlier." Kris mused.

"I didn't mind, but I must say you don't seem to enjoy it as you once did," Nicholas said, "And it is certainly becoming a bigger world by the day." He thought about the 6,000 new babies in just four hours.

"In that case I would like to discuss this further at dinner with your mother, but I think you should plan on meeting with the Council this week and seeing if we can get a consensus on this issue and assuming we will, officially declare you the next Santa Claus," Kris joked, "Great, another reason for a banquet, again."

"Sounds perfectly fine with me," smiled Nicholas.

Kris stood and looked closely at his son and said, "I would caution you about what you say, and who you say it to, nothing is decided until the Council meets and makes its decision. And I wouldn't go around buttering up the Council this week because they will see right through that ruse."

Nicholas laughed at his father's suggestion and said, "Now father you haven't raised a fool, I will be the vision of tact until everything is completed, regardless of the outcome."

And while Nicholas was approaching 94, he felt like a 16 year old who just got a new car and couldn't wait to take it for a spin. He had to go off and do some celebrating even if in private.

Later at dinner, Nicholas and his parents discussed the many toys needing to be made and how the list got longer each year. They talked about the four manufacturing areas being near capacity and how they will make enough to fill the demand.

"I have some ideas on how to fill the rest of the need," said Nicholas in an offhand manner.

"Well I would love to hear your ideas, as Carrow and I are nearly out of our minds, and we can't build the next manufacturing center fast enough," said Annie.

"Actually I would hold off on finishing that building for now, as I may suggest a better use for it soon," Nicholas said casually.

His mother looked at him and asked, "Would you care to share this with us so we might be 'in the know' about your plans?"

"Mother, you have my word that when I get everything figured out, I plan to lay out a whole strategy to both of you and the Council," Nicholas looked deeply at his mother, "I have a glimpse of what is coming and it is much bigger than even you fear. Unless we do some major retooling, we will not be able to keep up and my new legacy will be short indeed."

"Are you getting this information from that book?" questioned his father.

"Partially, but if you look around you can see the signs of what is taking place all around. Movie theaters, televisions, radio shows, telephones and telegraphs, transatlantic flights, and much more. All of this is going to revolutionize the varying cultures and countries into sharing more information, and we will be the only society cut off from the world," Nicholas did not mean to get so passionate, but he had been thinking of many of these same problems for years and his enthusiasm got the better of him.

His mother's gaze softened and she smiled and said, "The Council and I were worried you were taking things in stride, but I can see this is not the case. We have been having many discussions along this same discourse, but I will tell you that the Council is still divided and you won't have an easy time swaying some of the members."

Nicholas sighed, and said, "I will have so many things to show the Council and many new inventions and gadgets on a scale not seen since the start of our culture up here. But every one of them is a necessity if we hope to keep up, no, I mean keep ahead, of the rest of the world as we always have."

His father shook his head and said, "Now I remember why I need to retire, I don't have the drive and passion I once had "

His wife looked lovingly at her husband and said, "Well at least you passed it on to our son, and besides for nearly two centuries you have brought joy and love to children, I think you've earned a rest."

"Well look at Carrow, that old codger is 400 plus and he isn't retired yet, and neither is Ulzana," pointed out Kris, "And nobody is kicking them out."

Annie laughed and said, "Ahh, at last it comes out!

First, nobody is kicking you out, you asked us if Nicholas could please take the next year..."

Nicholas looked at his father with shock, he had no clue his dad asked the Council, rather than the other way around.

"...And secondly both Carrow and Ulzana are stepping down this year as well, and we will need to appoint their replacements after Christmas," Annie continued.

"You're kidding!" exclaimed Nicholas, "They actually are stepping away from the Council? I can't believe it."

"More importantly, you better not say anything to anyone, as only the Council knows this and they will know where it came from if they hear it elsewhere," scolded Kris.

"Father you may not be aware of this yet, but I can keep confidences with the best of them and keep many from everyone else," Nicholas said in a hurt tone, "There has never been any discussions at this table that had become idle chat around the North Pole from me."

Kris apologized, and mumbled something about getting old AND grumpy.

"Now MR. Santa Claus," Annie was staring at her son, "I would like to help you implement your new ideas with the Council, assuming they are as good as I believe they will be. You do have friends in the Council, which many you already know, but some you may not. There have been a good many discussions concerning everything from opening up the Pole to tallfolk, to working with more companies outside of the North Pole. And some of these have come from you talking to other Council members, but it is time to cease these clandestine discussions, and bring some of your plans and ideas to all of us."

Nicholas looked dumbstruck, he thought he had been so clever and his mother knew, or at least suspected all along, what he was up to in his movements.

"Now there will be a perfect time once your position has been made official, and I would suggest you wait for that moment, but if you want to let me in on some of these projects, I could help you get the right backing at the right time to see them through," Annie paused and waited for Nicholas.

He had always loved his mother deeply and had complete and total respect for her in all things, but even he was totally disarmed by her total grasp of the situation and strength about how to best handle it. He was very glad she was his ally, he would hate to have to fight her on anything.

"We can begin tomorrow," was all he needed to say.

Kris just sat knowing Annie was always in charge, and might forever be the CEO of the North Pole.

Chapter Twelve

Alas! How dreary would be the world if there was no Santa Claus!... There would be no childlike faith then, no poetry, no romance to make tolerable this existence.

- Frances P. Church

The Changing of the Guard

With amazing speed, everything changed for Nicholas Kristopher Kringle. The morning after the dinner discussion with his parents, he began to take his mother around and showed her the array of products and projects he was working on.

Annie was very impressed with everything she had seen, but Nicholas wasn't done. He had decided to show her his most important treasure. So using the time continuum to save his mothers tired feet, he took her arm and popped over to Aeon's cottage.

Nicholas was very glad he and his father tidied up the place, and he had kept it neat in his returns. He retrieved the book and showed her what he had already learned. She had already seen the plans for the miniaturization machine, but he still hadn't disclosed where the plans had originated.

Annie read with rapt interest the projections and future events Aeon had enlightened her son. She smiled greatly and just said under her breath, "At last!" when she got to Nicholas meeting his future bride.

When she had gotten to the same place Nicholas had, he gently closed the book and asked, "Well?"

"I expected that you had been up to some things, but I had no idea. Does your father know any of this?" she asked.

"Unfortunately, I believe father has some clouded judgments by living at the Pole for so long. That, coupled with the horrors he has seen, has put him and me at odds about how many good people there are in the world," explained Nicholas, "Plus he seems to be a little bitter for some reason when it comes to Aeon's book. From the moment he saw it, it was almost as if he was jealous."

"I truly believe your father hasn't a jealous bone in his body, but I think he has a strong love and concern for Aeon, and often makes comments about how none of what he does would have been possible if not for Aeon, more than any other elf."

"Then why does the mere mention of Aeon get him so stirred up?" queried Nicholas.

"Your father wishes everyday he could see his old friend and mentor, and I believe that while he is thankful that he had left you something, he has nothing but his memories to look back on," Annie thought about all she had learned from her son and said, "We are both very proud of you, and I believe that when you have taken over for your father, no parent could be prouder of you than he will be. I also think that before we spring all your ideas and plans on the Council, that you need to bring him into the loop first. Otherwise I fear he will be deeply hurt."

Nicholas nodded his head, "I guess I was just afraid he would take issue with all that I was trying to do."

Annie laughed, "You know he is not the ogre you sometimes make him out to be. Yes, he wants to protect the North Pole, but he realizes that the world is growing exponentially, and that tallfolk are going to play an ever-increasing role in what we do. In fact, many of the Council members have discussed this several times. I believe once they learn of your scanner technology, this may ease many fears about opening the Pole to the rest of the world. If they can be assured we would only have people that we could trust, then that would take a lot of the air out of the arguments."

"So when should we meet with the Council?" asked Nicholas.

Annie smiled, "Kris is talking with many of them today setting up a special meeting for this Friday. But, I believe that you are right, that we should wait to spring all this on the Council until after the banquet that will follow your induction as Santa Claus. Timing can be everything on this, and after so many years of waiting, what are another few weeks?"

"Well, I am going to have the teams I am working with continue with their experiments and scale models. I feel the better prepared we are, the more the Council will see the wisdom of what we are doing," said Nicholas, "I do have concerns about starting some of the buildings that will be needed for the miniaturization machine and possibly the Visiting Center."

Annie shook her head, "Of all the things I am pleased that you follow in your father's footsteps, impatience is not one of them. Leave the new buildings to me. I will talk to who we need to make certain that construction either begins or is modified as needed for your plans. After all, I am the CEO of the North Pole."

Nicholas gave his mother a hug and said, "And I have always been as proud of that fact as I am that you are my mother. I can't tell you how thankful I am that you are on my side and will be around to help me."

"Well you say this today, but let's see what you have to say once you meet Mary Theresa, which by the way, when are you planning to make that trip?" Annie asked slyly.

"Well obviously it will have to wait until after the 'changing of the guard'," answered Nicholas.

"Not too long after, I hope," replied Annie.

Nicholas laughed, "Now who's being impatient? Besides, I believe everything will happen exactly when it is supposed to."

Annie grabbed her son's hand and said, "Well, maybe there is hope for you, yet."

While Annie and Nicholas were popping into Aeon's, Kris was flagging down Frederick in town.

"Hello old friend," yelled Frederick, "How are you?"

"Fine, great even," Kris called back, "I need to chat for a moment."

Frederick grinned and said, "It is always a pleasure to talk with Santa, what would you like to discuss?"

Kris smiled at the irony, "How about what you just said? I need to call a special meeting of the Council, I think it is time to officially turn over the job of Santa to Nicholas."

"You mean this Christmas?" asked Frederick.

"I mean as soon as the Council will approve it. Between you and me, Fred, I not only think he is ready, but I am tired. I really wouldn't mind skipping the next few hundred years. But I did have some questions I wanted to ask you about the procedure," Kris furrowed his brow.

"You mean like what might happen to you and Annie after Nicholas takes your place?" smirked Frederick.

Kris shook his head and snorted, "How is it you and Annie always say what's in my head before I can say anything? You know sometimes it is quite annoying!"

Frederick couldn't help but laugh saying, "It is because your face is like reading a book, we all know when you are concerned, happy, wrestling with a problem, and so on. That is it, isn't it?"

"Yes, that is it, for instance do I have to give up my position with the Council, or Annie, hers? And would we have to leave the North Pole if we were no longer officially in charge. And lastly, do we need to vacate our home, or just turn it over to Nicholas?" Kris looked deeply concerned about all these worries.

"Good heavens, what have you been smoking?" Frederick looked aghast at Kris, "Do you think we would just put you and Annie out like so much garbage after nearly two centuries of service to the North Pole? What in the name of God made you think of such a thing? Well never mind, don't even try to explain it, just know this. First, you both will be members of the Council for as long as you wish to serve. Now as a suggestion, and I would be happy to put it before the Council later, but since Carrow and Ulzana are resigning at the end of this year, I think the best plan would be to have you both fill in for them and appoint Nicholas into your position as President of the Council. This keeps Santa Claus as the figurehead and you would finally get a chance to vote on some issues, as I know you wished you could on several occasions."

Kris just nodded and continued to listen.

"Secondly," Frederick continued, "That is your home until the day you both either leave this earth, which I pray is another few centuries, or leave the North Pole, which I pray is never. We will build another home for Nicholas if he requests it, which he has never mentioned to me. And lastly, old friend, I believe anyone that would suggest Annie step down from her position as CEO would be taken out and strapped to the front of the first train heading out of the North Pole! Everyone loves and respects her, and she still runs the most efficient set up anyone could ever imagine. And when things need changing, she is not afraid to take charge and change them. I predict some major changes taking place this year, and she will be the one to implement them."

Kris' mouth began to move, but nothing came out, he looked like a fish trying to breathe air.

This did not slow Frederick as he concluded, "And if you have anymore crazy ideas, my advice is that you just get them out of your head before someone puts you in a straightjacket and has you committed."

Kris finally found his voice and said, "What changes are you predicting?"

"That is not important for right now, I think we need to go back to your original idea and schedule this meeting for Friday," said Frederick, "Now I will go talk to Jackson, Whitey, Britney, Denny and Frieda. You go convince Carrow, Ulzana, Ella, and of course you may want to mention it to our CEO – your wife," he said the last laughingly.

They began walking together and talking about what kind of Santa Claus they thought Nicholas would make, and it was obvious from Frederick's comments, he thought a darn fine one.

The big day had come and Nicholas was as nervous as a cat in a room full of Dobermans. Kris talked about the first time he and Annie went before the Council all those years ago. But somehow Nicholas just couldn't relate and said that this was entirely different. Back then, his parents had no clue why they were brought up to the North Pole, now he was basically interviewing for the position his father held since the 1700's. And what would he do if the Council had voted him down? What position would he hold, if not as Santa Claus?

Out of respect for his father, and to not seem overconfident, he did not wear any of his usual Christmas clothing, but was dressed in brown slacks and a tan, green and brown shirt. His mother chuckled when she saw him, but he was completely and unusually, humorless.

The three of them walked over toward the Council chambers in silence. It was almost like the first one to talk would cause tremendous bad luck for the lot.

As they arrived at the massive doors, Nicholas was almost panicked wondering if he wasn't rushing things, after all what's another few years? As they entered the great hall, he was met by Britney Clearwater, who asked if Nicholas would please wait until such time as he was asked to join the rest of them.

His parents smiled at him reassuringly, and continued with Britney into the chamber. There were a few chairs around the hall which felt vast, as every footstep seemed to echo from wall to wall. He looked at the stained glass that Frieda had created, and this did nothing to make him feel any better. There was one large window showing his father in his sleigh with the reindeer streaking through the sky, another showed his parents guiding what seemed to be the entire North Pole from a hill, the next was a full size portrait of his father in his grandest robe holding a baby in his arms, and on and on. How would he really fill such huge boots?

It was over an hour before the chamber doors opened and Denny Sweetooth appeared from behind the door. He walked over to Nicholas wearing his almost permanent grin and shook Nicholas' hand. He said, "The Council has a few questions they would like to ask you since your father has asked you to take over his full responsibilities. I tell you the following as a friend and Council member, you should answer each question as honestly as you dare, and I would not withhold too much information, as the Council is aware of more than you might think. Your mother has told us that you have been working on a number of projects that will have benefits to your job. It would behoove you to show that you are not only ready to assume the duties, but that you have plans to expedite your duties in an even more efficient manner going forward."

His grin never left his face, and he ushered Nicholas to enter ahead of him. All Nicholas could think of was "It's show time!" and he uttered a small nervous laugh as he walked toward his destiny.

Everyone looked pleasant enough, except Carrow who never did, and most had smiles on their faces. Frederick began saying, "Well Mr. Nicholas Kringle, it is about time that we finally had a formal meeting with you. Let me say personally, that it has been a distinct pleasure watching you grow and take on new duties throughout the Pole. Obviously, you know why you are here today as your parents have said that they feel it is time that we appoint you as the eleventh St. Nicholas, or Santa Claus, as he has become known around the world. And while we are happy to acquiesce with their request, before we do this officially we wish to make certain you are ready for what lays before you. Therefore we have a few questions if that is acceptable?"

Nicholas answered, "It is not only acceptable but I welcome the opportunity for your questions."

Frieda Cutinglass was the first, she asked, "Your father has told us that you had some difficulty at first grasping the concept of the time continuum, may we assume you have resolved this issue?"

Nicholas smiled and said, "Not only have I mastered what my father has taught me, but I have been able to take it one level beyond and layer several multidimensional layers upon each other. This allows an almost exponential set of permutations and time and place windows for the same time period."

Kris shook his head and just muttered, "I wonder how he learned that?"

Next was Jackson Kilowatt and his question was tougher for Nicholas, "Nicholas, your mother mentioned you are in the process of creating a good many projects to assist both you and the North Pole in your task for the future, would you care to enlighten us?"

Nicholas looked at his mother and father. Then he thought for a moment and answered, "I am more than excited and anxious to share many concepts and ideas with this esteemed body. However, while I have had an opportunity to present many of my ideas to my mother, and I am pleased that she sees merit in those ideas, the time has not properly presented itself to discuss this with my father and get his opinions and consultation. I ask permission that this question be postponed until such time as I have discussed this with the current President of this Council, so that we may both present these ideas together before the Council."

Nicholas watched as his father smiled and nodded, and he watched his mother dab her eyes. The Council mumbled to each other for a few moments and Carrow announced, "It is so agreed, we ask that you get this accomplished by next Friday, as we too, are anxious to see what our new prodigy are working on all around the village."

Next up was Denny, he asked simply, "What do you see as the most important duties of Santa Claus?"

Nicholas was prepared for this as he had listened to his father for years and believed his words just as he had spoke them, "To bring hope and faith to all children wherever they may be, and to represent the North Pole with all the dignity and pride that I can muster. I will forever represent this village and bring the gifts that they provide to as many children as believe in us, in order to make their days brighter and to let them know they are loved by each elf, and by Santa Claus and his family."

"That is a fine answer, but it is not all inclusive," Whitey stated, "How about your duties to the North Pole and the elves itself?"

"I'm sorry you are of course correct," Nicholas blushed, "The only way to do what I just stated is to make certain that the North Pole stays up with the latest technology, and provide the guidance to involve all that must be done to make certain that we can keep the promise to the children and to ourselves in our quest, to meet the needs before us today and centuries from now."

"So am I correct to assume that you believe we will need to seek assistance from outside the North Pole to accomplish these things?" asked Britney.

"I think that the time has come that we expand our ideas and production methods to certain people in other parts of the world, and yes, I believe that we will need to invite certain tallfolk that have been properly screened and tested to the North Pole. After all, imagine if you had decided that no tallfolk could ever be trusted and never invited my parents up because of your suspicions." Nicholas said matter-of-factly, "I believe, as I am certain some of you do, that there are good people around the world otherwise why are we doing what we are for the children? There is always hope that people of the south will cease their endless hostilities toward one another, but not all are that way. And there are many great minds that we will need to soon take advantage of beyond our own borders. I will show the Council next week ways in which we may safeguard our way of life and still allow some tallfolk to share their ideas with us and some of ours with them. It is the way of the future and the only way we will be able to continue to meet the ideals we have set for ourselves."

Ella Communicado, who had stayed silent up until now spoke up, "Tell me Nicholas, if it is so imperative that we involve tallfolk in our operations and us in theirs, wouldn't it be better to limit what you are hoping to accomplish rather than continually try to keep up with the world and its madness?"

Aha, thought Nicholas, *definitely not one for expansion, now how to carefully answer her without being nasty.* Nicholas mulled the question thoughtfully and finally replied, "I see your concern Ella, however let me respond with a question, precisely which child would you refuse when we received their letter?"

Annie, Frederick, Britney, Jackson and of course Denny, all sported grins, Carrow, Ulzana, Whitey and Frieda just looked stone-faced, while Ella just shrugged her shoulders. Both his parents had their hands over their mouths, so you could not tell if they were smiling or not, but their eyes both showed what you could not see on their mouth, both were grinning.

There were a couple more questions as to whether Nicholas planned to continue using the reindeer and Amerigo, which he said he did, then they asked Kris if he thought Nicholas had mastered enough of the job to do it on his own, which he had said yes, and then finally Nicholas was excused so that the Council could talk among themselves.

He moved to the hallway again and waited once more. He wasn't certain how the vote would go for sure but he thought 6-4 in favor for him. Then he froze, what if this needed to be unanimous? He thought for sure Ella would shoot him down, and that might be all that was needed.

After what seemed another eternity but in reality was about 15 minutes, the door was opened again and this time it was Ella who was smiling at the other side and asked Nicholas to rejoin them.

He walked back to where he stood beforehand and stood before the Council, His father looked at him and said, "The Council has just two more questions for you and one of these is a point for clarification."

Nicholas thought that this might go forever, but only nodded his head.

"The first question is are we agreed that between now and next Friday, you will discuss the ideas you wish to present before the Council with me, and together we will make the presentation and their decision will decide if we will continue with each individual program. Am I correct in our understanding?" Kris asked.

"Yes sir, you are correct," answered Nicholas.

"Fine," responded Kris to his son, "Then the last question the Council has is when would you like your celebratory banquet to officially introduce you as the new Santa Claus?" his father broke into a very large grin as the various Council members yelled out their congratulations, and then went to shake the hand of the new Santa.

At first Nicholas didn't react, not sure what had just taken place. Finally the reality struck him like a thunderbolt, and he grinned ear to ear and started laughing in an uncontrollable, "Ho, Ho, Ho!" as he received hugs and handshakes and sometimes both from all the Council members and his parents.

Ella approached him and said, "I am sorry if I gave you a scare, but the Council wanted to see how you would handle pressure and they made me 'the bad guy'. I knew you would find a way to tactfully put me in my place, and you did."

Nicholas gave her another hug and said, "Thank goodness, I thought I was going to have an adversary from the start!"

Ella laughed and said, "Not at all, and if you would have thought about it, who deals with the most tallfolk next to Frederick? I am in communications all the time with them, and like you I know there are so very many that are good and loving. I am most certainly your ally on that score."

"By the way," Denny said, "You never answered the last question as to when you want your banquet, I have a lot of food to prepare and need to know when to prepare it?"

To this Nicholas answered, "Since you have all the work, you may certainly decide for me and trust that I won't miss my own party, ho, ho, HO!"

He later learned from his parents that while a majority would have carried the vote, Nicholas was unanimously chosen, and that every Council elder felt that he would do as well as his father, if not better, though no one dared say as much.

The word spread through the village with the speed of a bullet. And everyone ran up and congratulated Nicholas the moment they saw him. As he was now spending more time with his father explaining a lot of his ideas and thoughts, this was a little embarrassing, as they would tell his dad that they wondered when he would finally retire.

Kris took it all in stride and was gracious to the last. He actually was enjoying all the attention his son was getting from everyone, and he remembered everyone coming up to him when it was announced by the Council. He was pleased his son would finally have his day in the sun, and told him so.

"It still feels a little awkward having them call me Santa," said Nicholas, "It will take a little getting used to."

"Ha, yes I remember how long it took me. Every time they would call me that, I would look behind me to see if someone else was there," chuckled Kris, "How about we stop in for a cup of coffee at 'Mocha Joe's' and we can talk further about the idea of involving the people of the south with the North Pole?"

When Kris, Annie and Nicholas were alone, they would refer to tallfolk as "Southerners" or "People of the South" since the three of them were all tallfolk themselves. Even when Nicholas was 10 years old he stood well above all but the tallest elves, so referring to the rest of the world as tallfolks felt strange.

As they walked into Mocha Joe's the proprietor greeted them enthusiastically saying, "How are my two favorite Santas?"

Both men laughed and answered that they were fine. As they walked back to a booth in the corner they placed their orders with Joe and asked for privacy if possible.

"I will make sure that you are not disturbed, as I am sure you have some very important topics to discuss before this Christmas!" he said with gusto, "Please feel free to stay as long as you care to and just wave for me." with that he was gone.

"Okay, now explain to me why we will need to involve the southerners with our people up here," Kris began by getting right to the point.

"In order to do this, I am afraid I have to bring up a touchy subject between us," Nicholas looked directly at his father.

Kris cocked an eyebrow and asked, "What subject is that?"

"Aeon," Nicholas stated.

Kris just shook his head and said, "That is not a touchy subject between us."

But Nicholas could see him bristling and continued, "Dad, I know you are hurt because he left me that book. He also never even left a note to you saying 'goodbye', but he knew I would need help and quickly, so he left the book."

"What kind of help, you haven't mentioned that book since you found it that afternoon," said Kris, "I know that was far too thick to just have that one letter in it."

"Well I hope you can put your disappointment aside to hear what Aeon wrote me with an open mind," said a concerned Nicholas.

Joe came up right then and laid the two coffee drinks they ordered before them and again said, "No more disturbances, I promise!"

That broke the tension between them and they both laughed and thanked Joe.

"Alright, I am an open book, no pun intended, tell me what you know," said Kris.

Nicholas began to reiterate what he had learned as he had done with his mother. When he got to the point of the population exploding to 6 billion souls, Kris just quietly said "Six billion!" and shook his head.

Nicholas continued on about the birthing data that was now continuously compiling in what was now being referred to as the 'Hall of Records'. He then explained how the Santa Ambassador project was progressing.

After that he hit his father with the new miniaturization machine that would reduce all the packages until they could be resized at delivery with the touch of a button, and finally ended with the new ideas that would involve having toys made outside of the North Pole.

"Do you really think this is necessary to have others make our toys?" asked Kris, "After all, for hundreds of years the elves have managed to supply everything we have needed. Why rely on others now?"

"Father, what you have supplied has been what we thought was beyond measure at one time," began Nicholas, "How am I going to visit upwards of a billion or more homes with a toy or two for each. The difference is as when you were using only Amerigo, versus using nine reindeer. It comes down to a matter of what can and cannot be done. In order to meet that big a need, we must go beyond our borders."

"I don't believe it can be done no matter how many gifts you can get," said Kris quietly, "You won't be able to use the continuum to reach that many houses in one night. Unless you plan to do this over more nights."

"Actually, I can," Nicholas countered, "As I told the Council, Aeon showed me how to take your multi-dimensional model and layer one dimension over another so it exponentially increases what you can do."

"Hmm," said Kris, "So that old elf *did* have more to teach, just not to me."

"Dad, I think he knew that you had all you needed to accomplish what you did," Nicholas was worried this was becoming too focused on Aeon and his father, instead of the matter at hand, "Aeon knew I was struggling, and would continue to do so. if he didn't intervene. He had greater faith in you, and I am alright with that. Can't you be?"

"I had to discover the multi-dimensional continuum on my own. he didn't help me." growled Kris.

"I can only believe he knew you would figure it out when the time was needed, and you did," explained Nicholas, "I am not sure he even trusts me to marry properly without his help."

"What do you mean by that," said Kris, "Is he telling you whom to marry?"

"Well suggesting more than telling, but I do not wish to get into that now," Nicholas was getting frustrated, "We need to talk about how we can convince the Council that we must open our strict closed-door policy."

"We?" laughed Kris, "I am not sure I am convinced, yet. I understand your concern, but I believe Carrow will have something to say about what we can and cannot accomplish here in the North Pole, before we need to explore other options."

"Even Mom has said it would place too big a strain on operations up here," argued Nicholas, "And she's the CEO! Besides, if I had to guess, I believe I may have enough of the Council on my side to do this now if put to an immediate vote. Carrow is still only one vote."

"And Ulzana is two and Britney is three," parried Kris, "And that is just the ones I am sure of, you may have others that could swing either way."

"If you were to help and support me, then I could do it," Nicholas eyed his father, "Without your help, possibly not, no – probably not. The Council still looks to you as their leader. If you are not convinced, than they will waiver."

"You and I have seen the world together," said Kris, "We both know how hard the world is. There are so many, including a good many Christians, who know to do nothing but make others miserable, or enforce their will on them."

"And again I say that for everyone that is bad, we will know two, three or four that are good," answered Nicholas.

"So you keep telling me," scoffed Kris.

"And now I can prove it to you," Nicholas said. He had been waiting for this moment. The old argument would now finally be settled between them.

"What do you mean you can prove it?" Kris asked.

"Come with me to the Trade School, I have some elves I wish to introduce you to, and something I want to show you." answered Nicholas.

They both finished their coffees and said goodbye to Joe and walked up the hill to the Trade School.

Nicholas had warned Keeney, Macintosh and Ion to be ready for their visit. As they walked through the door of the Trade school, all three were standing by.

Nicholas introduced his father to Ion and Macintosh. His father had already known and worked with Keeney for years. *So much the better*, thought Nicholas.

The elves asked Kris to follow them to the newly formed Hall of Records, which was just two buildings over. As the group walked over, Nicholas explained his concern, that had begun with Annie, about delivering presents to children who had been consistently naughty. Especially as Black Peter had long ago retired, saying the world had gotten too big for him. He said he didn't want to reward bad behavior, and that he asked the elves to devise another way to track who was naughty and who was nice.

Keeney took over the conversation then and explained how Jackson had recommended Ion and Macintosh to Nicholas, he said how they were already working on machines to collect information and put it into a more useful form for the whole North Pole.

As they walked through the doors of the Hall of Records, Kris was warned to watch his step and not without reason. There before him all over the floor and running up every direction were coils of wire everywhere. It looked like a mass of snakes waiting to strike.

"We have just begun the new wiring process to bank all the scanners and computers together, and tying them into the birthing units and hospitals," explained Macintosh.

"Uh, I think you are getting a little ahead of my father, Mac," said Nicholas, "We need to bring him up to speed from the beginning."

"Oh, sorry, Santa," Macintosh stammered, "Perhaps we should begin in the scanner room."

"Good idea," agreed Nicholas. He led the group up the set of steps to his right. "Up here is the proof I was telling you about."

When they got to the top there were machines all around and a small room for demonstration purposes. Nicholas led his father inside and told Keeney to please explain the two types of scanners.

Keeney puffed up and with great pride said to Kris,

"It really is a marvel what we have been able to produce here. We have two scanner systems that we are busy putting into areas all over the world. The first is what we refer to as a general scanner. As a person passes by this machine it will either give us a red or green specter around that person. Green is good, red is bad. Now that is just for that particular moment in time. Later on it may get redder or greener depending on what that person has done that day. It may even change completely from red to green or vice versa, though that doesn't seem to happen very often."

Just at that moment several people walked by the scanners and monitors showed primarily different tints of green with just a one or two bathed in light red glow. "As you can see, Santa, most of those people are good with only a couple toward the red tint, and not too badly."

"What would cause a red tint or green?" asked Kris.

"It is based on their actions and feelings over the last 24 hours," Ion Crosswire had answered, "For instance, if someone had a bad argument with their spouse, it may show them red tinged until such time as they made up or sufficient time had passed, when they might switch back to green."

"Or if they did a counteracting action, such as visited a friend in the hospital, or donated to charity, it would probably change them immediately to green. Depending on the strength of the action they will have a higher tinge to where you may have trouble seeing what the person truly looks like," finished Keeney.

"Only 24 hours, that won't tell us how good or bad a person normally is," retorted Kris.

"Ah," said Macintosh, "That is why we also came up with the pinpoint scanners!"

Nicholas interrupted, "Dad, we knew we would need to two pronged system. This is, as we have shown you, a general 'snapshot' if you will of how people are doing. The next machine will take an entire persons history and assign a number to it using a plus- minus scale of fifteen. A plus 15 would denote a saint, the highest we have seen so far is plus 12. Needless to say a minus 15 is the devil on earth, and we have seen a few minuses in the double digit range, but thankfully most people are showing up in the plus 2 to 10 range meaning, as we suspected, most people are good, and many are better than just 'good'."

"How can you get their history just from them walking by?" asked Kris.

"It is a very complex equation which I am happy to go over with you, it involves some predictability and probability formulas, as well as historical data and propensity qualifications, but I can go slowly," answered Macintosh.

Kris just waved his hand and mumbled, "Uh, no thanks."

"The point," pushed Nicholas, "Is that we now have a way to track good people from not so good people, and we can implement this anywhere we wish. In fact we are installing general and pinpoint scanners all over the world. And this also means that before we invite anyone to the North Pole, we can know that person's propensity to do good or bad."

Kris just stared at the monitors of green and red and finally said, "This is one of the projects you were working on?"

"Actually, sir," Ion said nervously, "This became an offshoot of collecting data from all over the world, as are many of our projects we are working on. We are now directly connected into every hospital and birthing unit, so we know instantly when a baby is born, and not only their birthday, and whether they are a boy or girl, but their Christian name, how much they weigh, how long they are, what time they were born, their parents names and address and more."

"Would you not consider this an invasion of their private lives?" questioned the older Santa.

"We would only deem it so if we planned to use this information for nefarious reasons, but as we both know," responded Keeney, "this information will just help us do our job better and protect us from people who might have it in their hearts to harm us or cause problems. Strictly an information and defensive system."

Kris kept looking at all the green on the monitor and began to break into a smile, "So it is true, there are still more good people in the world than not."

His son walked up and put his arm on his father's

shoulders and said, "You knew it just as I did, you just needed a little proof. It is why we do what we do, to help people who want to be good to others, and we don't want to leave one behind if we can prevent it. This is your legacy just as it was our ancestors. And with pride and joy, I assume it as mine."

Kris wiped his eyes briefly and said it was time to get going.

Everyone stepped out of his way as he made it back to the steps. When he got to the bottom he shook Ion and Macintosh's hand and told them to keep up with the great work. He turned to Keeney and said, "My friend, I know it is your chosen namesake to keep an eye on all that happens around us, but as a personal favor I ask you to also keep a watchful eye on my son. He is my pride and joy, and he is going to accomplish many more great things than I can imagine. He will need someone to watch over him."

"You have my deepest promise, as I have watched over you all these years, so I shall do the same with pride for our new Santa Claus," Keeney never felt so honored in all his 375 years.

Kris and Nicholas walked off together. Nothing was said by either of them for a time. Finally, Nicholas could stay silent no longer, "Well?"

"I have been thinking a great deal since we left, and I believe you have merit in your arguments about meeting the demands of Christmas, and I may go along with the idea of working with Southerners, but why do you feel the need to invite families up here?" asked Kris.

"It started as I was watching the Santas around the retail stores near Christmas," Nicholas began, "I could not believe how little any of them knew. And not just about the North Pole and us, but about the whole reason we exist and why we do what we do. There was no tie in to Jesus Christ's birth, no understanding of the love we have for children, as He had. Let alone any of the feelings or thoughts of the elves. No one even seemed sure if Santa Claus was actually married, let alone how his wife may be running the place. And I thought, good heavens, if the 'Santas' don't know any of this, what about the rest of the world?"

Kris just looked down and shook his head.

Nicholas continued, "It is just not right, we are the embodiment of Christmas on earth, and we are not getting the message across, because one night a year popping in and out of houses is not enough to explain it to the masses."

"So your plan is to invite everyone up here and show them around?" Kris chuckled.

"Not everyone, but as you and I know, there are a good many people who are struggling personally, but do much good. I will soon be able to know every person's heart from the scanners and how they are doing, plus we will have a history of them and who they are helping in the data base. What if we invited families up solely to try and help them accomplish the good that is in them, and to be able to spread the word about what we want them to learn from the North Pole," Nicholas was into his full enthusiasm now, "Imagine the good we could do for them, and those around them. We could reward those who have been selfless and help them continue to help others."

"Does this have anything to do with what your mother is working on in that one section of the village?" asked Kris.

"I don't know, as she asked me to stay out of it. She said she will do what needs be done and when," answered Nicholas honestly, "But I suspect my ideas may have something to do with it."

Kris nodded, "Yes, I'll bet you are quite right. Your mother is a very passionate lady, and if she can see a way to help others, she will move mountains to do it."

As they were moving back through the village, Denny Sweetooth sauntered over and announced to them, "Well it is set, a week from Saturday is your banquet if that is quite convenient?"

Nicholas laughed and said, "As I promised, I will not miss my own party. Is there anything I need to help with?"

Denny laughed this time and said, "Oh my, no! How would it look if the guest-of-honor worked on his own celebration? But thanks for the thought."

Nicholas said almost to himself, "Good, next Saturday should work out fine and I can leave the following Monday."

"Leave?" both men asked and Kris said, "Leave for where?"

For a moment Nicholas forgot both Denny and his father were there, "Oh, I have some things to do outside the North Pole. I won't be away too long, just a few days."

Kris looked like he wanted to press his son for more information, but before he could Nicholas said, "In fact, I need to meet with some one from the village, father I hope you will excuse me, Denny you also?"

"Of course," Denny answered for both of them and asked if he could talk with Kris about the plans.

Kris felt suddenly trapped but had no reasonable way out and said, "Sure, why not."

Nicholas waved goodbye and sped toward the center of the village. He found the quaint two story cottage which had toys and dolls hanging from all the windows, eaves and doorways. He knocked on the door jam as the door was wide open. He heard someone from a distance say, "One moment, please."

A fairly tall elf with a thick head of dark brown hair and an angular face appeared at the door. He wore gold colored lederhosen over a colorful shirt of yellows and blues. He sported a short but bushy beard and his nose was long and thin. He looked at his visitor and said, "Well bless my soul, it is the new Santa Claus! What is the honor of your visit Mr. Claus?"

Nicholas ho, ho, ho'd loudly and said, "First, please call me Nicholas and none of this Mr. Claus stuff.

Secondly I understand you are one of the best toymakers in the North Pole, am I right?

"Well if I am to be honest, then yes, I reckon that's the truth," boasted Rory Mattle, "Do you need something special for someone special?"

"Not exactly," shuffled Nicholas, "But I would like to discuss a plan I have been formulating with you as the center of it. Is there somewhere we could talk?"

"Well forgive my lack of hospitality, I guess I was just surprised having you show up like this, please come in and make yourself comfortable. Would you care for some tea or coffee? I have some cookies I snagged off Denny yesterday if you'd like a couple?" Rory was very animated in his offerings.

"Thank you, but I am fine," Nicholas waved off the offerings, "I am kind of anxious to talk with you, however."

Immediately the jumpy elf took a chair opposite of Nicholas and sat down saying, "I'm sorry, again, as I said I am off guard with your sudden visit."

"Do you not get any visitors?" asked Nicholas.

"Oh sure, all the time from other elves," answered Rory, "They are always asking me to come up with this or that for their kids. And sometimes Carrow will come down to talk with me about some new ideas for the production line. And even once your father came to see me, I believe he wanted a special toy for your sixth birthday. I created a marionette clown for him."

Nicholas laughed again, "You mean you created it for me! I still have that marionette hanging from my bed post! For a very long while I don't think my parents ever saw me without it. Well thank you for the beautiful craftsmanship of that toy. It is still among my favorites."

Rory blushed at the compliments and just said, "Well gosh, you are welcome. I am glad you liked it so much."

"Loved it you mean!" gushed Nicholas, "Well, let me get straight to the point of my visit. I would like you to play one of the most important roles to the North Pole that any elf has or will ever be involved in. That is if you think you would be willing?"

Rory just gaped at Nicholas.

"May I take that is a definite maybe?" Nicholas smirked.

Finally Rory found his senses and stammered, "That is quite an introduction you just made. How could I possibly refuse, and what is it you need me to do?"

Nicholas put forth the idea given to him by Aeon Millennium from his book, but of course left Aeon out of the discussion. He asked at the end if Rory would be willing to travel with him a week from Monday.

Rory rubbed his beard and thought for a long moment, he then said to Nicholas, "Very interesting, very interesting indeed, I would be honored to go. Now, may I show you something?" Nicholas nodded. Rory got up and went to the back of his home/workshop, he emerged carrying something which he handed to Nicholas.

After studying the object Nicholas said, "She is very beautiful. I foresee that any girl would love her. What do you call her?"

"I named her after my mother Bild Lilli, she is made of the new material plastic and she is very durable," explained Rory, "I just finished her and was going to take her to Carrow. Perhaps we could take her to this company instead. I will have Stacy Buttons design a swimsuit for her to make her more modest for our presentation. Do you think this might work?"

"Hmm, I believe she might. She is quite a bit older than the dolls I have delivered in the past," Nicholas rubbed his own beard, "But I think you are right, let's hold off on showing her to Carrow or anyone else in the village. This little lady is going to be a huge hit, I can feel it through my whole being, and this could be what we need to springboard us with the Handler's and Mr. Matson."

"Now the more important question for you," said Nicholas in a very concerned voice, "How do you feel about being away from the North Pole for what could be several years?"

Rory shrugged, "As long as I am able to keep making toys, I am content to do so anywhere. Besides, if what you say is true, I could be one of the best known elves the Pole has ever seen, though truthfully, that doesn't hold a lot of sway with me. But to be considered one of the greatest toymakers does! If this is where I am needed, then

I am your humble servant for however long it takes."

"Very well," Nicholas said with a smile and shook Rory's hand vigorously, "Now I must ask you that for the current time, and probably until after the upcoming banquet, we keep this between us."

"I had already guessed that this would be a clandestine meeting," smirked Rory, "Again I am pleased you have come to me and will keep your every confidence."

Nicholas patted Rory on the back and said, "I will check back with you in a few days to see what Stacy has come up with and to make travel plans." Then he slipped out and headed back toward his home.

Nicholas found his mother in her favorite room, the kitchen. She was baking up a batch of bread which always made the home smell heavenly. The one thing that Nicholas and his mother shared was a passion for cooking. Ever since he was a young lad, he would play in the kitchen while his mother taught him how to mix things. He always had an aptitude for chemistry and enjoyed how mixing things would always change the consistency and flavor of food.

By the time he was of high school age his culinary skills were already admirable, and he made several of the family dinners, as long as time allowed in his studies. Even his father would rave about his son's prowess in the kitchen and some of the meals he made. This of course, only spurred Nicholas to come up with more elaborate meals.

This also increased his friendship with Denny and Pierre and the three of them would discuss recipes and concoctions all the while throwing ingredients into bowls and mixers. It was some of the best memories Nicholas had growing up.

He reached around his mother and gave her a good squeeze. She laughed and said, "Your father was just talking about you and what a nice day he had."

"He's home already?" asked Nicholas, as Denny was not so easily dissuaded when he had someone to discuss a party to plan.

"No, he called me on one of the new communications devises the Council is testing, she answered, "It is a cordless telephone laying right over there. We can reach anyone in the North Pole without being tethered to a cord."

"Incredible," sighed Nicholas, "Well did he say anything?"

"Only that he had a very interesting day with you, and then you disappeared," Annie said.

"I had to meet Rory Mattle and plan my trip to Southern California. By the way, who do I talk to about using standard transportation to Los Angeles Airport?" asked Nicholas.

"Who else, Ella Communicado," said his mother, "She will make all your plans and arrange everything."

"But she is on the Council! Won't she ask a bunch

of questions?" said Nicholas horrified at his mother's suggestion.

"The first thing you need to do is stop this 'me against them' attitude you have with everyone outside your little band of soldiers!" Annie scolded, "We are not your enemy, and the Council is not against you or progress, in fact quite the opposite. The second thing you need to know is that every time you involve a Council member, they don't all run to each other and tell the others what you said or did. And lastly, you need to remember the entire Council is behind you, but that will change if they feel you are working behind their backs."

"I'm sorry," Nicholas said sincerely, "I guess I have been acting like a spy in my own house. I promise I will quit trying to be so secretive. I just want to make certain everything works out as it should."

"Well remember you have some powerful allies now, which you won't have if they feel you don't trust them to make the right decisions," Annie said firmly, "And come Friday if you leave anything out when addressing the Council, I will make sure it is brought up."

Nicholas shrugged, "Alright, that's fair. Everything comes out in the open, but I hope you plan to be there for a very long time, because I am positive that they are going to be ready to fight me on a good many issues."

Annie scoffed, "Oh, I wouldn't be so sure of yourself. You don't know it yet, but a good many things you are about to propose, has been in discussion for a while now and the Council is leaning toward changes. It is you that needs to give them a chance, more than the other way around."

Just then they heard the door in the hallway open and Kris bellowed, "I am going to shoot my son for leaving me to deal with that rotund little menu planner!"

Both Annie and Nicholas broke into laughter and Nicholas called out, "Better not shoot me anywhere vital, or you will be stuck doing this all over again later!"

He came in from the hall and grabbed and kissed his wife. "Well that makes it all worth it!" he smiled, "And you," he said looking at his son, "What was so all fired important that you had to run like a jack rabbit who saw a coyote?"

"I'm sorry Dad, I had to meet with another elf as we have to travel down to Southern California the week after the banquet to meet with a company there," he looked at his mother as if to say, *the honesty and openness starts now.*

"Well next time give me a little warning would you?" grunted Kris, "You really have to leave so soon? Everyone will want to congratulate you again."

"I am sure I will have met everyone at least once by and before the banquet," Nicholas said, "They can wait to say it again upon my return." He then faced his father and asked, "My bigger concern is whether or not I have your support for my presentation to the Council tomorrow on the projects we have discussed the last couple days?"

Kris grabbed his beard and began stroking it slowly while staring back at his son, "There are some things I am not entirely convinced of..." he held up his hand as he saw Nicholas sucking in breath ready for an argument, "however I feel I have seen enough, and you have sufficiently justified your arguments for me to give my support of your endeavors to the Council."

Nicholas released the air he was holding in him and said softly, "Thank you."

"Is it safe to assume that you have no other surprises to unleash tomorrow that I would be caught unawares?" Nicholas eyed his son.

Nicholas laughed and said, "No promises, but no, I cannot think of anything else that should come up tomorrow."

Kris shook his head and said, "Well if anything does, I will just have to plead ignorance and stay quiet."

Annie teased her husband, "You never stay quiet about anything, and I am sure you will find your voice, but I think Nicholas is right, there shouldn't be anymore surprises and if there are they will surprise more than just you."

With that they spoke about what order and how to best present Nicholas' ideas to the Council.

The next morning was, as most were under the dome, a beautiful day with a few puffy clouds rolling over the village and a most comfortable 50 degrees Fahrenheit. During the summer as it was now, it would actually warm up into the 70's during the day, even outside the dome. However, here they could control on which days and times it rained, which was always scheduled for at night, and nothing stronger than a mild summer breeze would flow through the village during the day. That was not always so outside.

But this was a beautiful day both in and out of the dome. Nicholas, was a little apprehensive about the deliberations of the Council, but still felt optimistic about the final result. All would work out as it should.

The Council meeting was scheduled for 10:00 in the morning and Nicholas had arranged for Macintosh, Ion, Keeney and a couple others to meet him in the grand hallway at 9:30 to go over the presentations. It was 9:15 and Nicholas had already told his parents that he would see them there and was out the door heading to the Council chambers.

On his way over he saw Jackson and waved. Jackson came over and patted Nicholas on the back and said, "Best of luck today. I have been anxious to hear the official version of all your ideas, even though you have told me some of the concepts."

Nicholas had always felt that since Jackson had

helped him find Macintosh and Ion, that he had always been a forward thinking person like Nicholas. He trusted Jackson and had let him in on some of the things he was doing, but knew that even Jackson would be surprised by some of the other ideas and plans he was about to share. Still, he appreciated Jackson's support and told him so.

"If it is good for the village and Santa Claus, than it is good for all," Jackson said, "I hope the rest of the Council will be receptive to what you put forth today."

Nicholas shrugged, "We'll just have to see, but I believe everyone knows I have the North Pole and children and the success of our mission in mind."

Jackson laughed and said, "Whoa, save the political speeches for in there!" he pointed to the chambers up the way.

Nicholas just returned the laugh and said, "Just practicing!"

They walked up the path together and when they reached the door, Nicholas said, "Well I must get ready my friend, my assistants and I will need to leave you now."

Jackson caught the hint and said goodbye to Nicholas and the other elves, "See you soon," he smiled and moved on.

Just outside the door was a stack of boxes and packages that had been left there last night. As they moved the pile into the grand hallway, the little band started unwrapping and assembling the pieces that they would be showing the Council.

At 10:00 sharp, the door to the Council chambers opened again for Nicholas with both his parents standing on the other side. Annie looked at her son and asked, "Ready?"

Nicholas was. He marched in with his parents and was followed by his small army of elves and a series of scale models.

As he stood before the Council he began his speech in earnest. He talked about the challenges of the past and how they were met with new ideas, then he spoke of the future challenges and the ever exploding population and the use of radio and television and its growing effect on how information was being given and received. Without alluding to Aeon's information, he talked about how one day he would be visiting a billion or more houses on Christmas night.

He then talked about how he had vexed over this problem while learning the lessons of his father. He finished his introductory speech by stating, "I believe that with the help of the various elves in this room with me that we are prepared to meet the challenges and concerns before us. And with the Council's permission, I would like to introduce my helpers and then discuss the projects before you."

As he introduced each elf and their specialty he talked about how like the great pioneers of the North Pole, these elves would help continue and grow the influence of the elves and find good persons to plant the proper seeds to help sow a more peaceful world. As he got to Keeney Eagleye, he reminded the Council how carefully Keeney has watched over the Pole through generations of tallfolk and never let anything untoward happen to its residents.

After finishing his opening remarks he turned the presentation of the miniaturization machine over to Macintosh Gelfeeney and he demonstrated with his scale model how this would work. He took a ball and placed it into one side and turned on the scale model. As the ball went through into the machine it seemingly disappeared until he held up something smaller than a pea on the other side of the machine, which was the ball now in miniature form. The Council all began murmuring to each other and nodding their heads.

Nicholas stepped back to the front and said, "We can miniaturize anything and ship it down to the distribution centers for delivery on Christmas Eve.

Britney spoke up and asked, "So what would a person do with a ball that small?"

Ion started to giggle, but a quick look from Nicholas stopped him cold. He turned to Macintosh and just said, "Mac shall we finish this demonstration?"

With that Macintosh placed the miniaturized ball onto Nicholas' hand and pulled out what looked somewhat like a magic wand. He pointed it at the ball and pushed a button on the handle. Instantly the ball returned to its normal size.

"This is a temporary miniaturization machine,"

Nicholas explained, "It will shrink an object for as long as we wish. When I deliver the present and push that button, anything miniaturized including its wrappings will return to normal size."

Macintosh stated, "We have tried it on a number of different items. As long as it goes in together they will be miniaturized together and will be returned to normal size together."

The Council approved the full scale machine to be built at one of the manufacturing centers and Annie Kringle specified which one she thought might work best. Nicholas thought, *One down.*

Nicholas then turned to Keeney Eagleye who explained how the two types of scanners worked and where they had been employed. At the end of his presentation which included a movie taken at the Hall of Records that was shown to the Council, Kris cleared his throat and announced to his fellow Council members, "Both Annie and I have seen this technology, and we support the use of this for our own education, edification and defense. It is obvious the more we know about the hearts of others the better we can attend to those good and loving in the world."

There was some discussion about invasion of privacy, and wasn't the North Pole already going on the premise that everyone was good, anyway?

Nicholas stayed quiet as he felt his voice would be needed later, and this was a half-hearted discussion with no clear disagreement, but more of a clarification. Besides his father was doing quite fine convincing the Council. In the end, his father quelled the debate and the Council passed the scanners use as well.

Keeney felt he was on a roll, so he next discussed the data capturing taking place and the hardwiring into the hospitals and birthing units. By now they had now added death announcements to the mix so they could void any person who had been known to pass and expunge them from the data. Keeney admitted it was a little morbid, but said since they were now keeping track of everyone Christian born, that it might be a good idea to weed out those who had died, too.

This was treated more as a point of information to the Council to let them know that this was proceeding. It was Frieda who pointed this out to Nicholas and the elves.

She admonished Nicholas saying, "I understand that you are trying to keep us ahead with all this information, however any projects like this in the future needs to be brought before the Council before you proceed with them. We are still the governing body, and the North Pole is not your personal playground to do with as you please. As you are new, even though this information should have already been passed on, I am willing to let this infraction slide if the rest of the Council agrees."

The rest of the Council saw Nicholas get redder in the face and just grumbled their agreement. Nicholas wondered to himself if by winning that battle he had just lost the war.

Nicholas asked the Council if the other elves might be excused, as he had a couple more ideas he wished to bring before the Council that did not involve them before a decision would be reached. Carrow took it one step further and requested a recess until after lunch so they could all begin fresh.

Nicholas went to lunch with his parents and they talked about how it was going so far. "I am concerned about the scolding I got from Frieda and how it may affect my chances about the other subjects I wish to discuss," said a concerned Nicholas.

"That was just some saber-rattling on Frieda's part," said Kris, "She likes to remind people that she is 'in charge' occasionally."

"Especially if she feels that she should have had a say in something, first," added Annie, "Of course you caught the jab at us that we should have brought you up better to know this."

"Yes," said Nicholas, "I am glad that just fell on the floor and died." Then he chuckled and said, "I don't know her hardly at all. I am not that familiar with Britney or Ella, either. Though I must admit I like Ella, she seems to have a good sense of humor about her."

"Britney is a good egg, also," chimed in Kris, "In fact, they all are good inside. Frieda just likes to remind people that she is on the Council and was one of the original founders. Her artwork is everywhere and all of it is breathtaking."

"So I've seen," replied Nicholas, "Okay, so what do you both think are my chances for this afternoon?"

"Well your father and I will support you as best as we can," said Annie, "I really cannot say beyond that, much of what you are going to ask has been argued much without resolution, yet."

"I think the best you could do," thought Kris out loud, "is to present it with all the passion you have, and convince them why you think this is vital to the North Pole, as well as the tallfolk. Although, don't forget Whitey is very concerned about the security of the Pole, so don't make light of that fact. That may be your best chance. If they know how driven you are on this score, they may acquiesce to your wishes as the new Santa Claus."

"I think your father is right," said Annie, "Right now they are just as worried about upsetting you as you are about upsetting them. Although I wouldn't let that go to your head."

"Don't worry," chuckled Nicholas, "There are a lot more of them than there is of me!"

"We should head back," said Kris, "They should be reconvening by now."

"Yeah, and I don't want to be late for my own funeral," grumbled Nicholas.

"Just remember, they all want to see you succeed as we do. In fact, it would do them no good to upset you before you even got started," Annie explained, "There is no one but your father that can do this. No one else understands the time continuum as well as you, and as long as you believe you are doing good for Santa Claus and the North Pole, than they cannot accuse you of doing this for selfish reasons."

Nicholas thought about this for a moment then said, "I *am* doing this for the North Pole, if people lose faith in Santa Claus and Christmas and the message both brings, the results could be far worse than anything they could dare dread today."

Now Nicholas was ready.

As the Council returned, everyone seemed in a good mood, but also a little apprehensive about what was to come. As Kris banged the gavel and called the Council officially back in session he turned the floor over to Nicholas and said, "I believe you have a couple issues you wish to bring before this Council?"

"I do, thank you Mr. President," Nicholas responded, "There are two issues both related to the tallfolk of the south that I wish to discuss with the Council and two proposals I wish to get the Council's decision on." With that Nicholas began:

For hundreds of years, with the exception of two people, no tallfolk have been allowed to set foot at the North Pole and no one, except the elves outside the Pole, have been allowed to know anything about the goings on up here. I believe the time has come that we change these policies and here is my explanations as to why.

Even with all our technology and sophistication, we have come to a point where we will not be able to keep up with the manufacturing demand that will soon be upon us without assistance from outside the North Pole. In the near future we will soon be needing toys and presents for more than a billion souls on Christmas Eve."

"How could you know that?" asked Carrow.

"I know that there has been a population explosion," said Frederick, "but how do you arrive at that huge number?"

Nicholas knew it was time to release his secret weapon and did so, "Aeon Millennium." He said simply.

"Please explain," requested Whitey.

"Aeon knew I would be having trouble with the portion of the time continuum, as he must have come forward, or backward, in time to see me struggling. He then created a book that he left to me, alone. In it he explained a part of the time continuum that even my father hadn't stumbled upon, but would be necessary to master in order to reach the billions of people I will eventually service. It also included the schematics that made possible the miniaturization machine you saw this morning.

"There is much more that he has left me, but just as he would do with this Council, he said there was to be a time to introduce these new ideas, and he asked me not to jump ahead. I will hold promise to this and he has clearly marked dates on each of the pages so I will know when to advance to the next invention or information. While I already knew this in my heart before, Aeon also said it was vital that I convince the Council to open the Pole's borders and allow for a sharing of ideas between the tallfolk and the residents of the North Pole beginning now.

"If Aeon has foreseen this in his visits to the future, then he would not push this idea if he saw it would harm the Pole or its residents. I feel that this is vital to our survival if we wish to bring the ideas and morals that we hold so dear to the rest of the world. While the tallfolk may always be at war with each other, as we can now see with our scanners, there are far more good-hearted people than not. We MUST bring the information of peace and love and the teachings of not only Jesus Christ, but every prophet and peacemaker to these people, and we must lead by example.

"If we are to be as untrusting as those of the south, then what better are we? If we do not lead by example, then how can we claim to be different in our beliefs? Just because we do not war with each other here, does not prove that our hearts and minds are any bigger than theirs. But if we share our message with others, than we can teach them that there is a better way and we can hope that they will spread that message.

There are some brilliant minds out there that would easily rival our own. And by opening our minds to theirs, we will all benefit."

"Most of their brilliance is in developing new weapons," said Carrow.

"I truly believe that weaponry is often a by-product of the ideas others are working on, rather than as a purpose unto itself," replied Nicholas, "And I have been among these people. Yes they can be untrusting, selfish and uninformed, but if they have a chance for enlightenment and we do not provide it, then again I ask, how much better are we if we withhold this information because of our own distrust?"

"What exactly are you asking the Council to do?" asked Denny, "Perhaps we can better answer you if we know the question you are asking us."

"Of course, what I would like to propose to the Council is to build a Visiting Center at one end of the North Pole. We would keep this away from our manufacturing, research and development areas and away from the woodlands area where most of us reside to maintain separation and privacy from the tallfolk. We would build a grand inn where we would house certain families for a week. I would meet with them while they were here and we would try to assist them in their strife while educating them in the beliefs and love that we wish to share with others.

"We would encourage them to talk about what they learned from us and advise them that some things must be kept secret. We would introduce certain technologies that we feel may assist the greater good, and others we will keep to ourselves as we have always done in the past. We would only invite families that we know do good things and are selfless to others. It would be much easier to build on good habits and reward good people, than to attempt to change hearts that may not be receptive."

"Is that the true purpose of the scanners you have begun setting up all over the world?" asked Ella.

"It wasn't the purpose of them originally, but yes they would be used to help determine who we should invite," said Nicholas. "And if we invite a family, all the members must have the same moral fortitude or we will pick another."

"Would I be allowed to review your findings prior to inviting them to the Pole," asked Whitey.

"Of course, you would be an integral part of this," answered Nicholas.

Annie said, "You should explain the other part of this puzzle as you will be spending some time away from the North Pole this year as well."

"The other part my mother alludes to," sighed Nicholas, "Is that with the Council's approval, I will be setting up alliances with companies that could benefit us in securing enough toys and presents to appease all the requests we are already getting as well as future letters."

"Are you quite sure we cannot keep up with the demand you are suggesting." asked Carrow.

"Quite certain since I found the book, but I had concerns previously," answered Nicholas, "In fact my parents and I had this conversation several times before finding the book, and like you, could come to no equitable solution. Let me put it to the CEO of the North Pole, do you believe after the numbers I have shown you that we could keep up with the demand we are facing?"

Annie was pleased with the question and was prepared with an answer, "Considering that our own population has remained on a much slower growth path, and also considering that even though we are the model of efficiency in production, the sheer diversity of what will be required soon would force us to seek out these alliances. I would much rather deal from a position of strength and guidance rather than be desperate and have no choice in our dealings. But yes, either way, we will need to either import help or rely on alliances, if not both."

Nicholas felt this was a good time to cease discussion and let his mother, the CEO have the final word. He remained silent while the Council murmured among themselves. Carrow finally suggested that Nicholas be excused while the Council deliberated on his proposals.

As Nicholas began to leave, Kris said "Just a moment, please." Kris then turned to the Council and said, "Under the circumstances, as both these subjects will determine the role of the new Santa Claus, as much as all residents of the North Pole, I request that Nicholas be allowed to stay and listen to our deliberations. He has shared all his secrets with us, and I feel he is deserved of the same respect and information from us."

Annie quickly seconded her husband's motion.

"I agree as well," said Frederick.

So the Council allowed Nicholas to stay, and he sat silently but attentively as each Council member brought up what they thought might be dangerous precedents as well as wonderful discoveries and advances.

It was clear to Nicholas who was on the side of his proposals and he thought it might just be the majority, although Ella, Whitey and Denny could argue either side effectively, and did.

It was finally his father who slammed the gavel again and said, "It is well and truly time to decide these issues. If the Council chooses it may do so by written vote or spoken vote but this must be decided as either way will have serious ramifications to our immediate future and plans. So first let us decide written or oral?"

Oral was chosen by a slim majority, and Kris said, "Very well, now do we decide each issue separately or together."

Denny laughed and said, "In for a penny, in for a pound, I say they are inseparable and should be decided together."

This also carried by a slightly larger majority.

"May I have the Council's vote please?"

Annie started the ball and said, "I vote yes on the issues."

Frederick followed by a simple, "Yes."

Carrow then sat up straight and said, "I have little doubt that the leadership of this body will decide properly and in the best way for the entire elven race, however

Ulzana and I have decided to abstain from this vote. We wish to courteously abstain in this very important decision."

"So two yeses, and two abstentions, next?" said Kris.

Ella said, "I vote in favor."

Frieda said, "While I may be viewed as out of step with progress, I sometimes believe progress is not a good thing, I vote no."

Denny cleared his throat, "If one of our wisest has seen the future and does not perceive a problem with aligning with the tallfolk, than I believe our new Santa Claus and his heart and vote, yes."

Britney looked squarely at Nicholas and said, "I pray you know what you are doing as I have all my faith and trust in you as our new Santa, yes by me."

Jackson said, "The Council already knows my views as they have not changed since the very first time we brought this up for discussion, now and always, I am in favor – definitely yes!"

Whitey looked sternly at Nicholas and said, "I will go along with these proposals with reservations, but know that if a threat ensues from these new policies, I will make certain that they are revoked with the quickest haste. So I vote yes."

"I have a consensus," said Kris, "I have seven in favor, one against and two abstentions. The motions carry, congratulations Nicholas." He slammed the gavel again to emphasize the point.

Nicholas felt as if someone had just placed the world on his shoulders and it was heavy. He smiled and said, "I will do everything in my power to make you proud of the decision you made today." With that he weakly rose to his feet and asked to be excused.

"I do not believe there is any more business before the Council," said Kris, "I suggest we stand adjourned?"

Everyone nodded and Kris brought the gavel down for the last time that day.

The following Saturday, no one felt more like celebrating than Nicholas. He had officially become the new Santa Claus, and had already implemented the first of what would be a series of changes that would affect history in the North Pole and possibly the world.

The banquet in his honor was a rousing time with well wishing elves from all over the world who had returned to the Pole to meet the new Santa. Of course, a good many already had unofficially met him when he accompanied his father on his world tours at Christmas. Nicholas remembered them and was happy to see them in a more relaxed atmosphere. Even with the use of the time continuum, everything was under a great rush to move on to the next town, village or city when they would stop. Even so, the feast once more continued for days. While Nicholas had missed the previous banquets in his families honor, he was enjoying this one as if making up time.

Of course, Denny had once more prepared a sumptuous feast and the food seemed never ending. And being in the North Pole, as always, everyone could eat as much as they wished without ill effects or gaining any weight.

Sometime during the banquet the elves called for a speech. When Nicholas rose, he cleared his throat and as the din died down he said, "My dear friends and fellow bringers of joy, I appreciate everything I have here and all of you. But before I make my remarks, I believe it is only fitting that we first hear from the Santa Claus that brought so much joy to so many children and families and established us all in the hearts of so many, my father, Kristopher Kringle."

Everyone stood and a thunderous ovation took place that lasted quite a while. Kris finally stood and bowed then raised his hands to call for quiet. "We have made so much history together that it is hard to imagine the true and total affect we have had on the world today. I could not have done this without the help and support of my lovely wife, the Council and each and every one of you. I am so proud that my son is taking over the legacy and legend and will do incredible and mighty things going forward. I look forward to quieter years and helping our new Santa Claus in a consulting role. I thank you for all the glorious years of service, and hope you will be as wonderful to my son as you have been to me. God bless every one of you."

Again the crowd thundered their approval.

With that Kris sat down and Carrow Chekitwice stood up. He stated to the crowd, "Ever since we decided to invite Kris and Anne Marie to the North Pole those wonderful centuries ago, we have watched as they have fulfilled dreams and wishes throughout the world. We have seen Mrs. Kringle assume the responsibilities of the North Pole and work very hard to always keep the pace of our needs in check. Ulzana and I have always been, and continue to be, so proud of everyone and their efforts. So much so that it makes it very difficult to make this next statement. At the end of this year Ulzana and I will step down from the Council." Murmured whispers ran through the crowd and Carrow waited for them to die down, "We will still remain active in our roles as tailor and in manufacturing, but we wish to make room for the new Santa Claus, whom we have every confidence in, and we, like Kris, wish to live at least a little quieter life as well." He abruptly sat down saying all he wanted to say. Polite applause followed when they realized he was done.

This began a series of speeches from other members of the Council, each praising the work of Kris and Annie, excitement at the changes Nicholas would implement, and thanking the years of leadership from

Carrow and Ulzana, and some reminisced about the beginnings of the North Pole and the changes that took place over the centuries.

Toward the end the crowd again called for the new Santa Claus. Nicholas stood and again addressed the crowd saying, "Many things will continue as the legend has continued. And many things will change as the world, itself, has changed. I will do my best to keep the North Pole at the technological and theoretical edge, while instilling the age-old traditions that have been handed down to me over the centuries. I look forward to working with and for every one of you and pray that you will enjoy me as much as my father. As he said, thank you and God bless you all."

He sat to a standing ovation that continued as long as his father's had. He was pleased to see that the elves were accepting him as the new Santa and hoped it would continue until his retirement, whenever that may be.

Chapter Thirteen

The value of a man resides in what he gives and not in what he is capable of receiving.

- Albert Einstein

New Beginnings

The following Monday, Nicholas and Rory Mattle left for California. Nicholas had sent a telegram to Ruth and Elliott Handler requesting a meeting to discuss a new line of toys that he wanted to offer the Handlers and their partner, Harold "Matt" Matson. He received a reply saying Monday afternoon was fine by them and said that their executive assistant would pick them up at the airport.

This was either one's first trip in a commercial airliner, and both were pleased with the service and doting treatment they received on the plane. As beards were somewhat out of fashion in this era, Nicholas received many looks, bordering on stares, as if they knew him, but couldn't place him.

They arrived at Los Angeles airport within five minutes of their scheduled time and stepped outside into the beautiful California sun. Rory had never set foot out of the North Pole and he was one of the first elves born under the dome. He had never seen such a sight and was taking it all in. A car pulled up in front of them and a comely lady of thirty-something stepped out of the automobile. She had strawberry blond hair, a very pleasant shape and beautiful green eyes that matched Nicholas'.

"I am sorry if you have been waiting long, traffic was terrible," she said in a rapid speech, "I am Mary Atwater, and I am here to take you to Mattel."

"We just arrived on the curb, ourselves, so you are right on time." answered Nicholas, "Thank you for your assistance and timeliness." He thought to himself looking Mary up and down, *Aeon, you sly dog, she is lovely. A very interesting situation we have here.*

They shook hands and he noticed her skin was as soft a flower petals. He gave her a big smile and said, "Shall we be going?"

They loaded up the car with Rory getting in the rear seat and Nicholas up front with Mary. Nicholas and Mary talked almost the whole way there. He learned that Mary had moved out from the east, New York actually, and was finishing her degree in business from University of California in Los Angeles while working for the Handlers and Mattson.

She spoke about how she loved California, but truly missed the four seasons and especially the snow. She always felt winter was a beautiful season when the snow had just fallen and coated everything in a soft blanket of white.

She discussed that while it was difficult in a man's world, she had found a mentor in Ruth Handler and talked about how strong and confident a woman she was. Ruth and Elliott shared decisions and responsibilities and she mused about how, in her mind at least, they were a perfect couple.

"Even when they disagree about something," she continued, "They find a way to compromise and work it out. To me that is a true partnership."

Nicholas thought about how his parents were the same way. He never heard a cross word between them in all the decades, correction a century, of seeing them together and wondered how they always did it. He also wondered if he would be as easy to live with for Mary.

They arrived at the modest office and walked into the lobby area. Matt Matson greeted them there and walked them back to the small but warmly decorated conference room. Ruth and Elliott came in shortly afterward and introduced themselves.

Nicholas introduced himself as Nicholas Kringle and Matt said, "You mean like in Kris Kringle?"

Rory spoke a bit too quickly and said, "Yes, that's his father."

Elliott said, "You mean he has the same name as Santa Claus?"

"No," Rory said matter-of-factly, "I mean he is Santa Claus. Or at least he was until this year, Nicholas here is officially taking over."

Nicholas was not planning to be quite so abrupt, and had told Rory on the flight out, but everything just spilled out. While Nicholas held the same belief as all the people of the North Pole regarding 'sincere speech', there were times for a more tactful approach and he had planned this to be one of them.

"Believe it or not, my friend here speaks the truth," Nicholas said, "And whether you choose to believe it or not is not important. What is important, is that we wish to align with your company and have you help us provide toys throughout the world beginning with this one." he pointed to the bag Rory was carrying.

Rory pulled out Bild Lilli, and Ruth let out a gasp. "What's her name?" asked Ruth as Rory handed her the doll.

Rory said the name and explained it was his mother's.

Elliott and Matt just chuckled and Elliott said, "THAT is supposed to help our company? What little girl wants to play with a grown up doll? Nearly every child plays with baby dolls and infants, no one wants a grown woman."

"I am not so sure," said Ruth, "I watch our daughter play with paper dolls and their clothes all the time. Even more than playing with baby dolls. She spends hours with those 'grown up women' as you call them."

"Yes, but that's paper, not a real doll," retorted Matt, "What is she, a fashion model or something?"

Rory said, "She is precisely no more or no less whatever a child wants her to be. Whether a professional woman, a fashion model, a lady of the beach or anything else they can imagine."

"Actually as someone who receives letters all the time from boys and girls, I can tell you we have an inside track on what children ask for, and every indication tells us, this is the next major toy if we can find someone to build it," explained Nicholas.

"According to legend, I hear that you build all the toys in the North Pole yourselves," scoffed Elliott.

"That is true, but we are coming to a period where we have too many toys to distribute and we now need to seek outside assistance. Before we begin this line, which we could, we thought we would attempt to bring in an outside firm, but if you have no interest..." and Nicholas began to rise.

"Just a moment," Ruth stopped everyone in their tracks. "Perhaps you could tell us what your ideas were and how you saw us fitting into your 'operation'."

Nicholas sat down and began laying out the plans that he had worked on with his father and mother.

"So let me get this straight," said Elliott, "You want us to give you a royalty off everyone of these Lilli dolls we would sell, help you provide all the ones you will need for Christmas, and hire Rory here as a consultant to help us make other toys. Is that right?"

"And we would ask for influence in your company for as long as it will exist, in the management decisions made in the future to agree on the type of person you are bringing to make sure that they will have the heart of your company in mind," said Nicholas.

"You must be joking," said Matt furiously, "Why would we trust your judgment over our own?" He looked at Ruth and said, "You can't be seriously thinking of this proposal as anything but ludicrous, Ruth. For Pete's sake he and his friend here think they are Santa Claus!"

Rory corrected him, "HE is Santa Claus, I am only an elf. A very talented elf, but an elf nonetheless."

Ruth laughed and said to Nicholas, "Mr. Kringle, you must admit this all sounds a little far-fetched, wouldn't you agree?"

Rory was getting a little edgy and said, "Far-fetched or not for you, it is 'sincere speech' and every word true."

Nicholas put his hand on the elf's shoulder, "Before anyone gets upset or disrespectful," he looked at Matt, "Let me assure you I can prove what I say, and would be willing to do so if we can agree in principle."

Elliott said, "Our lawyers would have us committed and thrown in the loony bin before they would draw up the contracts."

"No contract," Nicholas said solemnly, "Just a piece of paper signed by me and two of the three of you, and witnessed by the others in this room. This is to be kept strictly confidential and no one is to know until you are either dying or turning the company over to others, at which time this agreement will be carried forth into perpetuity or until we release the company."

"Just like that?" snorted Matt.

"Just like that," answered Nicholas.

"Out of extreme curiosity," Ruth asked, "How would you prove your statements."

Nicholas smiled, "My dear Ruth, how would you like to go for a ride?"

Nicholas took out a small box and pushed a button on the side and spoke into it, "Forrest, are you here yet?"

They heard the box crackle and a voice on the other side answered, "I'm on the roof waiting for you just as you requested."

He asked the others in the room if there was a stairwell to the roof. They looked at each other and shook their heads.

"I expected as much," Nicholas said undaunted and stood up, "Okay everyone get a little closer together."

As they all hesitantly moved closer to Nicholas as if he was a wild animal, he looked at them and said, "Ready?"

"Ready for what?" asked Elliott.

But by the time he finished the question the five of them were standing on the roof. And before them was Forrest sitting in the sleigh with four of the reindeer attached.

"How in the heck...?" Matt trailed off.

"Where did these come from?" asked Elliott.

Forrest said, "Well we were in the neighborhood and just dropped out of the sky." Then he laughed at his own comment.

"Ready for that ride, Ruth?" asked Nicholas.

"You can't be serious!" exclaimed Ruth.

"Mary tells me you aren't afraid of anything," Nicholas grinned, "Can you prove it?"

Ruth answered quickly, "Except dying!"

"Nonsense, I have done this countless times, and off much bigger roofs than this!" Nicholas roared. He then traded places with Forrest and held his hand out for Ruth.

Elliot fairly screamed, "I forbid it!"

"Then join us," Nicholas chided, "There is plenty of room for three, and if you would care to come along as well, Matt, I just push this button..."

Suddenly a second seat in the back slid out allowing for more passengers.

"All aboard," Nicholas called.

Ruth began moving toward the sleigh and Elliott came up to her and said, "The man is a nut! You can't get in that thing, you'll both be killed."

"I don't think so," replied Ruth, "I think this may be the truth and I for one would love to go on a ride with Santa Claus."

After several minutes of debate with Ruth moving closer and closer to the sleigh, Ruth finally said, "Elliott, I'm going. Stay here if you want, but a chance like this may never come again."

She stepped in the sleigh with Nicholas.

Elliott said, "Well if you are going to die, than I am not going to hang around being a widower." And with that he stepped in and sat next to his wife.

"Matt?" Nicholas inquired looking at the man.

"Uh, no thanks, someone will need to remain to handle the final arrangements." Matt said shaking his head.

"Okay, On Streak, on Frosty! Now Dreamer, now Fireball, on my coursers fly faster than wind. Away!" and the sleigh took off while Nicholas expertly adjusted the thrust of the sleigh and they all flew smoothly away from the building.

Nicholas took them over the coast and up about ten thousand feet, so they wouldn't be so easily seen by those on the beach.

As they were sailing along Ruth said, "Why didn't you just come like this in the first place, why have us chase Mary down to the airport?

"Well first off, the shock might have been a little much, look how you reacted in the conference room to our statements, though I must confess, I had planned to be more tactful than Rory. But secondly, I have personal reasons that I can't explain right now." Nicholas explained.

"Well, yes, I can only imagine what our initial reaction would have been. You look different from the pictures of Santa Claus we have seen, you have much darker hair on your beard than I imagined," Elliott finally said.

"My father has the white beard, but mine is changing quickly, I expect another few years or so and you won't be able to tell us apart, except he is considerably older." chuckled Nicholas, "Well should we head back before Matt has you declared deceased and takes over the company?"

Ruth said, "I am very sorry we doubted you Nicho...I mean Santa, yes we can go back now and talk in earnest."

"Please call me Nicholas if you prefer, I only go by Santa at Christmas, then I have no say as everyone calls me that anyway."

Landing on the roof, Nicholas thanked Forrest and told him that he could return the reindeer as he would return using a more conventional way. He then had everyone huddle closer and returned to the conference room they had left.

"So is that how you get in and out of people's home on Christmas Eve?" Ruth asked suddenly sounding more like an excited schoolgirl.

"That's pretty much it," replied Nicholas, "Now regardless of what takes place between us, what has happened must remain between us, you cannot even tell Mary. This is our secret and no one can ever know my identity."

They all nodded and looked a little deflated. I am sure that they had thought about who they were going to tell first. Which is the trouble with secrets, it is only fun if you can share one.

Elliott was still not convinced that the doll would ever be a hit. And Ruth looked at Rory and as soulfully as she could she said to him, "I know you wish to honor your mother, and I am certain she is extremely proud, but I think this doll needs a more common name than Bild Lilli. May we have your permission to change it?"

Rory looked at her in return and felt himself melt before her. He said, "Even my mother said that was a terrible name for a doll. Call her what you will. But thank you for asking so sweetly, I can see you are going to have your way with me on disagreements. You just need to look at me like you did, and I will be in trouble."

Nicholas laughed out loud, and Elliott chuckled and said, "Yes, Rory, that is how she gets her way with me all the time as well."

"Actually," Ruth said staring at the doll, "I would like to name it after my daughter's nickname and call her Barbie."

After another hour of discussion and working on details, Nicholas asked if Mary could drive them to the hotel he had booked for himself and Rory? Then he asked two more favors concerning their administrative assistant. On the second when Elliott began to protest, he volunteered to cover any costs involved, which calmed him down.

They agreed, and though Ruth thought the requests peculiar, she didn't say any more about it.

Nicholas and Rory met Mary in the lobby again and she said she would be happy to take them to the hotel. Nicholas invited Mary to go to lunch for all the chauffeuring about, and Mary said that it wasn't necessary to buy her lunch, and that she had a good deal of work remaining at the office.

Nicholas pleaded and said he hated to eat alone and that Rory was not able to accompany them. He asked Rory earlier to please plan on having room service or eating at the hotel. Apparently, Ruth had mentioned something about it being alright to have lunch, and while it took a little convincing, Mary agreed to have lunch with him. She asked what he'd like to eat and Nicholas told her to pick her favorite restaurant in the vicinity.

After stopping at the hotel long enough to register, they said goodbye to Rory and headed off. Mary took him to an Italian restaurant which Nicholas thought perfect. They had an intimate booth in the back corner and Nicholas wondered if this had all been planned ahead of time.

They picked up the conversation where they had left off when they arrived at the office. Nicholas asked what made her leave New York for California.

"I have always wanted to see different places," she said, "California seemed to call the loudest. I have many more places I would like to see when possible. I am hoping that my next position will allow me to travel more."

"You don't plan to stay at Mattel?" questioned Nicholas.

"I love the Handler's, but I am finally in my last semester at UCLA, and will get my degree in January of next year. I am hoping, as difficult as it may be, to break into upper management myself at some firm," she said with force, "I want my life to really count for something. I have dreams of making a genuine impact and trying to get to the top of a worldwide corporation."

"That is a lofty goal," commented Nicholas.

"You mean lofty for a woman," she sneered.

"No, it would be lofty for either man or woman to secure the top spot in a major firm like you are talking about," replied Nicholas, "Competition is fierce and everyone wishes to be on top. Man or woman matters not, it is a lot of work and only very few can make it. I have no doubt if this is truly what you want, you will make it."

"Thanks," Mary smiled, "I'm sorry if I am a little defensive, but most men just make disparaging comments when I tell them I will be running a major company someday."

"Just remember you will leave all of those smart alecks in the dust when you get there, and they won't be so disrespectful if they know what's healthy for them if they still are." Nicholas chuckled.

Mary smiled at his comment and then asked, "Unless it's a government secret, what were you meeting the gang about at Mattel?"

Nicholas shrugged and said, "Nothing much, we have a couple toy ideas we thought they might be interested in and we just presented a couple prototypes."

"All that would have lasted maybe 15-20 minutes

tops with them, you were in there for a couple hours," she looked directly at him, "Are you thinking of taking over the company?"

"Absolutely not!" laughed Nicholas, "I have a very large and going concern where I am, and I was just looking to see if they were interested in helping our company help produce the inventory we expect we'll need by Christmas."

"So maybe I should apply at your firm next year?" Mary said slyly, "Of course, then you may end up working for me."

Nicholas just laughed and said, "We are structured a little differently than a traditional company. And technically, my mother runs the company now."

"So what exactly is your role in the company?" pried Mary.

Nicholas smiled, "Let's just say I mostly handle distribution and sales."

"Aren't those different departments in the company?"

"As I said, we are set up differently than most, but we would certainly qualify as a worldwide company," he mused.

They bantered back and forth in a very playful manner. While Nicholas found her a serious person, she definitely had a good sense of humor. He found himself liking her more and more as they talked.

Mary didn't seem to mind being with Nicholas either, she found him interesting and genuine in his approach to business, as well as good natured and well mannered. They spoke of dreams and the future. And while he had some almost science fiction ideas for the times that were coming, she found herself fascinated listening to him describe some of the crazy products that he said were just 'around the bend'.

She was amazed that with all their talking, that scarcely anyone bothered them and almost no time had elapsed. According to her watch, only 35 minutes had gone by, though she would have sworn that an hour and a half or more had passed.

When she commented on this fact, Nicholas just shrugged and said, "Time can be a strange thing sometimes."

She asked when Nicholas was heading back and where his company was headquartered saying, "I assumed it was in Seattle since that is where your flight originated."

"It's actually north of Seattle, and as far as when I will return, I have some things that I need to accomplish while I am in L.A. and then off to the Eastern U.S.," he decided to go for broke, "In fact, how about dinner tomorrow evening?"

She hesitated for just a moment then smiled and said, "That sounds nice, will I need to pick you up?"

"If you write down your address, I plan to get a rental car later and then I could pick you up," he said.

She did as he suggested and slid the paper over to him saying, "This is a little tricky and I live in one of those

subdivisions that has many twists and turns, perhaps I
better write down exact directions."

"Not to worry, I am very good at finding my way
around," he said smiling.

"Just in case, I wrote down my phone number if
you get lost, there is a gas station with a phone you can use
and I will guide you to the house," she said, certain he
would need to call her.

"Thanks, shall we say 7:30 tomorrow?" asked
Nicholas.

"That will be fine, but could I ask a favor?" she bit
her lip as she asked this.

"Go right ahead," he prepared himself as he said
this.

"Nicholas seems so formal, may I call you Nick
instead?" He laughed out loud, expecting almost anything
else in her question, "Yes, you may call me Nick, I
generally like to shorten names myself, which makes Mary
perfect, it is already short."

As they rose to leave, Nicholas released time once
more. The waiter, who was bringing their check, instantly
continued toward their table. Luckily her seat in the booth
faced the wall, so she never noticed that they were the only
ones moving in the restaurant. She took him back to the
hotel and bid him goodbye until the next evening.

When he got back to his room he called Rory's
room and they got together. He made a couple more phone
calls with Rory present and began talking about how they

would proceed with several products that they planned to introduce for Mattel and another company, Hassenfield Brothers in Providence, Rhode Island. This was his trip to the east that he was visiting later in the week. While in L.A., Nicholas also had a meeting with another company. Their up and coming president would someday be as well known as Santa Claus. While he was very busy building his massive park, Walt agreed to meet with Nicholas to discuss how his company might work with both the Handlers and the Hassenfields. Nicholas would soon create alliances between Disney, Mattel and what would eventually be known as Hasbro.

Nicholas didn't so much rent a car as borrowed one from one of the elves, who was based at the Los Angeles warehouse that serviced the North Pole. It was a new model and the elf had just cleaned it after receiving the request from Ella. The elves also mapped out exact directions down to the number of feet to Mary's driveway insuring their new Santa wouldn't get lost on his way. They further wrote out directions to a very nice restaurant that other elves managed. They thought Mary would like it, and it was guaranteed that they would not be needlessly disturbed.

While Nicholas was getting the car, the elves also made arrangements for Rory to stay with another family, until he could get settled on his own in Southern California. He was to begin at Mattel the next week.

Nicholas returned to the hotel and sat in his room

wondering if he was doing things as Aeon had foreseen. Time and the future was such a tricky and risky proposition. One wrong word or phrase, or a poorly judged movement, could throw everything out of whack and change the future forever.

While it had its temptations, Nicholas was like his father, and believed time travel itself was too dangerous to use except under the most direst circumstances. The results were just too disconcerting. He wondered if Aeon had already changed the future in his suggestion for Nicholas to meet Mary. What if Nicholas had met someone else some other time? Could he have altered his reality in another dimension by coming here purposely?

It also made him wonder where and when in time he would meet Aeon as he had promised. He had assumed it would be on one of the Christmas Eve runs, but he might just as well drop in on Nicholas while in bed at home, or even on the street here. He had no idea, which both frustrated and excited him.

The next day seemed to take its own sweet time progressing until it was time to go meet Mary. Nicholas paced for what seemed like hours waiting until he thought he would go mad. He thought to himself, *It's a shame I can't make time move faster like I can stop it. I am sure I would have sped it up by now.*

He was particularly careful with the elf's car, but like his father he was used to great speeds, and had a difficult time going anywhere close to the speed limit. He continually caught himself going much faster than stated on the signs and had to keep releasing the gas pedal.

As he worked his way through the traffic he thought about when and where might be the right time to 'come clean' about who he really was. If he blurted anything out too soon, he might chase Mary to another corner of the globe, or she would think him as crazy as the owners of Mattel initially had. And he didn't have Forrest and his team standing by to change her mind.

If everything went well tonight and things seemed to progress as he hoped, she would agree to another date and he might use a different tact by then.

The directions were flawless, and he could tell on Mary's face as she opened the door she was surprised he found her house so effortlessly. She invited him inside and went to get a jacket. The house was clean and orderly. He looked at the bookcase in the living room and saw something that made him smile. There among the books were old pull toys and nutcrackers from many years ago. When she came back to the room he asked her about them.

"They were gifts to my parents and aunts that have been passed down to me," she explained.

"They look almost new, didn't they play with them?" wondered Nicholas.

"Yes, they were just taught to take good care of things," she then looked at him and said, "Do you like really old toys?"

"I've seen quite a few of them," he smiled,

"Actually what I like is the joy they bring children and seeing them playing with them."

They walked to the door and Nicholas held it open for Mary. He said, "You have a very charming house."

Mary said, "Thanks, it is rented right now. I am hoping to have a home of my own someday, but that will have to wait until my salary grows a little more."

"Yes, or perhaps if you marry your future husband may have one." Nicholas held his breath.

"Maybe," Mary laughed, "But I haven't found anyone I want to play house with yet, whether he owns it or not."

Nicholas breathed out again thinking, *Well she didn't say she wouldn't marry, just that she hadn't found the right person.*

"Well I have it on good authority that you will like this restaurant we are going to," Nicholas changed the subject, "It is one of the locally owned favorites according to my sources."

"What's the name?" inquired Mary.

"It is called Chablis," answered Nicholas.

"Oh Nick, I have been wanting to go there for a long while now, that's great," Mary was genuinely excited, which pleased Nick immensely. She then asked, "How did you get reservations so late?"

"Excuse me?" asked a surprised Nicholas.

"That place is next to impossible to get into, it is one of the best restaurants anywhere around here. I've heard there is a two month wait to get in," she said, "How did you do it?"

"Well, uh, they must have had a cancellation, I think," he stammered.

Mary looked at him quizzically, "You *did* make reservations, didn't you?"

Nicholas said calmly, "I'm sure we're expected." Then again changed the subject, "So where do your parents live? Still in New York?"

"You might say permanently, they both passed away several years back," she said.

"I'm so sorry, Mary," he said sincerely, "Was it health related or an accident?"

"Both health related," she continued, "That was one of the reasons I moved to California. Too many memories living in the same town as where I grew up with them. You said your mom runs the company, is your dad still around?"

"Yes they are both in excellent health and are doing just fine," Nicholas said.

They pulled up before the restaurant and before Nicholas could get out, two valets jumped out and opened their doors. The first valet said, "Good evening Mr. Kringle, here is your ticket, everything is prepared inside."

Mary looked with wide eyes at Nicholas and said, "Mr. Kringle? It would seem you are expected indeed."

As they walked through the doors that were held for them, the Maitre D' came up to them through the crowd and said to Nicholas, "If you will follow me Mr. Kringle, I have your room prepared." He led them to an intimate dining area with a table set for two and candles already lit. It was like nothing Mary had ever seen.

As they were seated, two other waiters came up and offered menus and asked first Mary, and then Nicholas if they would like a cocktail, wine or other beverage. Mary asked for a glass of Merlot and Nicholas ordered a Guinness.

"A beer drinker?" Mary teased, "I might of thought so with that beard and mustache."

"Actually I rarely drink anything alcoholic, but on Christmas Eve it has become tradition for my father and I to drink Guinness, so I thought I'd see if it tasted differently here and now," chuckled Nicholas.

"Well, I don't drink much either, but I feel like celebrating tonight," she was taking in the ambience and then looked deep into Nicholas' eyes and said, "So exactly who is Mr. Kringle? Obviously you are much more important than you lead me to believe."

"Actually, you shouldn't read too much into this, the management of this establishment works with my family, and we are old acquaintances," said Nicholas nonchalantly. "Really, how old?" asked Mary.

"A very long time," Nicholas said slowly while thinking of how to change the subject.

"And how is it you just happen to have friends in Southern California being a Washington-based company?"

Mary was like a dog with a juicy bone by now.

"I never said we were based in Washington, I just said north of Seattle. And I also believe I mentioned we were worldwide, as well," Nicholas countered.

Thankfully, the waiters walked up again with their drinks and Mary asked what the specials for the evening were.

The first waiter smiled and said, "Whatever you are in the mood for Miss Mary."

Nicholas just put his hands over his eyes and looked down at the table.

The waiter then turned to his boss and said, "Just like at home, eh Mr. Kringle? Do you know what you would like?" "Umm, give us a couple minutes to decide. May I assume if we come up with the entree, then you will figure the side dishes to go with it?" he said as more a statement than a question.

"Yessir!" The waiter caught the gist of the comment and snapped to attention.

As he walked off, Mary just looked at Nicholas and said "Care to take it from the top?"

"Well now we know what makes this restaurant so special, don't we?" said Nicholas in a surprised manner, "Imagine coming up with whatever you are in the mood for? I wonder how they can do that?"

"Yes, I have never heard of that before, not even from people I know that have dined here," stated Mary, "At least they never told me of any such 'special'."

"Probably as surprised as you and me were and just forgot to mention it," Nicholas knew it was coming.

"And what was the comment he made to you about 'Just like home, eh Mr. Kringle?'" questioned Mary.

"I'm sure he meant just like at home, where you can prepare whatever you are in the mood for," Nicholas was somewhat prepared after the waiter made the comment.

"Hmm," Mary just said. She had decided that whatever the absolute truth was, she would have to hear it later. She instead began thinking about what she was in the mood for that evening.

Mary finally decided on rack of lamb and Nicholas ordered prime rib medium rare, and told the waiters to fill in the rest the way they thought it should be.

When the meals arrived, they ordered another round of drinks and dug into the beautifully prepared plates. Mary had commented that this was the best food she had eaten in a very long time. Nicholas accidentally slipped up and said, "It *is* just like at home, delicious."

Mary didn't comment, but filed the information away for later.

The rest of the evening was enchanting for Mary. She thoroughly enjoyed being with and talking to Nick. While some of the things he said seemed to not completely add up, she found that she could talk to him for what seemed like hours and it was always actually just a few minutes.

She talked about growing up in a small town in upstate New York called Canandaigua. She had said she had almost married there, and then found out her fiancé was seeing someone else while they were engaged. That had put her off dating for a while, and while she had been out a few times, she hadn't met anyone that had caught her fancy with all the cultural differences with the men in California.

She realized that she had said too much and then blushed at her candor to her dinner partner. "I'm sorry," she said, "You must think me the tower of babble going on so."

"I think it's charming," smiled Nicholas, "And I am enjoying learning all about you, immensely."

"Which speaking of, let's get back to you, do you mind if I ask how old you are?" Mary had been trying to figure that out much of the evening. It seemed Nick knew so many things about history and events, yet even through his dark beard he looked about 40ish.

"How old do you think I am?" Nicholas fired back, knowing too, that this question would be asked.

"That's not fair," protested Mary, "That beard and mustache make it very difficult to tell. And you seem to know so much for what I might guess your age to be."

"I am probably older than you may guess, but I'll bet you will be close," grinned Nicholas.

"Oh, alright," she gave him another close look and bit her lip again, "I hope I don't upset you, but I will say

46."

Nicholas sat back and with great aplomb threw his napkin on the table and said, "That is a perfect guess! See you should trust your feelings more often. Now my candid question, I hope you like older men, as I would say you are what...thirty-two?"

"Just turned in May, yes. Good guess, yourself," she said. Then she blushed again and said, "And no, I don't mind older men, especially since many of the ones my own age have been so disappointing."

The waiter came in and asked if there would be anything else and offered a baked Alaska, for dessert, which Nicholas almost made a comment he would have regretted, but stopped himself just in time.

"I think the lady and I are finished, thank you anyway. Just the check, please," said Nicholas.

"Oh, it is already taken care of Mr. Kringle," the waiter said with great pride.

"What? No, that is really not necessary!, Please let me take care of this," he insisted.

"Mr. Kringle, it is our great pleasure to serve you and your guest for all you do on our behalf," the waiter stated unequivocally.

Nicholas knew he was not going to win this dispute without creating a scene, so he acquiesced to the wishes of the owners and thanked them profusely for the honor.

Mary just said, "Must be some kind of acquaintances..."

As they left the doors of the restaurant, which were again held for them, the car was waiting in front and the valet refused any form of tip, but instead thanked him for the honor to serve "The Kringles".

For a moment Mary had a wild idea that perhaps Nick was some type of mob boss and that everyone might be doing all this for all the wrong reasons. But she looked at Nick's smile and eyes and put the thought out of her mind as ridiculous.

Nicholas wanted to ask Mary to go out again tomorrow, but knew he shouldn't be too over-eager. "How about getting together again the day after tomorrow?" he finally asked.

"What do you have in mind?" she asked.

"How about we make a day of it and visit Griffith Park and the zoo?" he decided to again go for it all.

"I love the zoo, but you forget I have a job, and class that evening, so I am afraid I can't," she said.

"I'll compromise with you, you take the day off and I will have you back in time to make your class," he quipped.

"I need the money for rent coming up, sorry," she said disappointed.

"I'll get you the time off with pay so you won't lose a dime," Nicholas was determined, now.

"You aren't extorting the Handlers are you?" Mary was seriously concerned now, her bosses were kind, but could be stingy and never offered Mary any time off with pay.

"Good heavens, no!" laughed Nicholas, "I just have a very unique arrangement with them and it would be a favor to me that I am sure they will honor."

"Well if it is alright with them, let's say 9:00 in the morning day after tomorrow," she said hesitantly.

"Consider it a date!" said Nicholas knowing that it was already approved by the Handlers as his second request.

They drove up to Mary's driveway and Nicholas opened Mary's car door and helped her out. He walked her to the front and waited while she fumbled with her keys. He took her hand when the door was opened and thanked her for a wonderful evening saying she was the most charming dinner companion he had met in a very long time.

Mary said she was extremely pleased that he asked her out, and that she looked forward to seeing him again for the zoo.

He left with a grin on his face and thought, *Not bad for a first date at all.*

Nicholas arrived promptly at 9:00 for his second date with Mary. He was pleased that she was also ready to go and that she didn't dawdle leaving.

The day was a perfect California weather day, sunny with an expected high of 75 degrees and a gentle breeze coming off the ocean. The traffic was crowded, but not overbearing and they talked easily on the trip into Los Angeles.

Mary lived in Long Beach, which was a little ways from the city. On a good day it was about 45 minutes to Griffith Park, on bad days considerably longer. Today bordered on good with just a few slowdowns.

They got to the park before 10:00 and strolled to the entrance. As they went through the gate Mary commented that it had been years since she had visited the zoo. She said that several new exhibits were recently added and she had put this on her 'need to do' list. However, between school and work, there just didn't seem time. She thanked him for whatever magic he worked with the Handlers, as they didn't hesitate giving her the day off with pay.

For two days Mary had vexed over who this Nicholas Kringle really was. His seeming hold over the Handlers, and the whole affair at the restaurant the other night, along with his endless confidence and good humor left her wanting to learn more, but concerned with what might be discovered.

Her dating exploits had been less than stellar and she had pretty much resigned herself to ending up an 'old maid'. This was part of the reason she decided that she wanted to excel in business. She figured if she couldn't be a great mother and housewife, than she might as well make her mark on the world that way. In this day, women never accomplished both, it was always one or the other.

She loved children and it disappointed her that she may never have any, but as she was getting older she knew her chances were becoming slimmer. At one point she even thought about changing her major from business to education and become a teacher.

But she liked the idea of accomplishing great things for a company utilizing her talents, so she stayed with the coursework she started.

Except for the part about dating, she shared much of this with Nicholas, whether she had meant to or not, she couldn't seem not to tell him her innermost wishes. It felt like it was being drawn, or more specifically, gently coaxed from deep inside her. It was not an unpleasant feeling, but certainly unsettling, as she felt she wouldn't be able to keep a single secret from this man.

As they walked around the bear enclosures several of the animals seemed to be as fascinated with them as they were with the animals. The two polar bears came as close as they were allowed sniffing the air as if they had caught a pleasant aroma.

Nick seemed to take it all in stride, but again Mary added it to the mounting oddities she experienced with this strange man. When she asked Nick what he thought caused the bears' behavior, he laughed as he stroked his beard and said, "Kindred spirits!"

Mary couldn't help but laugh as well and let it go. However, as soon as they came to the big cat enclosures a similar thing happened, and the cats began pacing at the front of their cages. Nicholas just shrugged it off and said before Mary could ask, "Must be getting close to feeding time."

Mary didn't believe the zoo fed the animals so early in the day, but again held her tongue. That is until they reached the compound containing various deer. They were bounding and leaping as if being chased by the cats they had just left. And the whole time coming up to the very front of their cages.

"Think they're hungry, too?" she said sarcastically.

"Probably they are just happy to have such a lovely day to bound around. I know I am enjoying it equally as much," Nicholas grinned as he said it. He seemed to be having a great deal of fun.

While watching the animated monkeys, a group of young children came up to the exhibit. After a few moments, Nicholas felt a tug at his pants. He looked down and saw a young lady looking up to him.

"Hello Santa Claus, do you remember me?" the young girl asked.

"Well good morning, Grace, and how are you?" Nicholas responded.

"I wanted to thank you for my dolly at Christmas," she beamed, "I take her everywhere with me, 'cept I am not allowed to take her to school or on field trips."

"I fully understand, but I am very pleased that you are enjoying her. Now you best stay with your class so your teacher doesn't get concerned." he said gently.

He noticed that the class was now moving toward him, instead. The teacher was leading the group to retrieve her lost charge. She said, "Now Grace, you know better than to bother strangers."

"He's not a stranger, he's Santa Claus and he brings me stuff," she said in her defense.

The other kids began yelling "Santa Claus!" and broke free of the control the exasperated teacher thought she had, all of them running toward Nicholas.

Several of them hugged Nicholas' legs and others shook his hand. He just looked at the two wide-eyed women and shrugged saying, "It's amazing what people think when you have a beard and white hair, isn't it?"

He hugged the children back and said, "Now you know if I am Santa Claus then you also know I expect you to listen to your teacher and pay heed to what she says. Now it is lovely to see you all and I hope you enjoy the zoo as much as I am. I look forward to hearing what you want for this year..." and the kids began shouting so Nicholas held up his hand for quiet and got it, "...closer to Christmas, when you come to visit with me. But this is not the time or place."

A couple of the children expressed disappointment at not being able to have a personal audience with Santa, but did as he requested.

"Enjoy yourselves, now" and he nodded to the teacher and said to her, "Now just remind them that I might be watching and they better behave."

With that the monkeys began a fresh set of antics and the children moved back toward the enclosure to watch the show.

As they moved away, Mary began the questioning, "Kringle? Santa Claus? How did you know that girl's name, and how is it you know how to deal so well with children?"

"Whoa there, Take it easy, okay which question was first?" Nicholas began acting a little exasperated himself, "As you know my last name is Kringle, so I have done an extensive fact finding of Santa Claus, who also uses the same name as mine occasionally. Second, when I grew the beard and mustache people began calling me Santa almost immediately, even though my beard is not white. Third, I heard the teacher calling their names before she walked over, and being in sales, I have a thing about remembering names. And lastly, I love children very much, and I relate well with them because I care so."

"Well you were obviously enjoying yourself, and that is wonderful that you enjoy being with them. Are you, or have you ever thought of, being one of those Santas in the department stores? I'd bet you make a great one?" she teased.

"Well it is my intention to talk to many of them and find out what makes them tick, but Christmastime is our busiest season, and I'm afraid I wouldn't be able to spare the additional time," as he looked back at the children laughing and pointing to the monkeys he said wistfully, "I hope those guys know how blessed they are spending time with all those children," he added wistfully

"Seems a shame that you couldn't do it, You sound like you would really like to," Mary squeezed his arm.

"Well I make up for it, not to worry. Besides, a few instances like what just happened, and it is like the real thing," he began to smile uncontrollably.

They covered the entire zoo in a few hours and stopped at one of the concessions to have lunch. Part way through their fare Nicholas said, "Not exactly like Chablis is it?"

Mary burst out laughing and said she had the very same thought. "I guess beggars can't be choosers when there is nothing else available," she quipped.

"Well I hope the animals have better luck, I feel I should make this up to you however with a better meal. I leave for the East coast tomorrow, but will return in a week. How about I take you somewhere truly special then?" he asked.

"First, you have already taken me somewhere special, and I thank you again for that," she smiled and said, "I can only guess what you might think is truly special. Okay, I'm game, what time?"

"How about we make it that I will pick you up at work at five?" he was already beginning to formulate the evening in his mind.

"Wouldn't it be easier if I went home first?" she asked, "Then I wouldn't have to worry about driving home later."

"As you wish, then 5:30 at your house," he relented. It wouldn't really matter to one who could use the continuum.

He decided there was no way he could pause time without it being noticed, so the day slipped by quicker than he had wished. He was just about to suggest that they head back when she said, "I am enjoying myself so much, I am seriously contemplating skipping my class tonight. I am caught up with everything and I can get the notes from another student. Would it be okay to stay a little longer or do you have another appointment?"

Nicholas' heart skipped a beat, he said, "My time is yours and I would be happy to stay a while more, besides we haven't seen the reptile house or the aviary, yet."

She bantered with him, "Is that the only reason to stay?"

Now it was his turn to blush and she could see it even through the beard. He lowered his head and mumbled, "Well no, I guess not."

She giggled like a school girl and said, "The reptile house is over there." She took his arm again and began walking him toward it.

They spent another hour plus at the zoo and then they went to a small restaurant for a better dinner as they were both left wanting from their lunch and exercise.

Mary realized over dinner that she had become fast friends with Nick and had begun caring more for him than she had any man since before New York.

Nicholas was already head over heels with this lady and was anxious, though cautious, to move the relationship along. He wondered if it was too soon to attempt a first kiss. The more he thought about it, the more he wanted it. He kept telling himself to go slow, that to rush anything might be to destroy it.

He waged this battle all through dinner and the ride home. He was not alone in his arguments with himself.

They arrived at her house and just sat in the car in the driveway talking. Neither wanted to leave the other and both were trying to figure out how to say goodbye. After about a half hour Mary said she had best get inside.

Nicholas came around the car and assisted her out. She decided not to wait until the awkward moment at the front door and leaned forward and kissed him fully on the lips. His initial shock kept him from returning her passion. He apologized and said he'd like to try again.

He held her closer and kissed her fully this time and she returned his with her own. When they broke apart, she said, "Well now I know what all that facial hair feels like. I must say, it is not as scratchy and uncomfortable as it looks."

Nicholas kidded saying he never kissed himself so he couldn't say. They kissed a couple more times and Mary said she *really* had to go, now. She said next week wouldn't come soon enough and he mumbled a similar thought. With that the door closed softly and she was gone.

He felt as if he had frozen himself in time standing and just staring at her door. With great effort he finally moved away. He felt as light as his reindeer and thought he could fly without them right there and then.

The days were getting shorter and Christmas was fast approaching. Kris was up again this night, walking through the house. For the last week he had been having trouble sleeping. He worried about Nicholas and the upcoming trip. He was agitated that his son picked now to start racing around the U.S., trying to establish alliances among the people of the south.

He wasn't sure how accomplished Nicholas was using the time continuum. He knew from Forrest that Nicholas had acquired the skill with the reindeer and sleigh and could ride Amerigo almost as well as him.

But Annie was busy building the new visiting center and since it was his son's idea, he thought Nicholas ought to at least be assisting his mother.

But most of all he was just worried. Nothing for himself to really do, and although Nicholas involved him with his immediate plans with the companies and structuring the agreements, he just sat around fretting like an old washer woman.

He came downstairs as he had been doing, and was heading for the kitchen when he caught a shape in the darkness. Since he lived in the North Pole he felt no dread from the figure, but was alarmed nonetheless. He went over to the nearest light and flipped it on.

There sat Aeon Millennium staring back at him. Kris just rubbed his eyes and stared back. Aeon finally broke the silence and said, "Hello Kris, how are you?"

"Is it really you?" asked Kris hesitantly.

"It truly is. You and I need to have a little talk. I picked a time when I knew you would be up and around, but alone. Why don't you take a seat so we can talk eye to eye? You know how I dislike staring up at you."

Kris sat in the empty chair nearest Aeon. He looked at Aeon as if he was a ghost. Finally Aeon said, "Quit looking at me as if I was Marley and you were Scrooge!" Aeon chuckled, "I apologize for startling you, but I thought this best. You have concerns and questions and I hope, and think, I can help you with them."

"Why did you leave so suddenly, I never even got to say goodbye to you," Kris began.

"Now you and I both know that those crazies would have wanted to throw another party and try to embarrass the heck outta me," complained Aeon, "And you, better than most, know I do not like parties, never have."

"Yes but I had to learn the multidimensional continuum by myself, and what if I hadn't?" Kris fairly whined.

"Ah, but you did and all on your own. I knew you would," Aeon said flatly. "But that is not what is really bothering you, so why don't you spill it."

"Fine," said Kris, "You left Nicholas an entire book with information about the future and apparently more inventions, and was I never even left a note."

"My old friend," Aeon said sadly, "You and I got to spend many moments and trips together. Nicholas is well and truly alone in his discoveries. And many of the things in that book, the Council is not yet ready for. You know how I work. But without some of these discoveries, the North Pole will lose a valuable edge to the outside world.

"In so far as why I left it to Nicholas and not you, it was to help you precipitate your retirement", Aeon continued, "You were looking more worn and tired than I was, and I knew I was getting worn out. Giving you that book would have been like throwing gasoline on a fire. You would still be trying to go now, just as you are thinking about doing, now."

"Only because I worry about Nicholas..." Kris began to say.

"Wrong, Kris, it is because you are worried that you won't be needed anymore and that makes you crazy after all these years of being the center of attention," interrupted Aeon.

"Well that may be partially true, but Nicholas seems to be going off half-cocked and trying to implement too much all at once. I don't even know if he can handle Christmas Eve by himself, yet," argued Kris.

"You were always attempting to find out what was coming next, so now I will tell you – at least part of it," said Aeon, "First, Nicholas will do just fine this and every Christmas Eve for the foreseeable future, and believe me I have seen quite a bit into that future.

"Secondly, you and Annie will stay busy and live many, many more years, although Nicholas' new wife will take the lead role just as Annie had done. And *Annie* won't mind a bit as she, herself, wants to step down.

"Nicholas will change as the cultures change. He will add a great many things and accomplish as much as you did during his reign as Santa Claus. He and Mary will have a full rich life, and you and Annie will become grandparents, though neither of you will be around long enough to see your grandson take over as Santa Claus, but trust me he will, and he will also do well.

"The North Pole will change considerably, and will need to be abandoned altogether some year, but not for many more decades. In the meantime, the new ideas and policies that Nick will implement will help keep the world from falling apart, and will spread the word of God's love just as you so desperately tried to do. He will change many lives for the better and introduce many inventions and ideas that will make the world a better place. Some I will introduce to him, but most will come from the combined genius of the elves here."

"You have seen all this?" sniffed Kris with a tear welling in his eye.

"I have, and you may rest easy. I'll tell you what, this one time and no other, you and I will travel forward to see your grandson as Santa Claus so you will have that memory to serve you," said Aeon.

"No," Kris said with resolve, "Since you have seen it, that is well and good enough for me. Besides, I wouldn't want to see something that Annie couldn't share with me."

"As you wish, though we could take her with us," he prodded.

Kris just shook his head and said, "She would feel as me, that the knowledge is sufficient."

"Then I will ask if there is anything else you will need to know as this will be our last time together for some time," asked Aeon.

"There are two things, the first is, are you a ghost and this visit is from another time, or are you still here and you just chose now to visit," queried Kris.

"Who's to say, I can't be certain myself. I know this memory so I think it is from the future, but truly it matters not, as I have given you sincere speech and you know my words to be true, regardless of the time in which they are spoken," answered Aeon, "And the second question?"

"Will man ever stop warring with each other?" Kris

was almost afraid to hear Aeon's answer.

"It will be many, many more years, but yes, peace will finally rule the land because ordinary people will finally insist on it. This is one of the most important reasons for Santa Claus and the elves to exist. While people will become further pulled away from God in the near future, they will return to their principles and eventually realize the futility in killing each other off, when so much more can be accomplished through cooperation. And the elves and Santa Claus will be a constant reminder of that fact," Aeon smiled and said, "In fact, your grandson will do more to bring about that change than you could ever imagine."

"I can't thank you enough for coming back and telling me all this," Kris rose from his chair, "Although I am truly sad to know I won't have the chance to see you again for a while."

Aeon shrugged, "I will visit Nick sometime soon, but it will be later. Let him know I will keep my promise."

"You called him Nick twice now, is that a name he prefers?" asked Kris.

"It is the name his wife calls him by, and there are a very few others who do," shrugged Aeon, "He is just plain Santa to everyone else. Now I will bid you goodbye, Kris. Always know that you are the closest thing I ever had to a best friend, and I shall miss you as you have missed me."

And once more, Aeon vanished before Kris' eyes and he was alone in the room. Kris would have no trouble sleeping ever again.

Nicholas went to the meeting with Walt Disney. The two men, both pioneers in their own right, began talking in concepts that would have left anyone else feeling like these two were speaking another language. But each one was not only staying up with the other, but matching idea for idea.

Because of the imagination and total belief in his own projects, Walt accepted Santa at his word and no proof was necessary. However, Mr. Disney did have a few questions about the elves and said he would like to do a movie about the North Pole and Santa someday.

Nicholas told him about how the elves didn't appreciate, or approve, of publicity and that he might be better off to stick with fairy tales, as the elves would be uncooperative at best.

At the end of the exhaustive session, both men had come to an understanding that would create a huge merchandising arm for Disney, and its new Disneyland Park, along with a huge boost for the two companies that Nicholas was helping Disney align with, while giving a nice royalty to the North Pole to help fund the efforts it would need from Mattel and the Hassenfield boys.

The meeting in Providence was less successful. Nicholas attributed it to too many egos and everyone trying to be the big dog in the room. They were not even impressed when Nicholas finally revealed who he was, including the sleigh and reindeer as he had done at Mattel. The father/son team of Henry and Merrill were riding high on the success of their Mr. Potato Head and felt that they didn't need anyone else's help in licensing or royalties.

Nicholas finally appealed to their greed when he laid the numbers he was projecting before them. The dollars and cents worked where common sense did not. He went away with part of the deal he sought, but would have to come back later to try and get everything he hoped.

He went home after that and gave a progress report to his parents. His father especially seemed pleased with the Mattel and Disney aspects. With regard to the Hassenfields his father shook his head and said, "Don't worry son, it may take some time but you'll accomplish everything."

His mother asked how 'the rest' had proceeded and Nick gave a full report minus a few details about that as well. Annie was genuinely pleased and was anxious to meet Mary. Nicholas asked, "How about next week?"

When he laid out his plan for his next date, Annie and Kris asked if he thought he was pushing the timetable to fast.

"Mom, Dad, you didn't see the way she kissed me," he blushed as he said this, "Besides it is getting close to

Christmas, and soon I won't have much time for courting."

His parents agreed with him on that score, and said what will be, will be. With that he said he would need to talk with Denny, Forrest and a few others to make preparations.

The following week arrived and Nicholas was ready for his big date. He rang the doorbell and Mary appeared soon afterward. She said, "I didn't hear a car, where are you parked?"

"Not very far, may I come in?" asked Nicholas.

As she opened the door wider, he produced a beautiful spray of flowers, pine branches and ribbons and bows around the arrangement and handed it to her.

"Oh Nick, it's lovely! Let me get these in water," and she began to move off to the kitchen.

"Uh, no need, just place them in a vase," he said.

"But they'll die!" Mary argued.

"Not these, they are specially treated, and will last several weeks before fading," he stated.

"Something else from your factory?" she asked slyly.

"Yes, may we sit down and talk before we head out?" Nicholas said seriously.

Mary thought to herself, *Here it comes. He doesn't want to see me anymore, or he needs to leave right away, or something else has come up.*

Then she admonished herself for jumping the gun and said, "Of course, let's sit in the living room."

After they were seated comfortably Nicholas said, "I need to confess something before we go out."

"I knew it," Mary blurted, "You're married!"

Nicholas just laughed, "Not as of yet, but as you said last week, I am more than I say I am, and you need to know all of it before we continue..."

Nicholas went into all the details of the North Pole, the elves, his father being Santa Claus, his mother being the CEO of the North Pole, and his taking over as Santa Claus beginning with this year's Christmas Eve run.

After about 15 minutes, Mary asked if he would care for something to drink.

Nicholas eyed her suspiciously and asked if she had been listening to anything he said.

"Of course, but you must be thirsty," she said completely calm.

"So you don't believe me, and you wish to go to the kitchen to call the police and have me taken away, right?" he said believing it.

"No my silly Nicholas," she giggled, "I guess I have a little confession to make as well, although after yours, all of this now makes so much more sense to me."She told Nicholas that a couple days after their second date, she went to Ruth Handler and talked to her about him. "I told her how happy I was about how well everything was going, but I admitted I was also concerned because I didn't know why everyone and everything reacted so strongly toward you. So I told Ruth many of the things that happened."

"I thought she would be worried as well, but instead she started grinning like the Cheshire cat and told me, 'Nicholas is extremely different from any other man you will ever meet. He has abilities I could never understand, but I cannot explain it now, because it would break a vow I made to him. But believe me when I say you can trust anything he tells you as the gospel truth.' I didn't really understand her comments until now, but I trust Ruth and I trust you," she finished.

"Well then I guess we are ready to go for dinner," he thought this was almost too good to be true, but decided not to question his good fortune, "Ready?"

She stood up and before she could take a step toward the door, they popped onto the roof where his rig sat with four reindeer and the beautiful black sleigh with red runners, upholstery and striping.

Mary gasped and said, "Oh Nick this is beautiful. Is this yours?"

"Well technically, it is my parents, you might say I borrowed the family car," chuckled Nicholas. He pulled a coat from the sleigh and said, "You may want to put this on, it gets a little cold where we are going."

She pulled on the luxurious coat and tied the sash. Then she stepped into the sleigh and asked, "And just where are you taking me?"

He got in after pulling his own coat on and said, "To meet the folks!" He snapped the reins and the reindeer sprang to life and the six of them took off immediately.

Mary grabbed his arm and the sleigh and fairly screamed, "My, that was quick!"

Nicholas laughed and said, "You haven't seen anything yet, hang on." As they gained altitude and Nicholas brought the sleigh into the slip stream, the sleigh shot passed the sound barrier. Mary couldn't believe the incredible speed at which they were traveling. Nicholas explained that while they would actually encircle the globe, it would take far less time than going straight to the Pole because of the speeds that they could attain inside the air currents.

Scarcely any time had elapsed when Nicholas brought the sleigh out of the stream and pointed below. "There's our destination," he said.

"Nick, there is nothing down there, except ice and snow," she thought he might be kidding.

"Don't let your eyes deceive you, and do not worry that we will crash, even though it may look that way," he tried to explain, "We have a protective dome that no one can see through or penetrate unless expected, as we are."

Mary covered her eyes as they aimed at what looked like the ground. When she finally dared look, she saw what Kris and Annie saw upon their first arriving at the North Pole. And she was equally excited over the beauty of it.

Nicholas drove the sleigh around village and pointed out many of the shops and places along the way. Excited whispers were shared by the elves as they went by, and more than a few giggles ensued afterward.

Nicholas pulled the sleigh to the front of the massive structure he called home. He helped Mary out of the sleigh and walked her up the steps opening the huge oaken door. Inside he took her coat and called for his parents.

Annie and Kris came from the back of the house and greeted their guest as warmly as anyone could, both hugging her and saying they hoped she wasn't to put off by Nicholas' announcement.

Mary stood flabbergasted looking at Kris. She then apologized and said, "So it is really all true and you are Santa Claus..." she trailed off in shock.

Both Nicholas and Kris Ho, Ho, Ho'd at the same time and Kris said, "I was, I am now retired and proudly turning over the reins to my son, Nick, as you call him."

"I am sorry, I didn't mean to offend by shortening his name," she said sincerely.

"Nonsense," Both Kris and Annie said together, and then Annie said, "It makes perfect sense, and it is certainly less stodgy."

Kris led them to the parlor and they talked for a

while until Denny Sweetooth sauntered in and announced, "Dinner is served!"

Nick introduced Denny to their guest, and Denny said, "It is an honor to make your acquaintance, Miss Mary." He was smiling even wider than normal.

They walked to the dining room and Mary commented about the size and beauty of the home, especially all the custom woodworking throughout. Kris told her that the elves never did anything halfway, and as they were the first tallfolk to ever arrive in the village, they thought the Kringles needed a massive edifice to keep them comfortable.

"There are no other normal size people here?" Mary inquired.

"Be careful what you call normal size here, to them we are the 'tallfolk', and no, you are only the fourth person besides the elves to ever be in the North Pole," explained Nick.

"Actually Nick is thought of as one of them, as he was born here in the North Pole," kidded Annie.

They sat down at a large but warm dining table that seemed intimate for its size. Kris said a brief but lovely blessing, which included welcoming Mary to their home.

Then Denny brought out some appetizers and set them in front of Mary. "I hope you will like these, I borrowed the recipe from Mexico," he said.

Mary took one and passed the plate. They were pieces of the most tender beef wrapped in a flaky type of dough with a mild salsa with just a hint of heat.

The morsel was fabulous and she told Denny so. Again, he smiled even wider than usual and bowed heading back to the kitchen.

The dinner conversation revolved around the history and legacy of the North Pole and the Kringles. Many questions were asked and answered about how things came about, and for how long the Kringles had been involved with the elves.

Mary looked at Nicholas and said in a rather stern voice, "So…you are not 46 then, are you."

Nicholas shrugged and said, "I said it was a perfect guess, I never said it was an accurate one."

Annie admonished her son saying, "Oh, Nicholas! That wasn't right."

Nicholas laughed while protesting saying, "I couldn't tell her then how old I was, she would have walked out right there and then! Either because she would have thought I was lying, or that I truly was too old for her."

"One thing you should know we don't age like normal people, Kris and I are both over two hundred years old," said Annie.

Mary tried not to show her total surprise at the statement, but even so choked on some water she was drinking. When she composed herself, she turned to Nick and asked, "So what does that make you 175?"

Annie laughed and said, "Oh no, we didn't have

Nicholas until we were both over one hundred! He is just one hundred himself this year."

Mary just looked at the three of them in surprise. She thought about how long she might expect to live in Southern California. Then she wondered how it would feel being around over a hundred years or more than her peers, admitting to herself that the prospect did not seem disturbing, especially if she looked like Annie at that age.

Then she began telling the stories about their two dates and soon had Kris, Annie and even Nicholas laughing out loud. Kris especially howled when Mary explained she thought his son was a mob boss at one point.

"Yeah," said Nick, "And my henchmen have names like Thunder, Lightning, Blaze, Torch and Frosty!" Which brought another round of guffaws from his parents.

During the evening Denny brought in one sumptuous dish after another, including turkey, beef, pork and fish. Each was in its own special sauce that fully complimented the entree. Mary just raved about each dish's subtle and distinct flavor. She had tried everything with equal relish. She said at one point, "I don't think I have ever eaten so much in my life and loved every mouthful!"

"Then you will appreciate that in addition to aging very slowly, we almost never gain weight no matter how much we eat," said Annie.

"NO!" exclaimed Mary, "How is that possible?"

"It just is," shrugged Kris, "Many things about

living up at the North Pole we have just learned to accept and not try to explain it, like not aging or gaining weight. But not many complain about it, ho, Ho, HO!"

After they had finished dinner, Kris and Annie excused themselves, saying how lovely it was to meet Mary, and that they truly hoped they would see her again very soon. Mary returned the sentiment and gave them each a hug.

"Well now I know why the whole world loves Santa and Mrs. Claus," sighed Mary. "Your parents are the loveliest of people."

"I have been truly blessed, yes," Nicholas said softly, "Well, would you like to see more of the village?"

"It is all so much to take in," Mary said wearily, "May I take a rain check?"

"Of course!" Nicholas answered, though he was disappointed to see their evening ending already. He retrieved the coat for Mary and placed it on her.

As they were leaving, Mary said, "I am absolutely loving this, but after working all day, and with so much to know and understand about you and your family, I am exhausted."

"I understand completely, I often forget just how unusual we are from the 'normal' world," Nicholas said truthfully.

They climbed into the sleigh and Nick took the reins and as they left the dome, Mary looked back to see only snow and ice behind her. She said, "It's no wonder no one has ever found you up here."

"And we try to keep it that way," added Nick.

It was almost no time at all when Nick gently landed on Mary's roof. He said, "Now I will need to bring you inside."

And with that, they instantly appeared in her living room. Mary teased him saying, "You know it is a bit disconcerting knowing that you can pop in and out of my house anytime you wish."

"Ah, yes, but I never would without your permission," he chuckled.

They sat on the sofa. Almost immediately she moved to him. He took her into his arms and kissed her deeply. After they broke she said breathlessly, "I may just have to give you that permission very soon."

"And I will take it and honor it," he replied quietly.

They kissed some more and began exploring a little more of each other. As things began heating up, Nicholas gently stopped and pulled away.

"Perhaps I should get going," he said and began to stand.

"Well maybe next time we can have dinner here, as I doubt you can outdo Chablis and Denny's fabulous cooking," she said, "Although, I am hardly up to the task of them, either."

"I cook - in fact - very well," Nicholas said matter-of-factly, "Denny, Pierre and my mother taught me. I really enjoy doing it, too."

"Well Chef Nicholas, I will get a variety of things and you may demonstrate your culinary skills," she laughed and said, "And I shall be your willing guinea pig."

They made a date for Saturday at 5:00, when she had no classes or work to interfere with their plans. Nicholas kissed her once more and said goodbye, then disappeared from her view.

Chapter Fourteen

Things never really change, they just evolve into new experiences and involve new lives.

- Anne Marie Kringle

New Endings

By the end of September, Nick and Mary had been seeing each other for many weeks. I will not talk more about how their relationship progressed, except to say they had become the very best of friends. Such a strong relationship must always begin and end with friendship.

Nicholas brought Mary up to the North Pole another time when the Northern Lights were in full display, it was then he asked her to marry him. She had said she needed to consider the proposal and asked him to ask her again next week.

Nicholas was disappointed, but knew Mary was wrestling with many issues. He agreed to her request but said, "As long as the answer is 'yes', I guess I can wait a week more."

Mary knew she had a deep love for Nicholas, but was worried about giving her life up in Southern California. She had made a strong impression on the owners at Mattel and thought she could work out a management position with them. And if not them, she was willing to move to another firm and begin her conquest there.

Mary also thought that while the North Pole was beautiful, it was so different from the rest of the world. It was a fantastic place, but she wondered how long the fantasy could last if there was nothing for her to accomplish?

And then there was Nick's age. Would or could she really live for centuries? What if she kept growing older and the rest of them did not? What would she do with herself if she did live that long? Annie seemed quite strong and was running the Pole just fine. Would Mary have any say in the goings on?

She decided the only person who could answer her questions might be Annie, herself. Mary asked Nick if she could talk with his mother, which he agreed to immediately and took her to Annie.

Annie told Mary she thought that there might be some concerns when Nick asked her to marry him. "I know for myself, if I hadn't already been married to Kris, I might have hesitated going off to the end of the world to most people," Annie confided.

They talked for more than two hours about Annie's life at the Pole, and what she wanted to do in the future. "I am ready to start turning things over to someone a little more energetic," Annie said, "Just as Kris is anxious to step away from the role of Santa Claus, I too, am anxious to relinquish the CEO role."

Annie also talked about how nothing could be closer to heaven on earth than being involved with the

North Pole. She explained about the elves and their infinite patience, about bringing joy to every child that asks, and she told Mary about what it was like to be married to the gift-giver and what Nick was like as a son.

When Nicholas asked Mary again one week to the minute he asked before, she accepted immediately, and they set a date for right after her graduation in January of the New Year.

Mary asked for, and received, two ceremonies. The first was up in the North Pole and the second was in Southern California so her friends, a few classmates, the Handlers, Mr. Matson and her coworkers could also attend. While the owners of Mattel knew Nick's secret, they were not as of yet cleared to attend the ceremony in the North Pole. However, they had already made the list for being one of the first tallfolk to be invited later.

Annie was getting closer to arranging that possibility for tallfolk, and was putting finishing touches on the new Reindeer Inn being built. They had added a new train station and were building a train for future passengers. They were also in the process of changing out many of the local shops to allow for people to get gifts from the North Pole. Although, they wouldn't be able to use money as an exchange, as Nicholas had come up with a better idea.

In the meantime, scanners were being placed in every major town and city. It was a massive undertaking, utilizing elves from all over the world. Luckily, they were wireless and only involved setting them up like maintenance boxes on telephone poles and light posts facing the traffic patterns and the like.

At the end of the first year, almost 65% of the population of the Christian world would travel past at least one or more scanners. And all the hospitals and birthing units were linked to the database at the North Pole, with reports of births coming in every second. The North Pole was on the edge of knowing what was taking place throughout the world, and now, as accorded to his legend, Santa really would be watching.

Mostly it would be Kris making notes and looking for particularly high number scores. Once identified, then Kris would make further investigations to see if they needed something in particular that could help others or themselves.

After learning enough about that family, and providing the rest of the family had a high number as well, then this family would be invited to the North Pole for a week and would meet with Nicholas or possibly Kris, if Nick wasn't available.

But most importantly, anyone brought to the North Pole would be requested to spread the word of God's love and taking care of their fellow man, and spreading love instead of forcing conflicts. This was something every being at the North Pole wanted.

Just as Aeon had predicted, Nicholas performed flawlessly on his first Christmas Eve trip and there was a major celebration to congratulate him a few days after his return, but before he performed his La Befana duties in Latin America. He was hugged several times by his parents who could not have been more proud of their son.

The elf that was chosen to accompany him was none other than Frederick Salsbury. As he had always wanted to accompany Kris on one of his trips, he was overjoyed at being the first elf to fly with Nicholas on his solo maiden voyage.

Upon their return, Frederick told everyone that would listen, which of course was every resident, about the exploits of the first Christmas Eve trip with the new Santa Claus. I will get into this in more detail at a later time, but it is important to remind you that Nicholas had officially taken over and had his first journey to explain what happened next.

When the time of the wedding came about, Annie was a nervous as anyone had ever seen her. She was continuously running from one end of the dome to the other. So much so, that her dog sled had been revived, as the Council was concerned she would worry herself into illness.

She ran to her greenhouse and worked with Celine Petalpusher on the floral sprays of which there would be a huge amount, then over to where they were working on the chapel where the ceremony would be held. She was desperately trying to finish the new inn so that Nicholas and Mary could be the first to try it out. There must have been 50 elves working on it, in order to complete the woodwork and finishing touches.

Of course, I was not immune to all the bustle as I was asked to be the official photographer for the wedding and to put a wedding album together afterward. Miss Annie would come around to tell me the latest shots she wanted taken, or to chase me over to the chapel to ask about positioning and where to set up. Or drag me over to the place where the reception was being held. I was also instructed to please be the photographer for the southern wedding, as well.

All the banquets before were held in the town square outside. It was the only place that could hold everyone. But Annie had decided that since the wedding would be held soon after our Christmas rush, that they could afford to use one of the manufacturing buildings. Especially since even the manufacturing buildings more closely resembled private residences with their woodwork and attention to detail. If elves were going to build anything at all, it had to be aesthetically pleasing, as well as functional, regardless of its use.

Annie was trying to plan the reception in the midst of creating the much needed Christmas presents. Carrow would grumble as Annie was running around with tape measures and pushing items around to look at angles and lighting.

Many residents suggested that she just use the town center as before, since they could control both the weather and temperature of the interior of the dome, they could guarantee that nothing could upset the plans weather-wise, at least. Denny was among them as he said he would need to bring a massive amount of items to prepare food in the manufacturing building verses just taking it to the town square.

But Annie wanted something that hadn't been done before. She knew she would only have one shot at doing a wedding for her son, and since Mary's parents were not around to assist Mary or help with the plans, then Annie would make certain that Mary would have a fairy tale wedding that she would never forget.

She was also helping Mary with the wedding ceremony and reception in Southern California, but there they were working with a top-notch hotel, and Annie was leaving most of the planning to them and the wedding couple for planning out food and utilizing the hotels best contacts for flowers, music, and the like.

Music was one thing she left in the capable hands of Carol Joynote. Since she had arranged to have the whole North Pole filled with beautiful music, which was already piped into the building for the reception. Carol would take care of the selections and then she had planned to bring in both a choir and an elven band to fill in after the dinner and for dancing.

Mary wanted and got a fairy tale dress to match her wedding ceremonies. Ulzana Stitchnsew made the most beautiful dress seen. It had a luminescence between the satin and the lace of the dress that projected a soft light. No one outside the North Pole knew how it existed, not even Mary, but she was never more proud of a garment in her whole life. She looked radiant even without the glow of the dress, but it enhanced her beauty that much more.

Even Nicholas' breath caught the first time she walked down the aisle. The first ceremony took place at the North Pole, as it was one hundred times the size of the California wedding. Every elf across the globe was invited to witness the new Santa Claus take his wife. As Mary walked toward her fiancé on that day everyone not only stood, but applauded the beautiful bride. Reverend Goinpeace officiated and talked about the love between them lasting 100's of years on earth and then eternally in heaven. Annie cried with joy, but even Kris welled up and let a couple drops escape.

The ceremony lasted 25 minutes, the reception three days. Parties continued day and night and even broke into other parts of the North Pole. Denny had created three separate shifts with many elves volunteering to help make food and clean up. When they finished their time, they rejoined the party.

After about three hours of well-wishers and food and drink at the reception, Nicholas and Mary retreated to the Inn and were not seen until the third day. They again spent many hours thanking the guests and moving around to various tables and circles. Mary was kissed so often that she was surprised she had a cheek left by the end of the day.

It was finally time to leave the North Pole for Southern California, with a stop or two along the way to some more scenic places of the world.

The newly-married couple finally arrived two days before the wedding and tried to relax so they would be fresh for the next go around. They spent the first day entirely in bed (or so I was told), and then Nicholas relaxed the next day, while Mary went to have her hair redone and do a little shopping.

Mary's last day at Mattel was the week before the first wedding ceremony, it was Elliott Handler who gave her away at the second ceremony, while Kris had given her at the first. During the second reception she and Nick spent a good deal of time with Ruth and Elliott. Mary knew it would the last time she would see the Handlers for a while. They spent that night in the hotel, and then began a three week trek to places too numerous to mention here. Anywhere Mary wanted to visit, Nick took her. By the end of the third week, they were both anxious to return to the Pole and home. They spent the last nights of their honeymoon on Fiji and flew off for home.

When they arrived at their home they called for

their parents, but the home was empty. They went up to Nicholas' old room and found everything had been removed and an envelope on the bed addressed to them both.

Nicholas opened the letter and read aloud to Mary:

Dearest Son and Daughter-In-Law:

We have gone on a second honeymoon, especially since we never truly had one when we were married, and you both inspired us to take one ourselves.

While we are gone a new slightly smaller house is being built for us in the newly developed visiting center. The elves have moved everything out of house that is personal to us and moved your room to the master bedroom.

We will be gone long enough for the house to be finished. This house will also serve as your "Visiting Center Home" once you are visiting people who are invited to come to us.

We will be anxious to return to you both, but know we will be enjoying ourselves immensely.

Love,
Mom & Dad

"I guess we have the place to ourselves, literally," Nick said.

"Oh Nick, I never expected Mom and Dad to move out," Mary lamented, "I thought we would just be together in this castle of a house."

"If I know my mother, she had wished all her life, prior to moving to the North Pole, for a home of her own. I think this is their wedding present to us. She had said something about having to wait until we were back from our honeymoon to receive it. They didn't whisper a hint at the California ceremony to either of us about the house or the 'honeymoon', so I'll bet that must be their plan," Nicholas considered aloud.

"Well that is more than generous of them," Mary said and began to cry, "Our own home, I can't believe it."

"As I told you once, perhaps the man you married would have his own home," chuckled Nicholas

"Yeah," Mary said wiping her tears, "But you had to marry me to get it!" And then she began laughing at the thought.

"Just one more reason, my dearest love..." he said as he kissed the remaining tears away from her cheek.

He picked up their bags and moved off to their new bedroom.

Nicholas and Mary were asked if they could fill in for their parents at the Elven Council meetings while they were away.

Mary found the meetings exhilarating and learned all she could about the North Pole's political system. The Council barely missed the elder Kringles, as Mary was such a quick study, and Nicholas had already attended a few meetings after becoming Santa Claus.

In their very first meeting, Carrow and Ulzana did as they said they would, and officially resigned from the Council. This left the Council with only six voting members until Kris and Annie returned, so the remaining Council voted temporary voting powers to the newly married couple.

Many issues were brought before the body including a few questions about new lines of manufacture and some issues of machinery needing to be used for other purposes for the New Year. Mary offered her advice and suggestions, which were approved without hesitation by the rest of the Council.

Some of the decisions concerned the new Visiting Center that Nicholas handled based on discussions he and his mother had worked on prior to the New Year. Again the Council went along unanimously with the suggestions and ideas Nicholas put forth.

When his folks returned to the North Pole, it was nearly April. They were greeted with open arms and good wishes from everyone. Annie and Mary embraced as if they had lost each other for years. Then Nick and Mary expressed how much they were missed, and thanked them for their lovely home.

Annie waved it off and said, "That monumental edifice was too large for us. And besides now we can be closer to the action instead of at the other end of the woodlands."

Nicholas said, "Well it was very generous of you, but I must say, your new home is equally beautiful, and I am sure you will love it also."

"We have little doubt as it is elven made just like our last," chuckled Kris.

The four Kringles walked toward the village from the stable area. They talked about the many places they had visited and the wonders they had seen. It was amazing the number of places the two couples had visited between them. Annie said she enjoyed visiting the many places, but told Kris toward the end that she thought her traveling days were over.

Mary made the comment that she thought she would never tire of looking at the environs of the North Pole. Annie agreed saying that she never had in almost two centuries of living there.

They walked the elder Kringles to their new home and visited for a little while. Annie said she was ready to lie down and rest a while. So the younger couple made plans with them to have dinner the next evening and said goodbye.

After a few days when things were more normal, the Council reconvened with the elder Kringles. Nick and Mary did not attend, knowing that there might be some sensitive discussions now that his parents were 'back in the saddle' with the rest of the Council.

After a couple hours, there was a knock on their door. Mary opened it to find Britney Clearwater on the other side. Britney said that their presence had been requested at the Council meeting. Mary hurriedly put on her coat and called Nick from his workshop.

They walked over and while she was pleasant, Britney would not explain other than to say their parents were fine. As they walked in the chamber they were met with smiles and greetings. As they sat down in the conference area Kris began the discussion.

"First let me thank you both for the admirable job you did in Annie's and my absence. I have received nothing but the most favorable reports about both your help and interaction," he said with obvious pride, "Which is why we have asked you to come. Annie and I had discussed this while we were gone and we have further talked to the Council about this. We wish for you and Mary to take over for Annie and myself in the Council."

Frederick interjected, "We have already voted on their proposal and you were unanimously approved."

Nicholas stood up and said, "Then as one of our first official requests, I would make a motion that my parents fill the vacancies left by Carrow and Ulzana."

Kris and Annie laughed and Annie said, "I told you that would be the first thing out of his mouth."

Kris said, "Son, while we appreciate your request,

we have already told the Council that we would like to retire and do fewer things around the village. We would just like to enjoy our remaining years doing as we please, and the Council has graciously said that we need never leave."

"Besides," said Annie, this would still leave two spots open to nominate elves that might be more suited to your future plans."

With that Annie and Kris stood up and Frederick said to Mary and Nicholas, "If you would please join us up here in the dais and take the place of your parents, we would be most grateful."

And so Nicholas and Mary hugged Kris and Annie and took their seats among the Council "officially" for the first time.

Chapter Fifteen

They err who thinks Santa Claus comes down through the chimmney; he really enters through the heart.

- Paul M. Ell

A Legend Continues

Much has changed since the 1950's, and much has stayed the same. Santa and Mary Claus, as they are known far and wide, did enact the new Visiting Center. And since that time many hundreds of visitors have been invited to the North Pole, and countless lives have been changed for the better because of it.

The Council reviewed dozens of elves to replace Carrow and Ulzana's seats, and after much deliberation, they chose Keeney Eagleye and me to fill the vacancies. Keeney for the knowledge he now possessed about tallfolk, and me, because of the historical enlightenment I could humbly provide. As I said when I came to them about the possibility, the past should always help shape the future.

Kris and Annie decided to keep more to themselves to prevent confusion among the elves and others. Occasionally when Nicholas was called away, Kris would fill in at the Visiting Center, and often would meet with Santa Ambassadors to help educate them on how to be good a Santa.

By the 1960's "Santa Clauses" were everywhere, a

very few were good imitators, but most lacked the true nature of our Santas, and should never have worn a red shirt, let alone a red coat.

But, there was little we at the North Pole could do about the spread of the commercial disease and greed that seemed to be the hallmark of the malls, stores and in the Santas, themselves.

We educate the roughly 5% of the truly good Santa Clauses. These Santas seek to instill the properties that we hope children will come away with after meeting them, which is mostly hope, faith and trust in God and their fellow man.

Nicholas has been Santa Claus for roughly seventy-five or so years. And is now talking about the day his two sons can help him. Mary gave birth to their first son at the age of 60, and their second boy at 65. They decided to wait to begin a family until their later years so they could enjoy them more, and put a new "spark" in their life.

Kristopher Frederick is now a young man and is as rebellious as his father was, but he is always filled with remarkable ideas. Nicholas Carrow is just seventeen, and is a truly loving and affectionate teenager. And while Kristopher can be argumentative, Nicholas can be stubborn to the point of obstinacy. Both are beautiful children and you can see Mary and Nicholas in each, and a little of Annie and Kris, too. Nicholas actually has streaks of white in his hair already.

Santa was on his rounds in 1972, and as he entered

a house he found a man sitting on the sofa that wasn't affected by the stoppage of time. Nicholas found this quite disturbing and ask the man how this was possible.

Aeon said, "I can jump into the same continuum you caused after initiating it, thereby not affecting my movements. I am the elf you have waited many years to meet."

Nicholas stood stunned for a moment and then surprised the elf by walking over, picking him up off the couch and hugging him hard.

"My you are a strong one!" Aeon said surprised.

Nicholas laughed and said, "Have you seen the size of the bag I now have to carry around? I could probably lift a small elephant if need be, ho, Ho, HO!"

He put the elf back down and asked him to wait while he finished placing the gifts he brought for around the tree and stockings. When he finished he sat down with Aeon. The two talked for what would have been hours, if Nicholas hadn't already stopped time. Nicholas had saved up 18 years of questions and was trying to get Aeon to answer everyone of them.

I, myself, cannot divulge most of their discussion, as it has to do with many inventions that Nicholas brought before the Council over the years. Much of which you tallfolk still haven't mastered, though you are getting closer all the time.

They did talk about the many changes that had taken place, and how some of these would affect the future even more. They also talked about how many of Aeon's predictions had come about. Aeon said, "That is because they are not fore-tellings but fact. I had witnessed them with my own eyes."

Aeon avoided the personal questions Nick had asked, and would not answer Nick's question about which son would eventually take over. "I will tell you this, however, your son will bring more changes to the world than you or your father have. Because of his determination and efforts, he will help bring about a lasting peace to the world, with the help of three other world leaders. None of whom are prominent yet," he explained.

"Will he open the North Pole to the public after that?" asked the current Santa Claus.

"This you need not be concerned with. Let us get back to the present or at least nearly present. You have done very well, and I am most proud of what you and Mary have accomplished," said Aeon.

"Have you been watching us?" questioned Nick.

"I have dropped in from time to time to see how things were progressing," Aeon shrugged.

"Why haven't you made yourself known?" Nick said slightly agitated, "Both Mary and I have wanted to talk with you so badly."

"Yes, and mostly about the future like you are doing right now," admonished Aeon.

Nicholas looked sheepishly at Aeon and apologized.

"No matter, I have told you all that I wish to disclose except one thing." Aeon relaxed his tenseness, "I waited for a time when you had all the confidence to do what you have done and to advise you that it is time for me and some others to leave this earth."

"But why? Carrow and Ulzana are still around?" asked Nicholas, "As are almost all the other elves. We have only had four elves pass away in the last decade."

"I have found yet another wrinkle in the continuum, which I cannot explain right now." Aeon said cautiously, "It is not of this earth, but it is a place nonetheless. I will take you and Mary there someday in the future, as I will take your parents in a few more years. It is for this reason I came to see you now. I need to explain that someday in the not too distant future, your parents will be coming with me. As will some of the elves that I believe I would like to have join me and the others."

Nicholas just stared at Aeon and finally said, "The others? Just where is this place? Is it heaven?"

Aeon chuckled low and said, "You may call it that, but in reality it is another stopping ground where time has limited jurisdiction over us, and can actually reverse itself. This is one of those inexplicable things that can only be experienced by those who will be there."

"But obviously you can return from it, because here you are. So my parents will return also, isn't that right?" pleaded Nicholas.

Aeon shook his head, "Again, it is not something I

can explain, except to say I have been allowed to become a type of 'spiritual guide' to this dimension, so that I am allowed every so many years to come and go, but I am the exception, not the rule. The next time I return, it will be for Kris and Annie."

Nicholas tried to ask more questions on the subject, but as often was the case with Aeon, he said nothing, or told Nick he must wait for the answer. Aeon said to Nicholas, "It is time we both return to our tasks, and you must forget much of what I just said for the time being."

When Nicholas returned from his Christmas Eve run, he had learned that Frederick Salsbury were nowhere to be found in the village. He had completely disappeared, and no one could find him. Nick had a pretty good idea where he might have gone, and with whom, but did not tell a soul, not even Mary. Kris found a note when they searched his home, but they dismissed it at first because all it said was, "Have gone off with a friend," and was signed "Love, Fred".

Nick knew he would miss Frederick, as the two of them had become close friends. But it was Kris who couldn't seem to let it go. He practically formed a one man search party to find his dear friend.

Finally, Nick went to his father and tried his level best to explain. Kris told Nicholas that Aeon had met with him and discussed another visit in 'a few years'. Nick knew that it would be to take his father and mother to the place he alluded to that night. Kris also remembered that Aeon said he might see him another time. He told his son about it.

Nick said that visit better be a long time off. At the same time he knew that Frederick was probably very happily talking Aeon's ear off, and they both chuckled at the thought. He said he had to get home and hugged his father goodbye.

Nick returned to an empty house. Even though Christmas just passed, and he hadn't even left for the Latin American countries yet, Mary was already changing out the assembly lines and making plans for the following year.

She had assumed the CEO post from his mother on the same day they took over at the Council. The one seemed part and parcel with the other. When his parents decided to make the change they went all the way. Nicholas had assumed the presidential duties of his father, and Mary the duties of running the village including the Visiting Center.

Mary loved having visitors come to the Pole, and whether elves or tallfolk, she treated them all like royalty. She was expecting their first group of this year in early February and was already excited about it. When she wasn't doing the duties she inherited from Annie, she was making plans for the arrival of the group with Denny and the new resort manager of the Reindeer Inn, Christel Bunkinstyle.

While she loved everything about the North Pole

and her life there, it was Nick she still loved the most. She had been Nick's best friend since right after their first meeting and the couple had remained that way all their long years together. Everyone who saw them together knew they would remain soul mates for life, just as Kris and Annie had.

Nick still loved cooking, and more often than not made their dinner while she was at the manufacturing center, visiting center or the greenhouse. Although she did almost all the baking, not that Nick couldn't bake, but she seemed to enjoy baking as much as he did cooking. And she was quite excellent at it.

Nick opened the large refrigerator doors and nosed around. He found some fresh haddock and retrieved it from the shelf. He prepared a special rub and had just applied to the fish when he heard the door open.

He rinsed his hands and dried them on his pants, which was his strange habit, when his wife walked into the kitchen.

"How's my wonderful hubby?" she asked.

"Much happier since my wife is home," he smiled and then kissed her.

"I saw your father on the way back about the next round of guests," she said, "And he told me the strangest tale. Something about another dimension where he believes Fred now resides?"

So much for plans to tell her another day, he thought to himself. He set her down at the small, but comfortable kitchen table and began to explain.

"How wonderful!" Mary exclaimed, "Just imagine, after this great adventure, we will have yet another one with our parents and close friends!"

"Yes, but I hope it will not be for quite a while, as I am still enjoying this one too much," he said in a serious tone.

"It will be a very long time, and by then you and I will be ready for it," she took his hand and squeezed it, "Now what is for dinner? I'm starved."

Nick got back to his meal preparations and thought just how blessed he truly was. He thought to himself, *Not for a very long time indeed, Mr. Millennium. I already have heaven on earth, and I wish to keep it just as it is a good deal longer.*

**Read an excerpt from the 2nd book
in the Santa Claus Trilogy**

Faith, Hope & Reindeer

Faith, Hope & Reindeer

Joe Moore

as told to by

Santa Claus

Chapter Five

The adults and children alike moved over to the windows as they all noticed the train decelerating. The view outside surprised them. They were going through a heavily wooded area that was thick with trees, and not only pines and evergreens, but maples, ash, oak and more.

Cory said, "This doesn't make sense. I thought all there was this far north was tundra and snow."

Katy said, "That's what the Internet site I saw said, too."

Indeed it was hard to fathom such a rich forest in the middle of the Arctic. When they saw the soft lights of dwellings their curiosity bordered on disbelief. Who could live in such a place? Then through the darkness they saw a small boy (or maybe a girl) leading what looked to be an elk through the forest. In the dim light none could make out any distinct details. Off in the distance there was a glow from what looked to be a large campfire, and more children moving very rapidly as if gliding across the snow in circles.

"Boy they must be of hardy stock to be outside around here," said Jim.

"I can't see any adults. Where are their parents?" questioned Brian.

"Maybe it's a birthday party or something," Susan added.

"Outside?" retorted Marshall.

Suddenly a wall of white covered the windows. As the

outside scene disappeared, the valet/waiter/porters appeared again and said they would be arriving at the station in about five or six minutes and everyone should start gathering their things.

They had gone into the tunnel that would take them to the village on the other side. Everyone asked about the woods and the dwellings and the children, the valets simply said all their questions would be answered at the orientation once they disembarked and were made comfortable at the lodge.

Surprisingly even after the very long day of travel, none of the Gradys felt exhausted. In fact, they each felt pretty good and didn't complain at the thought of an orientation meeting to learn about this strange excursion. Jared, for one, thought perhaps he would finally get some answers to his myriad of questions.

So he and his family went over to their table and started gathering jackets and belongings. Jared felt sorry to be leaving this magnificent train so soon, and would have enjoyed a much longer trip, though it was obviously not designed for sleeping. But then again, after the meals they prepared on board he thought maybe he hadn't seen the length and breadth of this train's secrets.

"Oh my God!" It was Heather who exclaimed.

As the train came out of the tunnel it was as if the white curtain was being drawn on a surreal Christmas scene. Heather was the only one to exclaim, as the rest seemed devoid of speech. A couple low whistles were the most that were heard, and Julie couldn't be sure if those hadn't come from the train.

Everyone's eyes seemed bigger than the sockets meant to hold them. They all tried to take in the full measure of what they were seeing. The scene even seemed to have gone over and above the dreams of little Patrick, as he stood on his bench in

Faith, Hope & Reindeer by Joe Moore

rapt fascination like the others.

It was finally Maureen who made the next comment, "Have you ever…?" was the most she could muster.

It was as if Julie and Jared had returned to their wildest dreams as children. Even then it was hard to imagine the variety of buildings and architectural styles that stood before them. And the colors!

Every color and roofline you could dream up was here. But the most amazing thing right off was all the children…except wait…they weren't children. They were dwarves… no that's not right either; they were…

"**ELVES**?" Katy asked out loud the question they were all thinking.

Chapter Six

"Welcome everyone, welcome to the North Pole!" said Conrad, Fred and the other valets.

"The North Pole?" asked Jared, Jim and Katy.

"Yup," answered Fred, "you are officially at the top of the world and in Santa's Village. Mr. & Mrs. Claus and all the people of the Pole welcome you. Now if you'll follow us over to the Reindeer Inn, we'll get you settled."

Everyone seemed to be in overload between the scene outside the window and the formal announcement of their location. Of course the children were as excited as kids can get and little Patrick was jumping up and down saying 'I told ya, I told ya!' over and over.

As they got off the train they were met with smiles along with "Welcome" and "Merry Christmas" from all the passing elves on their way to other places. The air was crisp, but certainly not the -12° they met in Fairbanks. This felt like it was at or around the freezing mark, and there was no wind or even a breeze to contend with.

It was cold but pleasantly so.

Cory looked up at the sky and said, "Well will you look at that." Covering the entire area as far as one could see was a dome like substance, and yet there were some billowy clouds inside at the top. A little ways off you could even see snow falling from one of the clouds.

Faith, Hope & Reindeer by Joe Moore

Maureen said, "Do you think they can make their own weather in here?"

"Since this place doesn't exist in the first place, I would guess anything is possible," laughed Julie.

There were high hills around the Village and houses and shops were on two different levels. Beyond these hills and shops were mountains that seemed to reach up and connect to the domed roof. Looking around there were shops and stores everywhere. Jared thought it looked like an old time Solvang, which is a little Danish town with multiple quaint shops and retail stores that he and Julie used to love to visit and stroll around.

Every store here was different. From the rooflines and trim down to the colors, shape and style of each structure. Some looked Russian or Cyrillic in nature, and he could swear that one was German, and the bakery he couldn't figure out. The roof and the towers looked like a big but gentle roller coaster from the front. Some buildings looked more like candy shacks or old hot dog stands taken to a much grander scale.

They followed one of the valets from the train car that was in front of them. The valets walked carefully keeping their eye on the guests with children to make sure they didn't travel too quickly.

They approached a large edifice that had so many gables and towers that its true size couldn't really be determined from any one direction. There were little reindeer statues mounted on the top of each tower. The building was a caramel color with smooth walls and windows everywhere. The roof was scalloped with dark red tiles that ended in soft curves.

A very inviting structure, as were the rest, each seeming to

Faith, Hope & Reindeer by Joe Moore

say "come on in and take a look around at your leisure". The valets grabbed the two large arched oak doors and opened the structure for their anxious guests. As they all filed into the expansive lobby they saw a fireplace large enough for a man to lie down inside with room to spare. However, on this particular day it had a large roaring fire going in it. The wood smelled of a hint of eucalyptus and it gave off enough heat to warm the whole lobby to a pleasant temperature. The room had seating all around and could comfortably sit twenty-five or more without leaving any one standing.

A sprite small lady came out of the back with a huge smile on her face.

"Welcome honored guests to the Reindeer Inn. My name is Christel Bunkinstyle and I am the Chief Resort Manager," the elf said. She stood approximately four feet tall, and had a long face with soft dark blue-gray eyes. Her nose was slightly longish and ended in a cue stick point. Her ears were long as well, but not pointed, as one would expect an elf's to be.

She said, "We will be having an orientation in the lobby in forty-five minutes, but you may all go up to your rooms to check your accommodations and register any questions or concerns about them. Your luggage will be placed in your rooms while you are at the orientation. Now all the room names are marked clearly on the walls and doors and you should have no trouble finding them on your own, however we shall take you to them personally for the first time."

She produced a two-inch gold sleigh bell from her pocket and rang it. Several elves filed in from three different ground floor locations into the lobby.

Faith, Hope & Reindeer by Joe Moore

Christel called out the name of each family and announced their room. "Billings – Donder, O'Reillys – Chestnut," with that Maureen, Jim and their three girls went trotting off with their 'bell-elf' leading the way. "Fredricks – Prancer, Wus – Vixen, Peters – Cupid," and Cory, Katy and Todd walked toward the stairs.

Katy said, "Excuse me, does she have our key?" indicating to the young elf heading off in front of them.

Christel said, "We don't have keys here. Terrible waste of time and energy."

Katy replied, "Well, how do you lock your doors?" Christel looked at Katy and smiled, "Dear, you are in the North Pole. You do not need to lock your doors or bolt your windows. We are all on the 'honor system' up here. And you may rest assured that no one will disturb your room, or steal from you. They wouldn't be here if they had even the smallest inkling of that in their heart. Enjoy the Cupid Room."

As they turned to go Christel returned to looking at the group and announced, "Gradys – Rudolph, Thomas – Alandale."

Jared, Julie and the kids marched behind an elf toward the stairs. "I'm William," the four and a half foot dwarf said, "You should really enjoy Rudolph."

Julie said, "I don't wish to seem ungrateful, but all four of us in one room? Is there any chance we could get a second room so the girls and guys can share a room together?"

William said, "Oh I wouldn't worry there, it's plenty big enough for all of you, you'll see."

The Gradys walked up onto the third flight of steps and there were two rooms on this floor, Rudolph and Pocatello.

"Pocatello?" Marshall asked.

Faith, Hope & Reindeer by Joe Moore

William said matter of factly, "Why yes, that's Rudolph's Father. Well here you go," as he pointed to the room adorning Rudolph's name and opened the door.

About the Author

Joe Moore may be a new author to the public, but the man has written millions of words over his lifetime. A former publisher, editor, advertising, marketing and sales executive he has done hundreds of campaigns and articles with thousands of proposals and stories for everything from fishing equipment to business magazines.

Moore has been a feature writer for several Southern California periodicals, and has written more than a dozen children's stories about Santa's elves that will soon be published in book form. He and his wife designed and built the North Pole with porcelain houses and hundreds of elves. This actually was the premise and inspiration for his Trilogy of Santa Claus. He has now published two books from the trilogy – *Believe Again, The North Pole Chronicles* **and** *Faith, Hope & Reindeer.* Look for the third book, *Glaciers Melt & Mountains Smoke* coming in 2014.

Moore is deeply rooted in his Christian beliefs. Without trying to drive the point home, he opens the reader's eyes to the knowledge that miracles happen everyday, and one should always count their blessings against those less fortunate. He feels that God helped him write these stories and feels He has a plan for all of us.

The fact that he bears an uncanny resemblance to our popular conception of Santa Claus is just the icing on the cake. Moore's hair and beard are naturally white and he has portrayed Santa to tens of thousands of children and adults for more than a decade. To most people that meet him, he IS Santa Claus and answers to that more than to his own name.

Joe hopes you enjoyed this first book in the trilogy as you traveled with Santa and Mrs. Claus on their wondrous journey of discovery and just what a difference even you can make to the world.

CPSIA information can be obtained at www.ICGtesting.com
Printed in the USA
LVOW07s0227131213

364990LV00005B/29/P